THE LAFITTE CASE

A Historical Mystery
by Ray Peters

A Write Way Publishing Book

Write Way Publishing
10555 E. Dartmouth, Ste 210
Aurora, CO 80014

First Edition; 1997

ISBN 1-885173-27-X

1 2 3 4 5 6 7 8 9

ACKNOWLEDGMENTS

Archdiocese of New Orleans
Hon. Lindy Boggs, M.C.
Chalmette National Historic Park
Clive Cussler
Contra Costa County Library
Peter Driscoll
Maureen Hirst
Historic New Orleans Collection
Jean Lafitte National Historic Park
John Paul Jones Museum, Kirkbean
Lafitte Study Group
Sir Gordon Linacre
Library of Congress
London Evening Post, 1779
Louisiana State Museum
Missouri Historical Society
National Museums of Scotland
Nature, 1961
Ray O'Neal
New Orleans Public Library
New Orleans States, 1928
St. Louis Public Library
Stewartry Museum, Kirkcudbright
United States Geological Survey
United States Naval Academy Museum
Yorkshire Post Newspapers, Ltd

CHAPTER 1

Flamborough Head, England
September 23, 1779

PRESENTED BY
Edw. Livingston, Esq.,
FEBRUARY 6, 1930

"We'll see action soon." Andrew Mason drawled softly, turning toward the large frigate bearing down on them, directly ahead. Painted black, she wore yellow stripes beginning at points from her bowsprit that widened along the gun ports on either side. With studding sails set at the extreme ends of her yardarms, she gave the appearance of a white-winged bumble-bee ready to strike.

"Aye," Jean Paul replied, anxiety knotting in his stomach.

"How old are you, then?" Andrew grinned through a mass of freckles under a shock of golden hair. Jean Paul eyed his fellow apprentice, envying Andrew's vivid hair. So much more gay than his own brown, tinted with red. "Fifteen," he answered, not wanting to lie to Andrew as he had when he signed aboard.

"Same as me," Andrew said. "I lied when I signed on."

The day was calm, rare since departing L'Orient over a month ago, and the first time, really, that Jean Paul had felt completely well. He had discovered soon enough, before the French coastline had disappeared under the sternsheets, that the motion of the ship was more than his stomach could bear. The first gale, encountered off the Skellig Islands of Ireland, convinced him conclusively that he was no sailor.

BonHomme Richard rode quietly, ominously so. Such a slight breeze blew from the southwest that her sails hardly bellied. There was none of the usual creaking of tackle, the snapping and popping of canvas taut to the straining point. Small waves crested and broke in the sea without sound. Even the seagulls, wheeling lazily behind the ship, quelled their usual squawks. There was only the soft wash of the hull through the blue water and the low murmur of voices as clusters of men stood idly about, nervously watching the large ship that bore down on them from the north, bows-on.

"Ye're French?" Andrew peered closely at him.

"No. American." Jean Paul turned to the coast that lay to the west, the lowering sun reflecting like green paint on the hills of England.

"Ye sound French. Like one what learned English after."

"I did. I lived in France all my life." Sunlight flashed on a window somewhere, from a cottage atop a long white cliff. "Most of my life."

"How'd ye come to do that?"

Jean Paul disliked the conversation. He turned abaft, seeking to change it. A tiny American fleet trailed along behind *Richard*, led by the frigate *Alliance*. American-built, she was nearly the size of *Richard*, commanded by the boisterous Frenchman Pierre Landais, who was resentful because he had been ordered to serve under an American. "That midget," he had once spit out under his breath, referring to Jones, the commodore of the fleet.

Alliance was braced on either side by the frigate *Pallas* and the corvette *Vengeance*, both ships French, both commanded by Frenchmen. It was hard, thought Jean Paul, to consider the fleet to be an American one. Especially since all the ships carried British colors at their mainmast peaks and at their sterns.

"Eh?" Andrew pressed his question.

"My mother was French."

"Your father, too?"

"He was Scottish." Jean Paul toned his voice to indicate he didn't want to discuss the matter further. "We're not making much headway."

"Aye." Andrew's smile flashed. He slapped the foredeck rail. "She's an old tub, ain't she?"

BonHomme Richard was French, too, like much of her crew and all of her marines. The planks of the old East Indiaman were worn and soaked with brine, slow and heavy in the water. She was hardly a nimble sailer, not quick to respond to her helm, and aggravated by the added weight because of her conversion from merchantman to warship. The heavy armament, especially the old eighteen-pounders mounted in the junior officers' mess, made her ride so deep in the water that the lower gunports couldn't be opened unless the day was especially calm. She lumbered unwillingly through the sea like a sodden log, especially in the light breeze southerly of Flamborough Head.

It must be especially fearsome, Jean thought, for the one hundred-odd British prisoners confined in the hold, captured in previous actions off the coast of Ireland. In that windowless dark, they must be aware of the readying for action, the uncertainty of their fate, the knowledge that their prison could quickly become their coffin. It was an unfair hell, even if they were British.

"She's the *Serapis*, Cap'n Pearson." Andrew muttered out of the corner of his mouth like an old salt, shucking the golden hair from his forehead. "Fifty guns."

Jean Paul's stomach knotted more tightly. He was afraid, for *Bonhomme Richard* carried but forty guns. And some were antiques. All were discards, and one was especially odd, described spitefully by the gunners as a "useless breech-loader."

"How do you know all that?"

"About the guns?"

"About everything. The name of the ship."

"I heard them talking." Andrew jerked his head in the direction of the quarterdeck, where Captain Jones stood with other officers, watching the approaching enemy.

The commander was conspicuously shorter than his aides Midshipmen Linthwaite and Mayrant, shorter even than purser Mease. Even in middle age, the captain had grown no taller than Jean Paul had in fifteen years. He was nevertheless impressive and in obvious command. Neatly dressed in a carefully tailored blue-and-white uniform, his coat bore shoulder epaulets that indicated his rank as commodore of the squadron. His face was clean-shaven under the tricorn hat, so closely that his cheeks glinted in the afternoon sunlight. His brown hair was neatly brushed back from under the hat and tied behind in a queue, glinting red in the sun.

"She's a beauty, ain't she?" Andrew stared at the approaching ship as if he wished she would hurry.

Jean Paul didn't think she was pretty at all. He wished with all his heart he hadn't decided to come on the cruise around the British Isles in the first place.

"Copper bottom," Andrew explained when a slight swell lifted the ship and her bows caught a flash from the sun. "Keeps the barnacles off, gives her another knot or two. All the new Britishers have them." He grinned at Jean Paul, proud of his superior knowledge about things of the sea.

Much of the remainder of the waning afternoon passed Jean Paul in a daze: Andrew chatting away; the beat to General Quarters by the drummers; Captain Chamillard issuing orders to his marines in French; the men clambering to the foretop under the command of Lieutenant Stack; the assemblage of the gun crews by Lieutenant Dale to their assignations on the lower decks; the "Line of Battle" signal ordered by Captain Jones, blue flag at the fore, blue pennant at the main truck, blue-and-yellow flag at the mizzen.

Andrew slapped the rail a final time. "To station," he said, making his way below to his post on the upper gundeck. The apprentices were posted on the gundecks to stand by, to observe, to help out only when ordered to. Jean Paul followed the shock of golden hair down the ladder to his position on the lower gundeck.

As he descended, he saw *Pallas* cut in astern, directly behind *Richard*. The "Line of Battle," explained by Andrew, was formed up in action against a lone ship such as the one approaching. Although *Serapis* outgunned each of the American ships, including *Richard*, only the first ship in line would bear the brunt of her broadside. That would be *Richard*, as flagship, of course, but while the enemy reloaded, the following ships in their turn would sail by and destroy the Britisher.

But then *Alliance* hauled her wind and set off independently for open water instead of following after *Pallas* as she should have.

Pallas dropped off astern and altered her course to the northeast. *Vengeance* didn't line up at all. *Bonhomme Richard* sailed on alone toward a vastly superior enemy that was now but a half mile distant. Jean Paul was puzzled, but he thought it might be some trick they were playing to fool the enemy.

At the first broadside, Jean Paul squeezed his eyes tightly shut. He pressed his hands hard over his ears and turned his head away from the thunderous blast of the cannon.

The enemy fired their own salvo into the American ship at almost the same instant, the British cannon balls slamming *Richard's* side as if the American missiles had snapped back on elastic bands.

The ship shuddered as if she had run aground. Her side bulged visibly inward. Some of the shot actually plunged through the wood, exploding jagged splinters into the air. The low-ceilinged officers' mess in which the guns were mounted filled with the smoke of war, the smell of blood and death. Jean Paul wavered on the sanded deck, barking his shin on the sharp edge of a water tub as he tottered. The tight knot in his stomach heaved upward and he gulped to keep himself from retching. Twenty men were crammed into the tiny space of the lower battery. Unlike Jean Paul, those that survived the first response from the enemy ignored the billowing smoke, the hurtling enemy balls, the whistling, flying splinters.

The cannon obediently awaited their next charge. Already run in from the force of their recoil and tight against their breeching lines, the smoking muzzles waited just inside the open gun ports. Swabbers leaped to work with long-handled sheepskin mops. Dripping with water from the tubs, the mops sizzled out wayward sparks.

"Load!" shouted the battery commander. Like dancers with near perfect synchronization, the swabbers withdrew their mops. Loaders moved forward, each with a fresh powder cartridge. After the quick insertions, they moved sharply aside for the rammers, who forced the packets far down into the breech. A wad of oakum followed, rammed down before the insertion of the ball.

Smaller than the bore, the ball bobbled into the dark maw, rumbling downward in its path, followed by another quick wad of oakum, which was securely rammed into place.

Jean Paul watched the macabre dance. With a ridiculous surge of reason, he wondered if the ball might bobble out just as it had bobbled in and he speculated that the last bobble out upon firing might well determine its final direction and explain the inaccuracy of these roundshot.

"Run out!" shouted the commander, waving his arms as if cracking a whip. At once, the crews dropped their swabs and their ramming rods to haul on the side tackles and roll the heavy cannon forward to poke their muzzles through the gun ports.

A pause as the gun captains sighted over their barrels. Each apparently determined that the target had shifted position since the last firing, for each signalled with his right hand that the stern tackles should be tightened to train the weapons a bit farther aft. They indicated with their left hands that the muzzles should be lowered, for the enemy had also sailed closer.

At once, a member of each crew prized under each barrel with crowbars while another tapped in wooden quoins to hold the position.

"Prime!" shouted the commander.

The gunners thrust fine wires into touch holes to pierce the flannel cartridges within the breeches, then poured mealed powder into the cavities before they stepped backward as one. The captains moved forward with their glowing slow matches.

Jean Paul stumbled backward, careful to avoid the bruising water tub. He turned to face the bulwark, pressed his hands over his ears once again and squinted his eyes tightly shut. He bent forward from the waist to protect himself from the impending blast, no longer caring if the crews thought him afraid.

"Fire!"

The blast was enormously greater than that of the first. The force of it pummeled at his backside like the kick of a horse, pushing him headfirst into the bulwark. The pressure of the blast pressed on his eardrums and he felt his head crack against a sturdy timber.

He awoke an eternity later to an immense ringing in his ears that throbbed in his head and hurt even his teeth. He found himself seated on the sanded deck, leaning back against the bulwark, for he had somehow twisted about when he fell. A touch to his forehead showed blood, but the roar in his ears obliterated the pain he should have felt. For a moment he rested, frightened by the noise in his ears that sounded as if he were swimming under a heavy sea. His hearing, he was certain, was lost.

His eyes were clear. Astounded, he saw two of the mighty cannon lying askew in their carriages, ripped apart as if giant hands had torn them asunder.

The exploding cannon had opened the deck above him. He glanced upward and could see into the battery of the twelve-pounders, and above that, fragments of the evening sky pulsing with flashes of light. He looked down again, where the swabbers and rammers and captains were sprawled everywhere about, their mouths distorted from that instant of pain before they died. Others, still alive, choked and gasped from the acrid yellow smoke, groping about the wreckage, their noses bleeding onto their shirts.

Then it seemed the *Richard* ran aground again, for the enemy poured yet another broadside into the broken ship. The balls penetrated more easily this time, exploding more jagged splinters that plunged themselves into the quick and the dead alike. Many of those still on their feet crumpled or were flung to the deck, their mouths frozen in screams, their vulnerable flesh torn by unrelenting iron or piercing wood. Unashamedly, Jean Paul retched again and again onto his torn and bloody shirt.

INTERVAL REQUESTED BY Ch. Rossiter
RESP. SUB., G. Choteau, Sec.
FEBRUARY 6, 1930

CHAPTER 2
New Orleans, Louisiana
February 6, 1993, 2:00 PM

"That's arsenic," Edward Livingston said when his grandson headed straight for the blue bottle of poison on the mantel. The boy's hand fell quickly away from the bottle, and Edward smiled.

"It's a murder case, then?" Mickey stared at the bottle. His name was actually Michael, but no one ever called him that. He simply didn't fit into the Michael mold.

"One of my clients was murdered, yes. But the murder was only incidental."

"Who're your clients?"

Edward pointed his cane. "His Excellency," he announced in his deepest courtroom bass, "the Emperor Napoleon Bonaparte."

Mickey reacted like a trooper. "Excellency." He placed one hand fore and one hand aft and bowed deeply, sliding his T-shirt upward, revealing an expanse of tanned, bare skin. Edward arched his bushy eyebrows, surprised and pleased by his grandson's courtliness.

"And the Admiral John Paul Jones." The cane swept to the other side of the room.

"Sir." Mickey's second bow was as deep as the first.

Edward tugged a watch from the pocket of his vest and arched his eyebrows higher. The watch, inherited from Father, always ran fast, as his father had. It was necessary to make allowances for both of them.

"Wow. I never been in 'The Secret Room' before." Mickey sauntered about the study with the loose-limbed gait of a teenager who hears the throb of a distant drum, his awkward knees imperiling precarious stacks of books.

The room had the aroma of a mildewed library mingled with the faint reek of pipe smoke. File folders and legal papers were everywhere, stacked on the floor and elsewhere in every available level space and some not so level.

A huge carved desk dominated the room like an exotic temple in a paper jungle. The two honored inhabitants ignored the intrusion as well as the mess, chiseled as they were from the finest Vermont marble. The emperor brooded imperially from the desk while the admiral watched with a lofty indifference from his position on the ledge of a tall window.

Edward bounced along behind his grandson, wielding the cane like a riding crop. Proud of his erect bearing and sprightly demeanor, he refused to allow himself to become depressed by his age, however advanced it might be. He tilted his head sharply upward to peer at Mickey, for the grandson had grown taller while the grandfather had grown shorter.

"They sure look real." Mickey touched a tentative finger to the point of Napoleon's hat. The stony Emperor glowered. The boy moved on to the admiral and traced a finger down the boyish marble nose. That interest was fleeting. He scuffed across the room to briefly inspect a wall covered with maps, then a framed photograph of three graves in a crowded cemetery.

"Who's the guy on the medal?" He peered upward at a

bas-relief face on a gold medallion that hung from a red ribbon above the fireplace.

"The guy on the medal is John Paul Jones." Edward pretended not to be bothered by the irreverence.

Mickey's head swung back and forth, glancing in turn at the bust and the medal. "They don't look the same."

"It's part of the mystery." *Score one for the prosecution.* Edward caned his way behind the desk to the Admiral Jones window, for his leg began to bother him from all the bouncing about. The old, wobbly glass distorted Audubon Park, across Walnut Street, which glistened shiny-black from the afternoon showers. In the middle distance, a restored streetcar rumbled along St. Charles Avenue like a remnant monster from the Industrial Revolution.

"Sure is a lot of stuff in here," Mickey said after the noise of the streetcar had died.

"It's a big case."

"What's that thing?"

Edward turned from the window. Mickey pointed to a dusty wooden structure that huddled in the corner of the study like a poor church. Clumsily made of wood and heavily ornamented, it was topped with an oversized cross.

"A baptismal font."

"Looks old."

Edward strode to the desk, trying not to wince at a new ache in his leg. He propped the cane against a drawer handle and settled into the padded black judge's chair that was the one extravagance he permitted in the study.

"It's from the Church of St. Louis in Jackson Square. Before the church became a cathedral."

Mickey turned from the font and stared overhead to a

yellowed portrait of President Madison, hanging by long wires from a picture rail near the ceiling. "I got to get home," he said off-handedly, as if he had already spent too much time in a boring museum.

Edward felt his cheeks tingle. Youth was always in a hurry. He lay the watch face up on the desk. "I want you to take over the case," Edward suddenly said, flat out.

"What?"

"I said—I want you to take over the case."

"What case?"

"This case." Edward swept his hand about the room.

"No way." Mickey's face was incredulous.

"Why not?"

"I ain't a lawyer, for one."

"You don't have to be a lawyer."

"It ain't my bag."

"You can make it your bag."

"Why don't you finish it?"

"I'm old."

"You ain't so old."

Edward peered at his grandson through the space between the top of his spectacles and the lower bushy limits of his eyebrows. "Sit down," he said gently. Mickey cocked his head to one side and looked at his grandfather as if he were nuts. "Take it!" Edward wanted to shout, but simply said again, "Sit down."

It was a command this time. Too stern, perhaps. Mickey hesitated, gathering himself to object. Edward held his breath and pointed to a chair before the desk laden with a haphazard stack of books. The boy sighed. He bent to shift the books to the floor, then dropped all at once like a loose sack of grain into the quivering chair. Edward breathed again.

"I don't have much time."

"What's the hurry?" Edward spun the watch idly about on the blotter.

Mickey didn't answer. He rolled his head back to gaze at the molded plaster rose on the high ceiling, allowing his long hair to drift over the chair back. Sandy-brown with a reddish tint, the hair was uncharacteristic of a Livingston. Inherited from his mother, no doubt.

"I'm sorry your father missed the funeral." Edward stopped the spinning watch.

"Dad does his own thing," Mickey said to the plaster rose, as if what his father did was none of his business.

"Do you?"

Edward watched Mickey's brown eyes. At least they were Livingston eyes. The family characteristics had skipped an entire generation, leap-frogging right over his father. Charleton more resembled a squat black-eyed bear with a black ponytail.

"Do I what?"

"Do your own thing?" Mickey didn't answer. Edward probed again. "Don't you even want to hear about the case?"

"Not really." Mickey glanced at the door as if planning an escape route.

"What are you interested in?"

"I guess, cars, mostly." Mickey combed long fingers through his mat of hair.

Edward seized the opportunity. "You any good at fixing cars?"

"I'm okay." Another quick glance at the door.

"How's school?" Edward employed the old lawyer's trick of dazzling the witness by a rapid change of subject.

"I'm through."

"Through?"

"It was boring."

"Didn't they teach you about cars?"

"Naw. Just old stuff."

"Old stuff like—"

"Like the stuff in this room, I guess." Mickey crossed one leg over the other and placed his hand on the bare ankle. His upraised foot waggled up and down in continuous motion.

Edward tipped back in his chair and looked away from the wriggling foot. "What will you do, then? If you're not in school? Get a job?"

"I already got a job."

"You have? Where?"

"The Eagle Point Café."

Edward knew the place. A beer dive near Carrollton. Overlooking the levee, it catered principally to the unemployed. "What do you—"

"I bus tables. For starters. Might work my way up to cook."

Mickey was already mired fast in the ruts of Carrollton. Following in the muddy footsteps of his father.

"I thought you liked cars."

"Couldn't find a mechanic job."

Edward fixed on the Livingston eyes. "Maybe you could take a look at the Pierce-Arrow for me."

The gambit worked. Mickey exploded to his feet. "You still have the old Pierce-Arrow?" His face lightened. The nervousness, the hesitancy, had gone. The foot, now firmly on the floor, was at last stilled.

"Still in the garage." Edward tried to conceal his exhilaration.

"What year is she?" Mickey visibly vibrated with enthusiasm.

"Nineteen twenty-eight. Same as always." Edward laughed.

"Does she run?"

"Hasn't run in years."

The weight of the long day settled like a specter on Edward's shoulders, however much he loathed to admit it. The room swirled; he forced his eyes tightly shut and swept the spectacles from his face.

"You all right, Grandpa?"

Edward opened his eyes and blinked. Mickey leaned anxiously forward. The dull gleam of the golden medallion over the fireplace glimmered like the morning sun.

He needed desperately to capture Mickey's interest, even if the interest was only momentary. Later, if Mickey became sufficiently involved, the car would become merely academic.

"Tell you what," Edward said, watching the glowing medal. "I'll make a deal with you."

"A deal?"

"If you can fix the car, you can have it."

"I—"

"That's one part of the deal."

"What's the other part?"

"You have to solve a riddle."

"What?"

"A riddle. You have to solve a riddle, too."

"What's the riddle?"

"It's right here, in this room."

Mickey's eyes darted all about.

"You see that medal? The one hanging over the fireplace?" Edward's quavering finger pointed.

Mickey swiveled, his shoes squeaking on the floor. "I see it."

"It's a replica. The original was authorized by the United States Congress for John Paul Jones, October tenth, seventeen eighty-seven, actually."

"So what's the riddle?"

"The riddle is that ... well, the original medal is lost."

Mickey laughed. "You want me to find it?"

"No. Just figure out where it is."

"How can I—"

"I'll give you clues."

"Why play games?"

"Do you want the car or not?"

Mickey thrust his hands deep into the pockets of his jeans. He slumped around the room, glancing at everything without apparent interest. Edward watched him go. He squeezed his fingers against the sides of the watch until his knuckles whitened. At last, Mickey halted and stood before the desk. "Maybe somebody stole it."

"No. The medal wasn't stolen."

"You're sure?"

"Dead sure."

"Do *you* know where it is?"

"Let's say I have an idea." He couldn't let Mickey know that he knew. "It's been missing for two hundred years."

That morning, the glimmering face appeared on the rising sun, then as quickly disappeared behind the filmy cloud. But before the image dimmed, the answer was his—

"Why should I figure it out?"

"Because you want the car."

"How much time do I have?"

Edward looked at the watch. "About four hours."

"Why four hours?"

"Because that's all the time I'm giving you."

Because, in four hours, the telephone call.

Mickey shook his head. "I don't have that much time."

"Why not?"

"I told you. I got a job. I got to get back to work. Anyway, Dad'll be awful mad at me."

A loyalty demanded by Charleton? Who had never shown such loyalty to his own father?

"Why would he be mad at you?"

"Anyway. It took you a long time, you said. And you're a lawyer." Mickey's earlier excitement had evaporated.

Edward rotated the chair to face the window overlooking the park. "Lawyers," he said, "aren't any smarter than anyone else. And you have a big advantage: Everything's assembled for you, all put together in this one room."

He rotated slowly back to see Mickey ease himself into the chair, gripping the arms more like a gentleman this time. Both feet remained on the floor, perfectly still.

"Okay," Mickey said. "Give me the clues. But I hope it don't take too long."

Edward gathered himself, greatly relieved. He slid the watch to the edge of the blotter with a quivering hand.

"John Paul Jones," he began slowly, "wanted to be an admiral more than anything else in the world."

"I thought he was an admiral."

Edward shook his head. "That was from the Russians. He wanted to be an American admiral."

"So how come the Americans didn't make him an admiral?"

"There was no such rank at the time in the American navy. Congress gave him a medal instead. And that medal became the most sacred, most precious thing that John Paul Jones ever possessed. He considered it to be his highest award. That's the first clue."

Mickey glanced surreptitiously at the door.

Edward pulled open the top desk drawer and withdrew a ring of keys. He held the cluster momentarily high above the desk, then pointedly dropped the mass into a heap on the green desk blotter.

Mickey watched. He waited. When nothing further was offered, his eyes fell to his feet.

Edward bent to open a lower desk drawer. He extracted a thick file folder, yellowed with age and worn with handling. He pushed aside the ring of keys and snapped on the green-shaded desk lamp, for the cloudy day was darkening early.

"Many years ago," Edward said, speaking more quickly now to maintain the precarious momentum, "your grand-mother and I took a ride out to visit the grave of Napoleon Bonaparte." He looked up as if he expected a challenge.

Mickey rose to the bait. "You drove out? In a car?"

If admirals didn't interest him, cars did. "The same car. The nineteen-twenty-eight Pierce-Arrow Saloon. It was brand-spanking new then."

"But you drove out?" Mickey looked near to laughing. "I didn't know that Napoleon was buried in Louisiana."

"A lot of people knew, back in nineteen twenty-eight. It was all over the papers."

"What does old Boney have to do with the medal?"

"A great deal. Just accept the fact for the moment. If you want to solve the riddle."

Mickey sat sharply upright. He folded his hands on his lap like an attentive schoolboy. "I believe it."

"Good." Edward ignored the pretension. "As I was saying, we drove out to the bayous to look for the graves. We were very surprised by what we found."

CHAPTER 3
Barataria, Louisiana
August 19, 1928

The little cemetery was like a circus, thronged with people.

Agnes fanned herself with the newspaper. "This where you wanted to have a picnic?"

Parked cars lined on both sides of Barataria Road, all the way from the foot of the bridge southerly. Some were pulled into the cemetery itself, dangerously near to the few headstones.

"Hotter here than at home." She sat on the extreme right side of the wide seat, as far away from him as possible.

Grown-ups and children alike scooped up handfuls of dirt and dumped them into paper bags and gunny sacks and buckets brought along for the purpose.

"Told you we shouldn't have come out here." She fanned furiously, leaning her head out the open window for air.

The day was stifling, like liquid fire, with humidity thick enough to bubble paint.

"It's the storm."

"What?"

"Why it's so hot. There's going to be a storm."

"What are they doing, anyway?"

"Souvenirs. They're taking dirt home for souvenirs."

"Foolishness."

It was foolishness. And destructive. And illegal. Edward thrust the car in gear and began to turn around in the narrow space left on the road.

"Where you going?"

"To report this."

"Foolishness."

It was better with the car underway, with the heavy air blasting through the windows. Edward roared back over the bridge, amused by Agnes' tight clutch on the door handle.

"They read the article, I guess."

"What?" Agnes held her hair with both hands to protect it from the wind.

"They read the article in the morning paper." He saw the article clearly in his mind, as if it had been stamped there:

GRAVES OF NAPOLEON, JOHN PAUL JONES IN LOUISIANA

NAPOLEON BONAPARTE, JOHN PAUL JONES, JEAN LAFITTE SLEEP IN
GRAVE ON BAYOU BARATARIA

The ancient burial ground lies on the high point of land that juts out at the point where Bayou des Oises flows into Big Barataria Bayou. There in a tangle of wild rose bushes, and tall grass, stands an iron cross—ancient, rusted, hand-hammered iron with a disc at the top and at the end of each branching arm.

He steered cautiously when a string of cars appeared, heading for the cemetery.

"I think I'm getting carsick."

He paid no attention, marveling instead how well the heavy car held to the pavement.

Now, for the first time, the celebrated story is given the world: alien bones lie in the tomb of the Hotel des Invalides in Paris, and in the tomb of the United States Naval Academy at Annapolis—where others were supposed to sleep.

"I don't know how we can afford this car, anyway, if things are so slow at the office." She had one hand on her hair and the other on the door handle.

It wasn't just a car. It was a Pierce-Arrow Saloon, and it was long and wide and heavy and black. Expensive. In the front, a massive chrome radiator braced by the distinctive Pierce-Arrow headlights, teardrop-shaped, that melded into the fenders with sophisticated opulence. The huge spare tire mounted at the rear of the trunk overhung almost too far, as if its weight could tip the car backward and launch the heavy vehicle at the moon. People *looked* when a Pierce-Arrow rolled grandly by. It was purchased from the proceeds of Father's insurance money, though Agnes didn't know about that.

"I didn't say things were slow at the office."

"Mrs. McFreeson did."

Old biddy Mrs. McFreeson. One of the leftovers from Father's office.

"She doesn't know about Marie Defenbach."

"What?"

"She doesn't know about the new case. It just came in."

"What's it about?"

"Can't talk about it. But it's a murder case."

Agnes would never have heard about Marie Defenbach. She would never have heard about Clarence Darrow, either, the celebrated barrister who was nothing until he took on that famous case. After Marie Defenbach, clients flocked to Darrow's office. Something like Marie Defenbach was exactly what Edward needed. A big case to establish his reputation once and for all.

And he had found it. The newsboy had delivered to his porch only that morning.

Big fat raindrops were just beginning to fall when Edward

swerved the car sharply from the road into the gravel approach
to a service station.

"What on earth—"

"I need to make a telephone call." Edward leaped from the
car and slammed the heavy door, penning all future objec-
tions in the car with her.

After the vexatious call to the Jefferson Parish Police Department, which helped not at all, Agnes sat in stiff-backed
silence and ignored him completely. He didn't dare speak
until he braked the big car at the end of the long line waiting
to cross the river on the Napoleon Avenue Ferry.

"I'll be pretty busy with the new case." His voice was loud
in the car after the motor was shut off.

"The Marie—whatever?" At least she was alive.

"Yeah." He was sorry he had initiated a conversation. All
of a sudden, he didn't want to talk. He wanted to think.

How would Clarence Darrow have handled it? Why, he
would have found one single shred of absolutely irrefutable
evidence. He would have savored that shred, toyed with it,
tantalized the jury with it. There was always at least one such
shred. There were sometimes more. But always, there was at
least one. And a good lawyer could prove anything. Anything,
if he was good enough.

Edward sat hunched over the wheel, watching the ferry
approach the slip, willing it to hurry, excitedly anxious to get
to work. Agnes spoke again, but he paid no attention to her
ramblings. He had just committed himself to become a pros-
ecuting attorney, for a case he believed would propel him to
the forefront of history.

CHAPTER 4

New Orleans, Louisiana
February 6, 1993, 2:18 PM

Mickey toyed with the telephone hook, idly clicking it up and down. One of the old pedestal varieties with a dial on its base, it hardly ever rang anymore, and had never rung often, even in the best of times.

"So you decided Napoleon was buried out there? By the Bayou des Oises?"

"The Bayou of the Geese."

Mickey's foot rose back up to his knee and began an incessant waggling. His hand fell from the telephone and draped over the bare ankle. "And the idea came from that newspaper article?"

Edward looked away from the nervous foot. He watched a young girl walk a black dachshund through the park. The tiny dog cocked his leg at every gigantic oak tree he encountered, never mind the futility of the effort.

"The newspaper article gave me the idea, yes."

"Isn't he supposed to be buried in Paris?"

"At the Hotel des Invalides." Edward swiveled back and reached across his desk to a rack of pipes that surrounded a dusty humidor.

"That's why you got a bust of Napoleon in here, because he's one of your clients."

Edward selected a large, curved pipe. He removed the humidor cover and plunged the pipe into the depths, working tobacco into the bowl with his finger.

"John Paul Jones. He's a client too, you said."

Edward withdrew the filled pipe from the humidor and

replaced the lid. He slid open a desk drawer and concentrated on a search for matches even though he knew exactly where they were.

"I thought John Paul Jones was buried in Annapolis."

"At the chapel of the United States Naval Academy."

Edward withdrew the large box of wooden farmer matches from the desk drawer and set it atop the file folder. He placed the pipe in his mouth and with shaking hands fumbled out a match.

"There's one more grave." Mickey waited.

"That of Jean Lafitte." Edward struck the match against the sandpaper side of the box.

"Jean Lafitte the pirate?"

"You know about Jean Lafitte?"

"Everybody knows about Jean Lafitte. All the kids used to play Lafitte games."

"Swords and everything?"

"We used sticks."

"Rescued damsels in distress, did you?"

"Beautiful damsels in distress."

"Pistols stuck in the belt?"

"Pistols all over the place."

"Chests filled with pirate gold?"

"We buried boxes everywhere. Cardboard ones. I don't know how they held up."

They laughed together, and the feeling was most pleasant. It was the beginning, Edward hoped, of a bonding. He had played the same games when he was a boy. Jean Lafitte the hero of New Orleans. The lovable legend of New Orleans that would never die, like Paul Revere in Boston or Robin Hood in Sherwood Forest.

Mickey slid his foot to the floor. He leaned forward and

rested both elbows on his knees. "What'd Grandma think about all that? Your trying to figure out those graves, and everything?"

"She didn't know anything about it."

"You don't think Grandma knew what you were doing?"

"Maybe she did. We didn't talk about it, though."

Mickey looked about, at the matching gold-framed portraits of President Madison and Andrew Jackson.

"Dad knew. He always called this The Secret Room."

Edward was aware that Charleton referred to his study as The Secret Room. The door was always locked and entrance was barred to everyone, without exception. Including Absinthe the cleaning lady, although her services might have been useful.

Mickey pulled himself to his feet and walked over to the fireplace. He stood before the mantel with his hands in his pockets and stared up at the medal. "So you believed the story in the paper?"

"Did I say I believed it?"

Mickey turned slowly. "If you didn't believe it, why did you—"

"I didn't say I *didn't* believe it, did I? I thought I already explained that to you. It didn't matter whether I believed it or not. What mattered was that I needed to establish a reputation. I needed a case. I needed a *big* case."

"So you sued somebody."

"There was no one to sue."

"How can you have a case? If there's nobody to sue?"

"I went to The Lafitte Society."

"That's a court?"

"Sort of."

Edward moved the matchbox aside and turned a leaf in

the folder. He ran a finger down the page as if pretending to look for an entry.

"They were like a court, I guess you might say. They were considered to be very prestigious, and passed judgment on all matters having to do with Jean Lafitte. Sort of a Supreme Court of Lafittism. Anything accepted by them would be found acceptable anywhere. If I could convince The Lafitte Society, I would have made my case. The world would listen to me."

"But what'd the Lafitte Society have to do with Napoleon? And John Paul Jones? Those guys didn't have nothing to do with Jean Lafitte, did they?"

"Well. The newspapers said Lafitte buried those guys there."

"And you proved it?"

"Lafitte didn't bury Napoleon. The Emperor died after Lafitte." It wasn't precisely true, but it would do for the moment.

"So it couldn't of been." Mickey slapped his hands on his thighs and strode to the wall of maps. He traced his finger along the broad curvaceous blue line of the Mississippi from New Orleans to the Gulf.

"I was just telling what the newspaper said, not what I said."

"You changed the story."

"Let's say that I found inaccuracies."

"How?"

"At first, I read everything I could find at the public library. From the very beginning, I found that things didn't add up."

"With the newspaper article?"

"With everything. I became very excited when I discovered many of the histories conflicting with each other."

"You laid all that on The Society?"

"I wrote them a letter, said I had new information about Jean Lafitte. I asked for a hearing."

"Did they give it to you?"

Edward nodded. "But I think they only did it because of my name."

"I thought you weren't famous."

"I wasn't. But the name Edward Livingston was."

"How come?"

"Edward Livingston was Lafitte's lawyer at the beginning of the nineteenth century. No relation."

"So they gave you a hearing. How'd it go?"

"Terrible. I met the toughest, meanest son-of-a-butcher that I had ever encountered."

CHAPTER 5
The Lafitte Society
Saint Louis, Missouri
February 6, 1929

Henry Stratmeyer crouched like a halfback waiting for the scrimmage whistle.

"Gentlemen." Edward avoided a direct look into the faces of the Society members ringed about the conference table, most certainly the halfback's. Edward's collar was too tight and he suffered an itch in the most unmentionable of places, but he nevertheless opened his presentation with precisely his carefully planned statement.

"There exists a considerable body of evidence to support the theory that the pirate we know as Jean Lafitte was in fact two people."

The crouching halfback didn't stir, but his quick smirk was as malicious and subtle as the blow of a sledge hammer.

Edward sensed the quiet rebellion in the room. Although he had prepared himself for the reaction, his spine stiffened to his tightened sphincter, his collar tightened, and the urgency of the itch intensified.

A streetcar clattered along Olive Street at that moment. In St. Louis, just as in New Orleans, conversation ceased until the rumbling subsided. It provided a perfect rhetorical pause, but it also gave the anticipated opposition time to gather its thoughts.

The instant that the rumble of the streetcar receded sufficiently to allow conversation again, Stratmeyer uncoiled himself and made his move. "We make a lot of baloney here in Saint Louis," Stratmeyer said, his shining bald head shaking as he spoke. "Some of it's good baloney. Some of it's bad baloney. But I've never heard baloney as bad as this."

Characteristic of the local inhabitants, he pronounced the "Saint" in Saint Louis as if it were spelled "Sent." Edward watched the man's hands. They flexed on the table top as he spoke, calling attention to heavy fingernails that were cornered instead of rounded as if he might have trimmed them with a meat ax.

Stratmeyer wasn't finished. His voice droned on like the tolling of a cracked bell. "We do not consider newspaper articles in this Society. Our business is restricted to original research. As a lawyer, you of all people should be aware of the lack of responsibility by the press. The idea that there were two Jean Lafittes is patently absurd."

"There's nothing in the newspaper about two Lafittes."

"That only shows you're heaping absurdity on absurdity. The newspaper article's bad enough." Stratmeyer bored on. "For example, the newspaper refers to 'an ancient chest of faded documents.'" He jabbed a crusty fingernail at the issue of *The New Orleans States*. "A chest of documents that cannot be made public." The malicious grin broadened, folding his cheeks like old parchment. "Proof, if proof exists, is in that chest."

"I'm well aware that—"

"When you find the chest, if there is a chest, you might be able to build a case."

"I—"

"Did you talk to the reporter?"

"I—"

Stratmeyer's voice rattled again, not waiting for a response. "Then you come along with this ... wild tale about two Jean Lafittes!" His words echoed in the panelled room. "Do you have any factual evidence? Or is everything you have rumor? Hearsay? Circumstantial?"

Edward grew exasperated and looked to the chairman to establish a proper procedural order. Was this how they ran meetings in St. Louis?

The green chair to which he had been assigned at the commencement of the meeting, identical to all the others, was at the foot of the table, cautiously distant from the nearest of the members. His was the only place not equipped with pencil and pad and glass of water, warning him that his position with the group was uncertain at best.

In the interest of economy, he had taken an upper berth on the Pullman, a mistake he would not make again. Sometime during the night, his suit had fallen from its insecure hanger and he had inadvertently slept on it. After he emerged from Union Station and stood awaiting a streetcar, wet St. Louis snow accumulated and melted on his shoulders. By the time he finally appeared before the Society, he looked like a hobo and smelled like a wet dog.

Edward felt his fury rise. His knees held rigid and his palms dried. Even as the chairman reached for his gavel, Edward moved in. "Sir," he crackled directly at Stratmeyer's shining skull. "Are you a lawyer?"

"No. But—"

Edward employed Stratmeyer's own tactic of interruption. "If you were a lawyer," he said in his best Clarence Darrow style, "you would realize first that all testimony is hearsay if the declarants are dead. In this case, which transpired well over a hundred years ago, there is no question but that witnesses are no longer among us. In the second place, since witnesses from that time no longer roam the earth, all evidence becomes circumstantial. If you were a lawyer, you would also know that, when hearsay evidence can be taken with reasonable confidence of its accuracy, such hearsay will be accepted as evidence in the court, and the jury may consider it."

Stratmeyer clenched his hands into fists, but Edward roared on. "I realize," he said, pacing to the other end of the room, "that this is no court of law. But, if it were indeed a court of law, the testimony I am about to give, if given the opportunity, would be fully acceptable."

Edward paused for breath and looked about at the members who had remained silent through the exchange with Stratmeyer. He was gratified that he had done some checking about the Society and its members, for it appeared that he might have some allies. One that he pegged, Professor Hunt from Washington University, was smiling, attentive.

But Stratmeyer represented the principal opposition, and could not be ignored. Stratmeyer sat now with his lips firmly clenched. Edward knew Stratmeyer to be a butcher from south St. Louis. His references to balony were consistent with his character—as were his fingernail.

Edward tipped his head back. He squinted his eyes almost closed and continued his short course in evidence. "Circumstantial evidence must be sifted through. Some of the chaff may be dismissed, for it may either be puffery or inconsequential. However, what remains must be closely scrutinized. Any information that cannot be disproven must be set aside. Later, if that information is shown to be important, it will be brought forward and sifted again. Since there exists only evidence that is circumstantial, it must then be sorted again until its grain is so fine that it is irrefutable. The infinitely greater sin is to reject evidence merely because it runs contrary to one's preconceived beliefs. For only then will justice not be served."

Stratmeyer's eyes were squeezed tightly shut.

Edward gathered himself. "I have studied the matter thoroughly. Although the evidence is limited, it can lead to only one conclusion: there could not merely have been one Jean Lafitte, there had to be two."

Stratmeyer's eyes were still clenched shut. "Did the two of them exist at the same time? Or—one after the other?"

"The two Jean Lafittes—as we know them historically, at least—existed one after the other."

"And when, might I ask, did this magic transformation take place?" Stratmeyer asked.

"At the close of the War of Eighteen Twelve. Right after the Battle of New Orleans."

"I move to adjourn." Stratmeyer raised his hand high and looked to the chairman.

"Mr. Stratmeyer," Rossiter answered, "you are out of order."

The butcher still held his hand up high, rutted fingernails and all. "Mr. Chairman, we are wasting our time with this charade."

Edward's knees began a renewed quiver. To conceal his

nervousness, he strode to the window and stared out while the Society argued with itself. Thus far, he had tossed a teaser before the group as a fisherman might drop chum into the water to attract the fish. Then would come the superior bait, with a hook attached. When he arrived at the window he thrust a thumb into his vest pocket and whirled to face the group. "May I speak?" he asked the chairman.

Rossiter smiled. "Certainly, Mr. Livingston."

Edward toyed with the looping gold watch chain across his vest. He began a slow pace around the room. "Just a few points to demonstrate that history can be inconsistent, improbable, even. The newspaper article claims that Jean Lafitte is buried alongside the Bayou des Oises. Such conjecture is plausible, for, after all, he lived and worked in the vicinity of New Orleans."

Stratmeyer, he could see, was gathering himself to object. Edward held his palm straight out like a policeman directing traffic. "Bear with me for a moment. I am merely reviewing the question. What about Napoleon Bonaparte?" Edward pursed his lips and cocked his head to one side. "Not likely, you might think. Yet, consider that a large French settlement existed in the south of Louisiana. There were many Bonapartists among them. There was a constant cry to rescue him from St. Helena. Many things remain in New Orleans to this day that honor Napoleon. There is the Napoleon house, where he was to live after the rescue. There is a death mask in the museum. But let me put Napoleon to the side, if I may, for the moment.

"What about the third body—that of John Paul Jones? Isn't the possibility that he, too, is buried beside the Bayou des Oises stretching things a bit too far?"

The eyes of the Society followed Edward as he roved. He

swelled his chest with confidence. His case was coming back on course, in accordance with his preconceived plan.

Stratmeyer lifted his hand once again. "There is no advantage in continuing," he said, his voice growing in volume. "This newspaper article is nothing but—"

Rossiter tapped his gavel. "We have granted Mr. Livingston an hour. He has traveled all the way up from New Orleans to brave our wintry weather." He smiled at Edward. "It is incumbent on us to hear him out."

"Why are we talking about Napoleon and John Paul Jones? Our purpose here is to study the life and times of Jean Lafitte!"

"The newspaper article, I believe, suggests a direct connection—"

"We don't consider newspaper articles! This is a waste of—"

Rossiter banged the gavel hard this time. "Mr. Stratmeyer! We are not considering the newspaper article alone. We are attempting to hear the testimony of Mr. Livingston."

"Point of order!" Stratmeyer still had his hand in the air.

"It's possible," Rossiter said to Stratmeyer, waggling the handle of his gavel like a cross school teacher, "that others present are not of your conviction."

"That's why we need a vote." Stratmeyer flexed the fingers on his upheld hand.

"You're out of order." The gavel tapped on the table. "Mr. Livingston, you may proceed."

The Society's secretary lifted his head from his notes as Stratmeyer begrudgingly lowered his hand. The secretary faced Rossiter. "Does all that go into the minutes?"

The chairman nodded. "I would think it advisable, Mr. Choteau. Did you miss any of it?"

Choteau glared at him for even the suggestion that he might not have recorded any word spoken in the room.

Rossiter smiled. "Mr. Livingston?"

Edward nodded at the chairman. "We were asking, if I recall correctly," he said, stealing an admonishing glance at
Stratmeyer, "why John Paul Jones? Why not Benjamin Franklin?
Why not John Hancock? George Washington? Were they not
heroes of the American Revolution? Why John Paul Jones? The
old legend known in the swamps and reported in detail by the
newspaper is so far-fetched, so unlikely, that it must be granted
some degree of validity simply because it is so absurd."

He had gone too far. Stratmeyer stirred, creaking his chair.
"Are you trying to tell us that, simply because the tale is so
ridiculous, it must be true?"

A thin creature chimed in with a high squeaky voice that
demanded attention simply because it was so pitiful. He spoke
directly to Edward. "The fact that the story is absurd could
hardly be considered academic proof."

Stratmeyer spun to him. "Thank you, Reverend Jordan."

Ah. That's who the man was. It was amazing that a minister, a man whose occupation relied so heavily on his voice
should have such a hesitant, unpowered delivery.

Edward bowed his head, as if he had notes written on his
shoes. "In Egypt, the pyramids exist. We know they exist. Yet,
we have never been able to determine how they were built. At
the time of construction, man had not yet invented bronze.
The workers had only soft copper to use for tools; tools too
soft to work the stone. They had not yet invented the wheel.
How were the pyramids built?" He lifted his face to the group.
"Yet, we know that they were indeed built, for they exist. But
the Hanging Gardens of Babylon do not exist. We read about
them, but have never seen them. Therefore, some among us
may doubt that they ever existed at all. But we must say, in all

probability, that the Hanging Gardens did exist, must we not? Or were they simply the figment of a romantic's imagination?"

The Reverend looked puzzled, uncertain. But he nodded, as if he accepted the analogy. Edward folded both hands behind his back and paced the room like a tourist in a museum.

"The newspaper article states that Jean Lafitte was born near New Orleans. That alone is upsetting to those who believe, for whatever strange reason, that he was born in France. Nevertheless, the French position is every bit as circumstantial as is the New Orleans one. On the face of it, there is no reason to believe one over the other. There is also a statement in the newspaper that Lafitte was the illegitimate nephew of John Paul Jones."

Several of the members shifted their positions at that remark, re-crossing their feet, moving their hands, wrinkling their faces. Edward recognized the body movements of disbelief. He changed his manner to a soft, instructive tone.

"Is it so impossible for Lafitte to have been born in New Orleans?" He halted his pacing for emphasis. "Let us back up to John Paul Jones. John Paul, which was actually his original name, had a brother named William, who was a tailor in Fredericksburg, Virginia. Now, Fredericksburg is a seaport, and is but a hundred miles from Williamsburg, not a far distance, even in colonial times. Brother William traveled on some occasions to Williamsburg. Not only was Williamsburg the capitol of the colony, but it was the center of trading activity, which tailors visited in search of fine imported English wool for their clients."

Stratmeyer could keep himself bottled no longer. "How did you come by these tidbits? You have proof, I suppose? Not that it matters."

Edward spun to him. "Original research, Mr. Stratmeyer. Exactly what you insist on."

"I don't see it."

"It's here. In my briefcase. Copies of documents from the library at Williamsburg, and from the museum at Fredericksburg, which I collected with my own hands. Would you like to see them now?"

Rossiter glanced at his watch. "That won't be necessary at this time, Mr. Livingston. You may proceed."

Edward resumed his pacing. After a very long pause effected to indicate he needed time to collect his interrupted thoughts, he continued. "The French had been emigrating to their colony Acadia, in what is now a part of Canada. In seventeen thirteen, at the end of the War of the Spanish Succession, France ceded this colony to Great Britain; it became Nova Scotia, New Brunswick, and Prince Edward Island. The British began to ease out the French settlers; they called it the Expulsion of Seventeen Fifty-five. It was called by the French '*Le Grand Derangement.*' Many of the settlers were herded onto ships and transported to English colonies that lay to the south, from Massachusetts to South Carolina. One shipment was sent to Virginia. The governor of Virginia would not accept these refugees. He detained them in camps until seventeen sixty-three. Comes now," Edward said, turning to Stratmeyer with half-closed eyes, "one William Paul of Fredericksburg. This handsome, well-dressed tailor sought companionship. A Scot from Kirkcudbrightshire, he spoke with a most pleasing accent. In the camps, he finds a pretty French maid that he takes a liking to. A maid cold, hungry and abandoned by her nation of birth. Seeking surcease from her torture, she eyes this glib local. Renewed hope abounds. She dallies with him, as they say."

Stratmeyer muttered but made no move.

"During the course of their dalliance, she becomes impregnated. However, her hopes for a continued alliance are at once dashed. Her courtier disappears, as courtiers so often do. She finds herself abandoned. She staggers back to her lonely tented cot by the harbor."

Edward saw the Reverend Jordan's lips working.

"Word of the Acadians' plight eventually reached the ear of Louis the Fifteenth, then King of France. He refused to sign the treaty ending the Seven Years' War until the English agreed to deliver the survivors of these camps into his personal care. Accordingly, the Virginia group was repatriated to various French coastal seaports. And it is thusly," Edward continued grandly, "that the legend of Jean Lafitte quite literally is born in New Orleans."

Stratmeyer grinned. "And what year would that be?"

"It was seventeen sixty-four."

Stratmeyer made quick notes on the pad of paper before him. "I don't suppose you have a birth certificate?"

"A fire struck New Orleans on March twenty-first, seventeen eighty-eight that destroyed over eight hundred buildings, including the cathedral where the records of birth were kept."

"A lucky break," Stratmeyer said almost before Edward had finished. He tapped the pad of paper with his pencil. "If your story were true, Lafitte would have been too old—"

"You forget." Edward took great pleasure in interrupting him. "There were two Jean Lafittes."

Edward reveled in the silence.

At last, Rossiter spoke, in a soft, respectful voice. "Mr. Livingston, do you have anything more at this time?"

"Much more, Mr. Chairman. This is but the beginning."

Rossiter fingered his gavel. "I'm afraid your time is up. If the Society pleases, you may be contacted when next an opening appears on the agenda."

It was not the time to object. "Thank you, Mr. Chairman." Edward bowed to the group and gathered up his briefcase. He noted that they busied themselves with pencils and papers and glasses of water and avoided looking at him. Like a jury who has found the defendant guilty.

CHAPTER 6
New Orleans, Louisiana
February 6, 1993, 2:30 PM

"It doesn't sound like you did so good." Mickey strolled across the study, his devil-may-care gait and bounding knees again threatening the piles of books.

Edward leaned back in the padded chair. Was Mickey at all interested? Or was this second effort to be as frustrating as the first? He slid away his spectacles and closed his eyes.

"You all right, grandpa?" Edward opened his eyes. Mickey leaned over the desk. "You okay?" he repeated.

"Fine." Edward replaced his glasses.

"Maybe you need to take a nap. Because of the funeral, and all."

There were no melancholy thoughts about the funeral, no regrets. It was, after all, a blessing. Even Agnes had looked forward to the end of her suffering from the cancer. She had been so near to dying for so long that the event, when it had at last occurred, was virtually undetectable. The funeral was a celebration of life, not a mourning of death.

"I'd rather go on with our discussion." The funeral was finished, behind him. Time to move on.

"About the Society? I'd think you'd want to forget about it. Did you ever get to any more meetings?" Mickey straightened. One knee began to beat time with that mysterious drum again.

"Oh, yes. Many more."

"Who were those people, anyhow? You said one was a minister." Mickey walked casually to stand before the baptismal font.

"They were just ... some people ... interested in the life of Jean Lafitte."

"The pirate who'll never die."

"He wasn't a pirate, actually."

"So what was he?"

"A smuggler."

"Then why does everybody call him a pirate?"

"People in New Orleans prefer their history to be romantic. They like pirates. Not smugglers."

"I thought Lafitte captured ships. Doesn't that make him a pirate?"

"Not if it's done as privateering. Privateering is done under the flag of a consenting government. There's a thin line of difference, but privateering is legal."

"Why is this thing here, anyway?" Mickey leaned to peer closely at the font, hands on his hips. "Does it have something to do with Lafitte?"

"He was baptized in it."

"Really?"

"I can't prove it. Not yet, anyway; maybe I never will. In New Orleans, everything and anything was associated somehow with Jean Lafitte, like the stories that George Washington slept in every bed north of Virginia."

"It came from France, then."

"No. I told you. Get out of your mind that Jean Lafitte was born in France, whatever they said in school. That font came from the St. Louis Cathedral right here in New Orleans."

"So why do they say that Jean Lafitte was born in France?"

"Until very recently, that's what everyone thought. Now we know that he was born in Haiti. At least, the Jean Lafitte everybody knows and loves."

"He was born in Haiti and baptized in New Orleans?"

"No. The Jean Lafitte born in Haiti wasn't baptized in this font."

"Right. There were two Jean Lafittes, you said. The other one who was baptized in the font."

Edward prodded himself to his feet with the cane. "Jean Paul. Born in New Orleans."

"How'd you figure that out, anyway?"

"Very early in the course of my investigation," Edward said slowly, "I decided that there had to be two. If not, the one had to be schizophrenic. I couldn't convince myself that he had a dual personality, so I started with the premise that he was actually two people." He paused to give Mickey time to react. "On close study, I found two very distinct personalities. One was clever, organized, disciplined. The other was the opposite: unruly, disordered, clearly undisciplined." He studied Mickey's face. "Rebellious," he added, recalling Charleton and his ponytail. Edward risked more. "The one accomplished great things. The other, only mayhem."

He peered through the wavy window glass to Audubon Park. It rained heavily now. The girl and the dog had gone. Wet Spanish Moss on the trees sagged the branches almost to the ground.

Mickey came up to stand beside him. "I can see why The

Society had such a hard time with that. Could you really prove it all?"

"A good lawyer can prove anything."

"So how did this ... new Lafitte get together with John Paul Jones?"

"He wasn't Lafitte at that point. His name was Paul—Jean Paul, after his father."

"I thought his father's name was Jones."

"The family name was Paul. The 'Jones' in 'John Paul Jones' was added after."

"Why?"

"Nobody's sure. There are lots of stories. It's one of those historical footnotes, largely immaterial. It probably occurred in seventeen seventy-three, when John Paul was accused of killing a seaman in the West Indies. Maybe he changed his name to avoid prosecution. It's not one of the details that historians like to dwell on. The reason for the name change was 'lost in the mists of history,' as they put it."

"Like some of yours."

"Perhaps."

It was a good point. Too bad he hadn't thought of it during one of the sessions before The Society.

"Anyway. Were you sure his name was Jean?"

"Not actually, but the name was highly probable."

"Why?"

"Analytical reasons. William might have boasted to his girlfriend about his brother, who was named John. He might have said John was a great sea captain, although he was only sixteen at the time. She was French, you will recall. She might have been inclined to name her son 'Jean,' which is, after all, the French version of 'John.'"

Mickey nodded, as if at least that much could be accepted. "How'd you get him on the boat with his uncle?"

Edward squinted his eyes almost closed. "The Cajuns—Acadians—were relocated to Louisiana. The weather was hot and muggy, there were swamps and alligators and mosquitoes. Not at all like their native France, and certainly not like Nova Scotia. Jean's mother wanted to go back to France. She had an illegitimate child to raise. Prospects were bleak for marriage. The settlers in the new area were busy with their own lives, their own problems. There might have been relatives in France that could assist if she returned to her native land. A lot of ships moved back and forth in those days, supplying the colony of Louisiana from the mother country. She found passage on one of them. As could be seen from her willingness to consort with the tailor from Fredericksburg, it is not impossible to imagine that she bought passage from an accommodating captain."

"Any proof of all that?"

"No more than historians can prove the reason John Paul changed his name to John Paul Jones."

Mickey appeared to accept that explanation, as well. "So now, Jean Paul is in France. Where is John Paul Jones?"

Edward was happily in his element and delighted with Mickey's question. "The French were our allies in the Revolutionary War. They hated the British as much as we did, and promised to give Jones a large vessel and a squadron of ships so he could make a nuisance along the British coast. He went to L'Orient to pick up the ships, but they weren't ready. In fact, there were no ships for him at all. He wrote a letter to King Louis the Sixteenth. After that, things started to move. The authorities found a rotten East Indiaman that was such a poor sailer nobody wanted her. Jones took the old tub because it was all he could get. He still had to fit her out, and he went all over France doing it, taking anything he could get. The biggest problem was the guns. The French wouldn't give up any of their good stuff, just the junk.

"Fortunately for our side, some of that junk proved to be extremely valuable. One of the cannons was an old breech-loader. Without that breech-loader, Jones might never have become known as 'The Father of the American Navy.' And we might very well have lost the war."

"Breech-loader?" Mickey glanced at the model cannon on the mantel. "Was that something good? I thought you said he got junk."

"The French thought it was junk. But breech-loaders were very handy on board ship, for they could be fired much more rapidly than muzzle loaders. After each firing of a muzzle-loader, it had to be run inboard, swabbed, reloaded, run back out. The breech-loader avoided all that, for it could remain in place while being re-loaded. About like the difference between a single-shot rifle and an automatic."

"Doesn't sound like junk."

"It wasn't. But breech-loaders weren't highly thought of, which is why the French gave it to him. There were problems with the breech; they often exploded or leaked hot gases into the faces of the gunners. In those days, armorers couldn't manufacture the precise fittings that they were capable of later."

"But this one was a good one. It didn't leak, I guess."

"The facts bear that out. The breech-loader had an additional, very important advantage, in that it was much more accurate than a muzzle-loader. Instead of a ball rolling up the muzzle and flying off in whatever direction it happened to bounce as it left the bore, it tended to fire straight and true."

"I can imagine what Stratmeyer thought of your breech-loader thing."

Edward smiled, remembering. "The newspaper articles said that Jean Lafitte invented the breech-loader. The reporter hadn't done proper research, for it had actually been invented centuries before."

"So Jones got this fancy gun. How did Jean Paul get on the boat?"

"The boat," Edward responded firmly, "was christened *BonHomme Richard*, after Benjamin Franklin's book. Jones also needed a crew. When a fresh-faced lad of fifteen applied for a position as a powder boy, Jones took him on."

"Especially since the lad was his nephew."

"He wasn't aware of that, probably. He later denied that he had a nephew on board, although there exists evidence to the contrary."

"What evidence?"

"*Richard*'s roster, for one thing. I provided a copy to the Society."

"And Jean Paul was on it?"

"He was listed as Mark Paul."

"Why didn't he use his real name?"

"He wouldn't have wanted the captain to know. As I've said, 'Jean' was the same as 'John.' It wouldn't do to have a powder boy with the same name as the captain. You will recall that the captain's name wasn't really Jones."

"Stratmeyer must have been out of his gourd."

"It was a tough push. I decided that I had to put on a performance, become an actor. I felt that I had to present a scene so vivid that I would surround them with it, immerse them in it, make them feel part of it. I had nothing to lose. It was," Edward grinned, his head back and his eyes squinted shut, "a stellar performance. It was so good that I felt I was actually on board *BonHomme Richard* myself."

CHAPTER 7
Flamborough Head, England
September 23, 1779

RESUMPTION OF PRES.
by Edw. Livingston, Esq.,
FEBRUARY 6, 1930

The throbbing in Jean Paul's ears was unceasing, unrelenting, punctuated dully by the booming of cannon, the screaming shouts of the men, the agonized shrieks of the wounded. They sounded so indistinct, so far away. Flames licked through the acrid smoke on the gun deck. Jean knew that however tired he might be, he must escape the smoky ruin. Head down, he struggled to his feet and found the ladder to the decks above. He emerged onto the waist of the ship into another version of hell.

As he stepped into the twilight, *Serapis* thundered yet another broadside. *BonHomme Richard* shuddered from the impact. Overhead, grapeshot whistled through the canopy of sails, smacking into masts, crippling yardarms, cutting braces that slithered downward and slapped on the deck like wounded snakes. Head down, he sobbed against the ladder as a new flurry of grapeshot whirred over the quarterdeck and sliced into a huddled group of marines.

Pallas was far away from the fight, just visible in the gathering darkness. More than a mile distant, she sailed about as if on an evening's pleasure excursion. Even more puzzling, *Alliance* was nowhere to be seen.

Jean Paul felt *Richard* list slightly and lose way, backing her topsails. *Serapis*, that enormous black and yellow bumblebee, stood close on the starboard. She appeared untouched by *Richard*'s first broadside and most certainly unmarked by the futile second. Her sails filled partially from a slight southerly breeze and she pulled ahead, causing all guns on both sides to fall silent for lack of target.

He looked to the quarterdeck where Captain Jones stood, Sailing Master Stacey at his side. The helmsman spun the wheel and *Richard* slowly swung her bow to the right. Her topsails filled and she moved ahead, crunching into the port quarter of *Serapis* with the grinding sound of tortured wood. The clatter of muskets and the popping of grenades resumed from both sides.

Richard's topsails backed and she dropped clear of her enemy. A puff of wind filled the sails of *Serapis* and she veered right to attempt the deadly raking position. Another cannonade flashed from both gundecks at once when her guns came to bear.

Richard's topsails filled and she chased after her tormentor, forcing the cannon to fall silent when they faced only the open sea. Again the two ships collided with a force that would have tumbled Jean from his feet but for his grip on the ladder. Muskets clattered and grenades spat until Captain Jones ordered his sails backed to haul *Richard* off astern.

The two ships maneuvered silently, neither in a position for firing. A gunner scampered up the ladder, forcing Jean brusquely aside. He ran to the Captain. Jean saw Jones nod, then the man trotted back to the ladder and disappeared below. The remainder of the old eighteens would be silenced lest others explode and sink the ship.

Richard curved about to come upon the portside of *Serapis*, now but a hundred feet distant. Again the enemy guns flashed. Jean ducked his head under a rain of tackle and braces from overhead. The helmsman spun *Richard*'s wheel, sluggishly bringing her bow about, for the mainsail braces had been shot away. At the same moment, *Serapis* moved to the left, thrusting her jib boom over *Richard*'s poop deck to nestle in among the mizzen shrouds. Both ships trembled violently from the impact. The topmen held tight as the masts swayed wildly.

"We've got her now!" Jean heard Captain Jones shout, surprised that the roaring in his ears had lessened so he could distinguish the words. He saw the Captain grab a line from the jib of *Serapis* and take a turn around a cleat, tying her fast.

Serapis dropped her port anchor in an attempt to shake free from her foe, but the light wind swung the two ships around until her starboard anchor hooked stoutly into *Richard*. The two ships were bound together, side by side, bow to stern. The most dreadful cannonading began.

There was such noise that Jean again put his hands over his ears and bowed his head. *Serapis* had brought her fresh starboard guns into play. The mighty booming of her eighteens overwhelmed the puny blasting of *Richard*'s remaining twelves.

For fully an hour they pounded away at each other, two fighters locked in a deathly clinch. One was strong and powerful and decidedly superior. One weakened, slowly fading. On the quarterdeck, Purser Mease commanded *Richard*'s few puny nines, tiny swivel cannon capable of shot no more effective than hurled pebbles.

From time to time *Serapis* was hardly even visible through the clouds of yellow smoke that hung listlessly in the still air, lit only by the blasts of her mighty cannon.

Fires started. They blazed through the wreckage, up the tar-encrusted mast of *Richard*, sweeping even through her sagging sails. One by one, *Richard*'s twelves became silent, until only the mighty thunder of the eighteens of *Serapis* ruled the bloody sea.

A hail of grapeshot whistled past the quarterdeck, tearing out the flagstaff with its huge American ensign, dropping it over the stern into the wreckage-strewn water. One by one, the quarterdeck gunners fell, even Purser Mease, who writhed in the debris clutching his bloodied head.

Only Captain Jones remained upright on the quarterdeck. He strode to the portside and struggled with a small cannon that had so far been unused.

It was the French breech-loader. Nothing else remained.

That desperate act meant that the situation had become hopeless. Jean pushed away from the ladder and picked his way aft, cringing when a shadow appeared over his shoulder. The white sails of *Alliance* sailed close by *Richard*'s bow.

At last! Captain Landis had come to the rescue, nearly too late!

It was a false hope. A new hail of grapeshot rattled in from that direction. *Alliance* had fired a raking broadside, the most devastating of all, directly into her own flagship! Jean saw men twist and fall on *Richard*'s forecastle. His throat choked. He faced his captain, seeking explanation, but none was offered. Lieutenant Dale rushed up.

"Sir!" he shouted. "The entire battery of twelves is out of action!"

Captain Jones stared at his lieutenant's perspiring, exhausted face. Before he could reply, John Gunnison ran up and stood anxiously at Dale's side.

"Sir!" he exclaimed, his voice barely audible over the din of firing. "There's four feet of water below! The prisoners want release!"

Captain Jones sank onto a piece of shattered timber, his hand still resting on the breech-loader. He calmly ordered Lieutenant Dale to go below and take charge of the pumps and assist with the plugging of shot-holes. "There's little you can do here," he said.

A young sailor appeared before him, eyes wide with fear. "For God's sake, captain!" the sailor shouted. "Why don't you strike?"

Jones stared up with a calm eye. "I will never strike," he said. "I will sink first." With that, he pushed himself to his feet and left the quarterdeck.

Jean was sick with fear, for the battle was lost. He wondered what held *Richard* together. Nearly the entire starboard side of the ship had been demolished, exposing to view the jumbled twelves each time *Serapis* flashed her thunder. Enemy shot had so torn *Richard* apart that they had actually blown out the other side. He could see balls from *Serapis* splash into the sea some hundred yards beyond her portside, having passed through the shambles and touched nothing. Flames licked everywhere, even smouldering the topsails. Her stern was smashed to pieces. The quarterdeck sagged alarmingly and appeared to be in imminent danger of collapsing entirely. He leaned over the shattered stern rail. The rudder hung askew below him, hanging but from a single pintle, ready to drop off. The flag had disappeared. Three hours of pummeling had reduced *Richard* to a mass of blazing splinters, kept afloat by God only knew what.

Through the waves of smoke, he dimly saw his captain on the forecastle, collecting a cluster of marines, perhaps to attempt the ultimate desperate act, that of boarding the enemy.

A white shadow reappeared. *Alliance* had returned. Again Landis boomed his guns at *Richard*, smashing in her port quarter. *Alliance* curved away, but was not yet through. Once more she returned, and smashed her cannons at the marines on the forecastle. Half the men went down and the rest scattered for protection into the waist of the ship.

Miraculously, Captain Jones was still on his feet, apparently untouched. But the boarding party, *Richard*'s final hope, existed no more.

Jones descended the ladder from the forecastle and picked his way across the deck. Men appeared from everywhere, running, waving their arms; the English prisoners had escaped. They scrambled onto the deck, shouting "Quarter! Quarter!"

Jones ignored them but halted midships when he saw one of his own gunners, accompanied by carpenter Gunnison, wave a lantern over the side and scream "Quarter!" Jones withdrew a pistol from his belt and took aim at the gunner, but the weapon either misfired or was empty. He grasped the pistol by the barrel and flung it at the gunner, toppling the man to the deck, the lantern into the sea.

A voice came from *Serapis*, fortified by a speaking trumpet. "Sir," said the voice. "Do you ask for quarter?"

Captain Jones bounded to the quarterdeck and stood beside Jean. "No, sir," he shouted. "I do not!" Then he lifted his chin and bellowed even louder: "I HAVE NOT YET BEGUN TO FIGHT!"

Richard's cannon had met with little success, but her sharpshooting marines had done better. They lay about on the deck, hidden behind bulkheads and stanchions, slowly eliminating the fighting men in *Serapis'* tops. Finally, only one of the enemy's snipers remained, then that one too was hit, and his shadow crumpled and fell. The sound of musketry all but ceased. A sailor from *Richard* slid along a yardarm, carrying with him a canvas bucket full of grenades. The watchers on *Richard* saw the sputtering fuses drop from his hand, then pop on the enemy deck. At the last, they saw a grenade disappear into an open hatch, followed by a mighty roar from deep within *Serapis*.

Jean saw his captain smile for the first time on that fateful day. "Help me with that, lad," he said, gesturing toward the breech-loader mounted on the portside rail.

They tugged the gun up from its socket and struggled with it across the deck, finally dropping the swivel pin into an unused socket on the starboard rail.

"That crate," he said to Jean, indicating a long wooden box behind the mizzenmast.

Jean flung open the lid of the box. He saw in the flickering light that it was filled with cartridges not unlike those for the twelves, but smaller, and with the balls attached. He lugged one to his captain.

The breech-loader was of considerably different construction than the muzzle-loaders. More finely made, its thin tube was banded about with straps of heavy iron. Its cascabel was longer, as if that aiming device were more significant. The tube was open at the thickened end where the explosion took place. Jean slid the cartridge into the tube, not knowing what he was about.

His captain slipped a wedge-shaped slab of iron behind the cartridge and bent at once to sight along the tube. His right hand made a quick movement atop the piece and the little gun fired, making hardly a discernible sound through the booming of the eighteens from *Serapis*.

But the result was spectacular. A flash of explosion erupted at the base of the *Serapis'* mainmast. Exploding shot! The heavy timber, three feet thick, was badly splintered.

"Another!" Jones roared, already slipping out the wedge.

Jean spun to the crate and collided with Purser Mease, who stood with a bandage on his head and a cartridge in his hands.

"Faster!" Jones shouted.

The little gun never seemed to miss, either because of its remarkably accurate fire or because of the Captain's aim, or perhaps because of a combination of the two. The firing was extremely rapid, perhaps ten times faster than that of a muzzle-loader, Jean thought. In a quarter of an hour, they had nearly emptied the crate of its cartridges. The gun had become so hot from the firing that Mease removed the bandage from his head and placed it over the gun to protect Jones' fingers.

Serapis' mast weakened. Splinters smouldered from the explosive charges. The entire length trembled with each impact and visibly began to crack.

The voice from the deck of *Serapis* through the speaking trumpet was scarcely believable. "Sir!" it shouted. "I have struck!"

Jean stared at his uncle with awe.

Surely, he thought, John Paul Jones must be the greatest sea captain yet born.

RESP, SUB., G. Choteau, Sec.
FEBRUARY 6, 1930

CHAPTER 8
New Orleans, Louisiana
February 6, 1993, 2:58 PM

"How did you do that?" Mickey's jaw sagged.

"Do what?" Edward opened his eyes, a little surprised to

find himself seated at his desk in the familiar study with the familiar books in their cases and out of them, the familiar maps on the walls.

Mickey watched him intently. "Tell that story about the battle. Almost as if you had been there."

"I was there." Edward reached for his pipe. "Are you familiar," he asked, striking a match, then watching it until the flare subsided, "with *déjà vu?*"

"Yeah, I know that. That's when you think you've already been there. Almost as if you've already lived it. It happens with me sometimes."

"It happens with most everyone," Edward said. "It's French for 'already seen.' You feel that you've already experienced something. That you've already been there, as you said. The ability to experience *déjà vu* has never been explained. Yet it exists. Many aspects of the human mind are as yet not fully understood." He struck a match and grinned at Mickey while the flare subsided.

"So this was *déjà vu?*"

Edward shook his head. He puffed on the pipe, drawing the flame into the bowl. "It's a reverse of *déjà vu*. Instead of looking ahead, you look back. *A priori.*"

"What went on before."

Surprised, Edward wriggled his eyebrows. "You know the term?"

"I studied Latin at Carrollton. *Per angusta ad augusta.*"

"Through difficulties to honors."

"It was our class motto. I chose it."

The schools at Carrollton were better than Edward had given them credit for.

"Your literal translation is correct. The prior. From a legal standpoint, the term means something slightly different, but that doesn't matter. When some people experience it, they think it's reincarnation."

"I thought that's when you lived an earlier life, were born again."

"Same thing, whatever you call it. Most people don't think about *a priori*. General Patton's a good example. He was an avid student of military history. He studied old battles so much he actually thought he had fought in them, had lived an earlier life. But that's exactly what *a priori* is. Being there. Living it. It has to do with cause and effect. The root of any lawyer's attempt to reconstruct a case, to dwell so thoroughly on the circumstances that he actually transports himself into the minds of the subjects."

The relit pipe tasted as terrible as before. Edward gave it up, lay it back in its holder. "I was actually there, on board that ship. I smelled the sea. I felt the movement of the deck under my feet. I heard the booming of the guns. I saw the blood ..."

Mickey stared at his grandfather as if the old man had become senile

"Do you believe that?" Edward grinned.

"So. You actually saw them fire the breech-loader?"

Edward felt he had his grandson hooked. The temptation of the Pierce-Arrow had become academic.

"Like I said. I was there."

"What'd the Society think?"

"They liked it, I gathered. Anyway, I was able to provide absolute proof."

"What proof?"

"Legitimate historians agree that Jones started firing one of the nine-pounders himself, after his other guns had been silenced except for an occasional nine, and after most of his men had been put out of action. It is firmly established that he began firing the gun at ten p.m. Captain Pearson surrendered at ten-thirty."

"What does that prove?"

"It proves that the gun was a breech-loader. In seventeen seventy-nine, a muzzle-loader had a rate of fire of one ball every six minutes. A breech-loader, on the other hand, could fire a ball every two minutes. Faster, even, if the handlers felt a greater urgency. In a half hour, Jones could have fired a muzzle-loader only five times. He would have been able to fire a breech-loader fifteen times, at the minimum. And, because of the inherent inaccuracy of the muzzle-loaders, he probably would have missed the mast half the time if his gun had been of that type. After all, the mast was a relatively small target, only three feet in diameter at the base. That means he might have had hits on the mast only two or three times. A nine-pound ball would not have endangered such a solid, rounded timber with only three hits. They probably would have just bounced off, anyway. Fifteen hits, however, could have done considerable damage."

"Sounds like a pretty thin argument."

Edward shook his head. "Not so. All by itself, perhaps. But the argument is only one thread in an entire net of evidence that must be taken as a whole."

"Maybe the mast was hit before, by the big guns." Mickey was dug in. He had the makings of a Stratmeyer.

Again Edward shook his head. "Only one salvo came from *Richard's* eighteens before they blew up. And that battery was too low, barely above the water line. The twelves were on the deck above, but the ships were so close together that even those could not have elevated sufficiently to hit the mast. Analytically, there was no way that any of *Richard*'s big guns could have struck the mast."

"Didn't Jones ever fire the eighteens before this battle? To test them? Find out if they'd blow up?"

Edward shook his head. "The eighteens were so close to the waterline that the gunports couldn't be opened unless the seas were unusually calm, like at Flamborough Head. *Richard* would have been swamped."

"What about the nine-pounders? Couldn't they have damaged the mast of *Serapis* earlier in the battle?"

"The nine-pounders were used to clear sharpshooters from the deck. They were too busy to shoot at the mast, and wouldn't have been effective if they had. Analysis shows that it couldn't have happened as the historians prefer to think."

"You said some guy had crawled out on one of the yardarms and dropped a grenade into a hatch."

"That guy was a Scot named William Hamilton. Historians claim his action was the straw that broke the camel's back. They claim that his one grenade made Pearson give up."

"Not you, though."

"The grenade made a big bang because it exploded some English powder cartridges. But when Jones inspected *Serapis* after the battle, he found that the explosion hadn't done very much damage. *Serapis* was still a sound ship, he said. Twenty Englishmen were killed in that explosion, which wouldn't have much effect on a total crew size of three hundred and twenty five. Altogether, Pearson only lost a total of forty-nine men, including those killed by the grenade."

Mickey twisted his mouth doubtfully sideways.

"On the other hand," Edward said, "a hundred and fifty

Americans had been put out of action by that time. Out of a total of three hundred and twenty two. Jones had lost nearly half his men."

He waited for the next challenge.

Mickey folded his arms and looked away, at the gold medal over the fireplace. "So," he said. "*Serapis* was still in good shape. *Richard* was shot to pieces."

"Already sinking."

"And you think Pearson gave up because Jones shot down his mainmast."

"No. Some historians make that claim, but it's wrong. The mast didn't fall until after Pearson surrendered. In any case, the loss of the mainmast wouldn't have been a good enough reason to surrender. It may have been crippling, but not fatal. Ships frequently lost their masts, both in battles and in storms. Jury-rigged masts were common. Ships were equipped to deal with that."

"So you're saying that Pearson was chicken."

"Far from it. Pearson was no wimp. He had served in the Royal Navy for thirty years. He was described as 'cool and skillful.' He was so highly thought of by the Admiralty that he had been given one of their newest ships. Before the beginning of the battle, he nailed the Union Jack to the staff with his own hands and told his crew that he would never surrender. He had under his feet a capital ship, a new frigate, served by a well-disciplined crew. Only two miles off his own coast, he faced a rotten barge that was converted to a ship of war with inferior firepower whose main guns exploded. Her crew was a motley assortment that included eleven different nationalities."

"So you think," Mickey countered, apparently still unconvinced that history could be so easily overturned, "that the battle was won because of this puny little gun?"

At last. Edward grinned with relief. He had brought Mickey right down to the final stroke. In true Clarence Darrow fashion, he struggled to his feet, accentuating a rhetorical pause with motion.

"It wasn't the gun all by itself," he said, amused by the confusion on Mickey's face. "It was the awesome mystery of the unknown, the superb accuracy, the phenomenal rapidity of fire. Pearson must have felt like the Mongols when they first witnessed the power of gunpowder." Edward waved the cane grandly in the air. "Like the Afrikaans when they first saw a machine gun in action. The English, when the first V-one rockets streamed overhead. The Japanese, when the atomic bomb exploded at Hiroshima. It was rockets, jet engines, radar. It was a secret weapon. Man's greatest fear is that of the unknown."

He stood wavering, allowing the silence of the study to emphasize his great dramatic moment. Mickey, he thought, looked as impressed by the argument as Pearson must have been by the gun.

They stared each at the other for some moments before Mickey broke the lovely silence. "How come," he asked, "Jones never said anything about it afterward?"

Edward caned his way to the window. The sunlight was gone. The clouds had thickened over again, threatening more rain. "John Paul Jones," he said, speaking close to the window pane, "was a very vain man. He had won a great victory, and was not the sort to give credit to any man or any weapon. He wanted the history books to remember him as a man of valor, snatching victory from the jaws of defeat through sheer determination and superior seamanship. He wanted to become America's first admiral. He made only a brief mention of the battle in his writing, as if he preferred not to go into detail. And it was one of the most significant sea battles ever fought."

"You need to find the gun. To prove your story."

"It would be irrefutable proof. But the wreckage of *BonHomme Richard* is lost. If it is ever found, the history books will need some re-writing."

"*Richard* won the battle, but she sank."

"It's a unique historical fact that the ship which surrendered had destroyed and sunk the ship that conquered her."

"From what I recall from history, Jones didn't need the gun."

"The schoolboy's story. The story the patriots would have us believe. It sounds better if Jones won through sheer courage and determination. But it doesn't ring true."

"I like the schoolboy story."

"We can't be too naive. The historians have no good reason for Pearson's surrender. Although they are quick to speak of the might of England's 'Wall of Oak,' the invincibility of the Royal Navy and the hopelessness of the American situation, they provide no rational explanation for the victory. They claim that it was because Pearson's mainmast was in danger of falling, and if it did, one of the other American ships might have captured him."

"Makes sense."

"Does it? If the mast fell, and he couldn't maneuver properly because of it, couldn't he have surrendered upon being attacked, should an attack have occurred?"

"Did Pearson say anything about the gun afterward?"

"He might not have recognized it as a breech-loader. He did admit, however, that his mainmast had been the target of some remarkably accurate fire near the end of the battle."

"What happened to him? He must have been in a heap of trouble."

"They made him a knight."

"Even through he lost?"

"The British never admitted that Pearson lost. They only say that a great sea battle was fought off Flamborough Head. Since Pearson was made a knight afterward, it would appear obvious to the British schoolboys that the British ship won."

"And Jones really did say," Mickey asked, "'I HAVE NOT YET BEGUN TO FIGHT'?'"

"He might have, or he might not have. There wasn't anybody standing around to keep notes. He said something like that, probably. More than likely, the media changed it around later to make it fit a headline."

Edward heard Mickey get to his feet. After a moment, he appeared at the window, hands in his pockets. "I still haven't figured out," Mickey said, looking down at his grandfather, "where the medal is."

"We're nearly there," Edward replied. "But first," he said, grinning, "I have to tell you what happened when I attended the funeral of John Paul Jones."

CHAPTER 9

Paris, France
July 20, 1792

PRES. BY Edw. Livingston, Esq.
FEBRUARY 6, 1931

Jean Paul staggered to a halt. In the Rue de Tournon stood a hearse. All black, even its wheels, befitting its duty. The hearse had a genteel dignity once magnificent but now old, tired. Brass glinted dull in the sun. At the corners, worn black paint revealed weathered wood beneath.

Jean Paul leaned against the corner of a building at Rue St.-Sulpice, ignoring the filth of the building wall. He had arrived too late.

The conveyance came to life, jolting forward and back over the cobblestones, harness creaking and rattling each time one of its horses rebelled against the maddening flies.

The lone passenger rode with it, forward and back. Silent, uncomplaining.

Heat and stink hung in the tepid air like a deadly fog, vibrating in the waves of sun on the cobblestones. Paris reeked.

Jean Paul's clothing was idiotic for July. The long coat to his calves, tight weskit under, capturing perspiration, containing it in a soggy mass. On the front of the coat, rows of brass buttons almost too hot from the sun to touch. Stifling black boots to the knees. Traveling clothes. Goodbye clothes. Funeral clothes.

He loathed Paris, the filth and grime and flies, the heat and stink. Not like L'Orient—even the thought of the place brought to mind refreshing sea breezes, cool screeching of gulls, the clean nautical look of shops, the persistent masculine perfumes of oakum and yesterday's beer.

Paris was shoulder-to-shoulder buildings stacked six stories high, heaped higher even with mansards. Paris was uncountable boots and uncountable hooves pounding uncountable years on worn cobbles, grinding together garbage and manure until the filth had turned to cooking mush under the steaming sun. Paris was flies, swirling and buzzing and swarming, feasting on inescapable rot.

And hearses. And death.

A small detachment of grenadiers fretted in slovenly disarray before the hearse. Suddenly, a furious drum roll and the soldiers stiffened to sagging attention, muskets swaying across their shoulders, tricorn hats with tricolor cockades nodding. The drum slowed to a mournful cadence, stepping off the booted feet in ragged unison.

The hearse jerked forward, jolting from smooth cobble to smooth cobble behind the sharp clattering hooves of the four black horses, their sides glistening under the cloying sun. Then two carriages moved past, loaded with folk dressed in black costume with white jabot and ruffled cuffs, white lace handkerchiefs mopping at their foreheads.

Behind the carriages trudged a handful of mourners on foot, servants, apparently, judging by their dress. Two shopkeepers in plain black clothing; a few small boys, such as those that make a game of any procession; a sailor, clad in loose pantaloons and flowing shirt once white, limping over the uneven stones with great difficulty, his face flushed red from the sun.

Jean stared. The sailor had a mane of golden hair tied into a queue at the back of his neck. He trudged along in step with the beat of the drum, head down, ignoring the group of chattering boys he followed.

The sailor was Andrew Mason.

Jean Paul pushed himself from the shade of the building into the blast of sunlight, flinching when the heat rammed onto his shoulders like a heavy yoke. He fell into step beside his former shipmate.

Andrew made no acknowledgment. Not until the little procession crossed the wide Rue des Fosses St.-Germain did he speak. "Thought you was dead."

Jean Paul turned to the red face, surprised to find it still mottled with the freckles of youth. Was it all so long ago? Thirteen years. They had both been lads of sixteen then.

"And I, you," he said, the words thick in his throat.

They trudged in silence until the turn onto Rue Dauphine, where the rows of tall gray houses reverberated the tapping drum into a confusing chaos. Parisians stood respectfully on both sides of the street, watching in silence from forged iron balconies.

Andrew's mouth wrenched when the limping foot slipped on a loose cobble. "Thought I was dead, meself," he said. "Missed it all."

"Missed what?"

"The fight. Knocked me cold, when the guns blew."

"You were with the twelves?"

"Aye. And you?"

"The eighteens."

"Luckier'n me." Andrew tapped his deformed thigh and looked directly at Jean Paul for the first time.

Again, silence, except for the drum, the clattering hooves, the chattering boys. The procession wound across the Quai des Grands Augustins, past the monastery to the Seine. On the Pont-Neuf bridge, a great banner stretched: LA PATRIE EN DANGER.

"They got their own troubles now," Andrew said, nodding at the banner.

"Just like we did. A revolution."

"Which side you on?"

"No side. I'm getting out before it starts for real."

Andrew looked surprised. "Are you?" he asked. "Where you going?"

"America."

"Think the fightin's done there, do you?"

"Hope so. Don't want any more fighting."

"Flamborough did you in, did it?"

"All I'll ever need."

"Saw him just afore he died," Andrew said, abruptly chang-ing the subject. He had an easier time of it now, on the smoother surface of the bridge. "Face all yellow, couldn't hardly see his freckles." Andrew grinned, then sobered. "His middle so puffed up he couldn't button his weskit no more."

Jean Paul choked, unable to reply. Although the air felt cooler over the river and the sun was falling lower in the sky, his forehead still bubbled with perspiration. He drew his sleeve across his face, careful to avoid the brass buttons. "Did he—" Jean Paul said hesitantly, feeling the need to speak, "was his hair—"

"Hair still like allus," Andrew cut in. "Tied in the back, just like mine. Never turned gray, neither. His hair stayed the same—red brown—like the color of sunset at Flamborough."

The road rose slightly after crossing the bridge, and An-drew had some trouble with the grade. The small boys fell silent at last. The only sounds were the mournful cadence of the drum and the creaking of harness. Not until they reached the Porte St.-Martin did they speak again, during a halt for inspection by the customs guards at the city gateway.

"Did they," Jean Paul asked hesitantly, "take him to hospital?"

Andrew snorted, dragging his crooked foot over a slippery cobble.

"What about the American ambassador? Didn't he—"

"Ambassador weren't even there. Had a dinner party, they say."

"Is he ... here now?" Jean Paul gestured to the carriages ahead of them.

Andrew snorted again. "Another dinner party."

Again Jean Paul lost his ability to speak. How could the Americans—his Americans—show such a lack of concern over the death of their greatest hero?

The drum rolled, the harnesses creaked, the hooves clattered. The cortège was on its way again. The Rue St.-Martin became a country road, bordered only by a few scattered houses, gardens and vineyards. Right turn into a narrow road, then right again onto Rue Granges aux Belles. At the corner, a tiny cemetery, unkempt, overgrown with weeds.

"What is this place?" Jean Paul gasped.

Andrew's voice rumbled low. "Where they puts them ain't got no money."

Again, Jean Paul was unable to speak. They trudged through the weeds behind the carriages to an open grave.

"So," Andrew said, resting his weight on his good leg while the black-clad folk alighted from their carriages. "Where you been? Since I seen you last?"

Jean Paul watched the doors open at the rear of the hearse. "L'Orient."

"Sailing?"

Jean shook his head.

"What then?"

"*Un marchand*. Shipping firm, on the docks. I get sick at sea. You know that."

Andrew chuckled. They watched the coffin removal from the hearse while the mourners gathered around the grave.

"Who are these people?" Jean Paul asked.

"Frenchies, mostly. They paid for everything, I hear. Coffin and all."

Jean Paul turned to him, aghast. "You mean the American Legation—"

"Not a penny." They sidled closer to the pitiful few mourners gathered around the minister. The small boys had disappeared.

It was over. Only Andrew and Jean Paul remained in the gathering dusk, watching the pair of laborers finish filling in the grave. They mounded the excess dirt, then, with a quick glance at the two remaining mourners, threw their shovels over their shoulders and plodded back along the Rue de Recollets in the direction of Paris.

"I'll take him with me," Jean Paul said resolutely when they were alone.

"What?"

"I'll take him with me. To America."

"Why?" Andrew was round-eyed.

"It's where he belongs."

"You're crazy."

"Maybe. It's what I'm going to do, though."

"He's buried! How you going to—"

"I'll dig him up."

"How you going to get him to—"

"You forget. I work for a shipping company."

"It'll cost you—"

"They're giving me free passage to America. I don't think they'll mind if I take along a ... box."

Andrew kicked at the loose mound of dirt. "Well," he said. "The digging shouldn't be so bad, anyhow." He placed an arm around Jean Paul's shoulders. "I'll find some shovels. You find a wagon."

RESP. SUB., G. Choteau, Sec.

FEBRUARY 6, 1931

CHAPTER 10
The Lafitte Society
Saint Louis, Missouri
February 6, 1931

Stratmeyer was incredulous, and said so. "I submit that your story is wildly fictitious. You made it up."

Edward stood at the window overlooking the Mississippi. The river rolled brown and sluggish beyond the white snow-covered bank. Edward leaned forward, almost touching the cold pane with his forehead. "All of it, Mr. Stratmeyer?"

The man named Peter Steinbach spoke for the first time. "We're wasting our time here," he said, echoing Stratmeyer's frequent observations.

Even Rossiter had lost some of his composure. "Mr. Livingston," he said, "that was a very well-knit tale. But ... do you have any proof whatsoever?"

"Many proofs, your— Where would you like me to start?" Edward turned to Stratmeyer. "You indicated earlier that it could not have happened at all. I merely showed you that it could have happened."

"That doesn't prove anything."

"Prove? What's proof? Can we even prove that John Paul Jones died, for example?"

"Don't be ridiculous."

"Please, Mr. Stratmeyer. Indulge me for a moment. Can we?"

"There's a death certificate."

"Possibly. I haven't attempted to obtain a copy, should there be one."

Stratmeyer laughed. "So now you're going to tell us he hasn't died?"

Edward allowed himself a grin. "I felt there was no real need for that. I did obtain, however," he said, withdrawing a paper from his briefcase, "a copy of the burial certificate." He handed the paper to Stratmeyer. "Dated, as you will see, fifteen July, seventeen ninety-two. Attested by the Reverend Paul-Henri Marron, who officiated at the service. Also Major J.C. Mountflorence, the only representative present from the American legation. Also Colonel—"

"Enough." Stratmeyer slid the paper along the table back to Edward. "We have proof he was buried, if not dead." No one in the room laughed. "Unfortunately," he continued, "you have no such documentation for the rest of your story."

"What part," Edward asked carefully through tight lips, "of my story requires documentation?"

"All of it."

"Come now, Mr. Stratmeyer."

"All right. How do we know that this—Jean Paul, you call him—even attended the funeral?"

A small voice spoke out. Peter Steinbach again. The man had turned into a reservoir of courage. "Mr. Livingston," Steinbach sat hunched over his notepad as if his heavy glasses were not as strong as they should be, "I find," he said, dropping his pencil onto the table, "that a period of thirteen years ensued between the time of the Flamborough Head battle and the funeral of John Paul Jones. Yet, you give no accounting of the activities of Jean Paul during that period, except that he had been employed by a shipping company. Can you elaborate on it?"

"Mister ... Steinbach, is it?" Edward asked pleasantly.

The man nodded. Edward tried to avoid patronizing him.

"Little is known about the gap. History, however, is filled with such gaps; because such gaps exist does not mean that what remains should be dismissed. In time, the missing places might very well be filled as new information comes to light. Sometimes, the information does not appear. For example: little is known about the boyhood of Jesus Christ, but that doesn't deny his position as the Son of God, does it?"

Steinbach shook his head vigorously, dangerously jeopardizing the spectacles.

"Some of those gaps," Edward continued, "may never be filled. Yet, as with a contract, simply because one or more failings exist does not mean that the entire document must be discarded."

His gaze roved about the group, unavoidably patronizing now. But if Steinbach had accepted the argument, and if the majority of the Society seemed satisfied with the explanation, Stratmeyer did not. He pushed his nose hard to one side with a loud satisfying sniff before he spoke. "I do not find the story acceptable in the slightest, regardless of how well you acted it out. Do you have any proof that Jean Paul was at the funeral?"

The question was staggering, and marked a milestone. Stratmeyer had accepted the fact of Jean Paul, and was now merely questioning his appearance at the funeral of John Paul Jones. It was time to shift the focus of the offensive. Time to ease off.

"None whatsoever," Edward said carefully. "Jean Paul's presence at the funeral is conjecture on my part. There were former shipmates of Captain Jones at the funeral. Accepted historical accounts bear that out. The names of those individuals are not recorded. There is, however, no evidence to attest to the fact that he was *not* there."

Stratmeyer threw an arm over the back of his chair. "You have stated that this nephew—Jean Paul—served on board

BonHomme Richard. You have submitted to us a roster of the ship's crew, which did indicate that a powder boy with the name of Mark Paul served on her. However, I believe Captain Jones said elsewhere that no nephew of his was on board. As a matter of fact, I believe that Jones even denied that he had a nephew at all. How do you account for that?"

His tone had become cooperative, helpful. Edward guessed that he must proceed with caution. "John Paul Jones, it is well established, was very vain, a characteristic not uncommon among short people. He wanted no circumstance about him that could possibly sully his career. It stands to reason that he would not admit to an illegitimate nephew."

Stratmeyer, by way of emphasis, hung his head deeply against his upraised arm, so his voice came out muffled. "But you have no evidence that a nephew—illegitimate or not—was on board *BonHomme Richard.*"

Time to change course again, get tough. "What is it you require, Mr. Stratmeyer? Something like an affidavit? A sworn statement to a judge?"

Rossiter leaned forward in his chair, massaging the handle of his gavel. "There is no need to—"

"On the contrary, sir," Edward interjected. "It happens that I have precisely such a document." He forced himself to keep from smiling. It was time for his *coup de grâce* of the day. Slowly, ever so slowly, he walked to his place at the foot of the great walnut table, leading the eyes of the assemblage, which followed his every move. As casually as possible, he withdrew a paper from his briefcase. Just as casually, he fluttered it across the table to Stratmeyer.

"A copy of an affidavit. Taken before an English Justice of the Peace and attested to by the Mayor of Hull. Given by some of the English who were prisoners on board *BonHomme Richard* and released when it appeared the ship was in danger of sinking. Some swam to shore and the authorities took down their statements. The document states that a nephew of John Paul Jones served aboard his ship."

Stratmeyer picked up the paper and began to read.

Edward couldn't resist a rhetorical jab. "It is written in the old style, common during the period. The letter *S* appears as an *f*." He smiled. "It was the way of the language."

The group waited in silence until Stratmeyer had finished his reading. At last, he laid the paper on the table. "This proves nothing," he said. "It is no more than a statement by an English sailor. The fact that it is sworn carries no weight whatsoever."

"The document," Edward said for the benefit of the other members, and lifting his gaze to the ceiling as if in exasperation, "is a copy of a statement taken on the twenty-fourth of September, seventeen seventy-nine, by His Majesty's Justice of the Peace Humphrey Osbaldiston." Edward paused and strolled back to the window for dramatic emphasis. "The affidavit attests to the examination of seven seamen, including one Thomas Berry, an Englishman, who had served aboard the ship, as he called it, '*Le Bon Homme Richard*,' and had escaped to the shores of Flamborough Head after the battle.

"Included within the statement is an accurate account of the descriptions of the ships involved and their marauding journey from L'Orient around Ireland and Scotland, to the ill-fated battle off Flamborough Head."

"Some of it's baloney," Stratmeyer said. "Like about Jones' statement when Pearson called on him to surrender."

Edward whirled to face the group, all of whom were watching him closely.

"Berry describes the retort of John Paul Jones when the captain of *Serapis* called out for the American to strike." Edward couldn't help smiling. He removed his right thumb from the armhole of his vest and held his index finger dramatically high. "Berry stated that Jones replied: 'That he might if he could; for whenever the Devil was ready to take him, he would rather obey his summons, than to strike to anyone.'"

His finger still held high, Edward advanced on the group, smiling more broadly. "It is well," he said, "that such a cumbersome statement never became the motto of the United States Navy. And it only serves to show that Berry was methodical. After all, how do we really know that Jones ever said, 'I HAVE NOT YET BEGUN TO FIGHT'?"

"However," Edward went on, feeling the wind in his sails, "that is not the point. The point is that he said to his *nephew*," and he paused for effect, "'that damn his eyes he would not blow his brains out, but he would pepper his shins,' and actually had the barbarity to shoot at the lad's legs. Isn't that what it says, Mr. Stratmeyer?"

Stratmeyer glared. "That's what it says, all right. But why would Jones have shot at his nephew?"

Another milestone. Stratmeyer appeared to accept the fact that Jones had a nephew on board his ship.

Edward rehooked the thumb. "It is recorded that Jones raised his pistol and fired at a seaman who had screamed for quarter just as the battle looked most bleak. In the confusion of battle— and it is agreed by all that this was a most horrendous battle— it is entirely possible that a frightened seaman would not know the direction of his ire. In any case, the pistol misfired."

"And you expect us to accept this document as proof that Jones had a nephew. And that he was on board *BonHomme Richard*." The old butcher *wanted* to buy the story.

"You accepted the burial certificate, didn't you? As proof that Jones was buried in the cemetery at Paris? You asked for evidence, and I have provided it. I am unable to provide any living witnesses who served on the ship some hundred and fifty years ago. So I have provided the next best thing, as valid as the burial certificate. Perhaps more so. Even in a modern court of law, such a document as this serves as substantial proof of the facts. From a legal standpoint, it is given pedigree standing, the identical degree of acceptance as if the originator had stood in the dock and personally testified."

Stratmeyer slid the affidavit across the table to Rossiter. "Still," he said, "you have no such documentation that Jean Paul attended the funeral?"

Back to that. Edward felt that Stratmeyer hungered to believe. He allowed a smile. "France was, at the time of the funeral, in the midst of their Revolutionary War. It was very grand of the French to provide such service as they did provide for a foreigner. I do not think that we can disparage them for failing to keep track of the names of those that attended the funeral."

Stratmeyer nodded. The loose threads were beginning to make cloth.

"Mr. Stratmeyer." Edward slipped his thumbs under his vest and strode toward the window. "On the attendance at the funeral," he said courteously, "I merely countered your argument. You said, earlier, that certain things could not have happened—"

"I don't recall saying that."

"I am merely indicating to you that they could have."

"But it doesn't prove that Jean Paul dug up the body afterward."

"Not at this point. However, I will prove to you that the body of John Paul Jones did not long remain in the cemetery."

CHAPTER 11

New Orleans, Louisiana
February 6, 1993, 3:19 PM

The telephone rang a harsh intrusion. Edward let it ring a second time, then a third, before he lifted the heavy receiver.

"Hello?"

"Mickey there?"

It was Charleton. Edward heard the frenzied patter of a sports announcer in the background, sounds of laughter, a cheer. Charleton was calling from a sports bar.

"Yes. He's here."

"He's got to come home."

"Right now?"

"He's supposed to be at work."

Mickey stood at the window, peering across the street at the park.

"Do you want to talk to him?"

"Naw. Just tell him to come home."

"Maybe he should take the day off. Spend the night here."

"He'll lose his job."

"He has a good excuse."

A roar of cheering came over the line. The excited announcer raved about a home run. Or a touchdown. Or whatever.

"I didn't know about the funeral," Charleton said after the noise died a little. "I was up to Baton Rouge."

"What about the note? I sent a note."

"Didn't get it. Like I said, I was up to Baton Rouge. The job got rained out. I come home. That's when I seen the note. But it was too late then."

"It was your mother's—"

"I know it was my mother's funeral! There was nothing I could do. I'll just have to send some flowers."

Edward heard more cheering, the stomping of feet.

"Can't hear so good here," Charleton shouted. "Tell Mickey to come home. 'Bye." Then a click, peaceful quiet, a dial tone.

"Did you hear that?" Edward rattled the receiver back on its hook.

"Yeah." Mickey still looked out at the park.

"He was calling from a bar."

"Harvey's, I guess. It has the closest telephone."

"He doesn't like your being here, does he?"

"I guess not. I can't spend the night."

"Because you'll be in trouble with your father?"

"I got to get to work, too."

"You can call, get the day off."

"I'll lose my job."

"You have a good excuse."

Mickey sauntered away from the window. He stood before the desk breathing through his mouth.

"If you stay the night, you can look at the car in the morning."

"Guess I'll have to forget about the car."

"Forget about the riddle. You can have the car anyway."

"No. A deal's a deal."

"It's all right. I want you to have the car. Forget about locating the medal."

Mickey shifted his weight from one foot to the other. "Why is it so important today? About the riddle? Why can't we finish this some other time?"

Edward didn't trust himself to speak. He closed the file folder and busied himself with the pipe, then put it down, afraid he'd make a fool of himself because his hands shook so badly.

Mickey leaned against the desk. "How about next week, maybe?"

"It must be today. This afternoon."

"Why?"

"You'd better go. You can take the Ford. Keys are in the kitchen."

"Why does it have to be today?"

Edward toyed with the watch. "You're in too big a hurry."

"You can tell me why it has to be today. How long will that take?"

Everything was in such a rush. Agnes' passing, the arrangements with the hospital, with the undertaker. Notices to be prepared, mailed out.

"Five minutes."

"Let's have it, then." Mickey fell into the chair.

Five minutes. Edward gripped the watch.

"The Society has a meeting today," he began, working to keep his voice calm. "I was scheduled to appear. I should have called them, to tell them I couldn't attend, because of the funeral and all. But I didn't."

"Why not?"

"Everything just got too hectic. I decided to put calling off until today. Thought I'd do it this afternoon."

"So why don't you call? Right now?"

"Because ... things changed. Twice, today. Once in the morning. Once in the afternoon."

"What things?"

"The most important ... thing ... happened this afternoon. When I went out to Carrollton to pick you up, take you to the funeral. Actually, I went out to pick up both of you. You and your father. Your mother too, if she wanted to go. But your father and your mother weren't there. It boiled down to just you. And when we rode off, out of Carrollton to the funeral home, I changed my plans." Edward rolled himself back from the desk. "I'm not sure I can say this in five minutes."

Mickey waited, his mouth closed.

"I had a tough father. He was so tough that, in grade school, whenever I wrote about him, I always capitalized the word Father. The teachers constantly corrected me, but I did it anyway, because that's the way I felt about him. He chose everything for me. The college I would go to, the courses I would take. He chose my career. He set me up in practice with him, painted my name on the door. He chose my wife, even."

"That doesn't sound so bad. You were married for a long time."

"A long, long time." Edward sighed.

"And that thing about your career. It don't sound like he did so bad by you. Sounds like he just wanted to help you."

"I guess he did. But maybe he helped me too much. I was never able to do anything *I* wanted to do." A lifetime of drawing wills and deeds of trust was definitely not what he'd wanted to do, although such hum-drum work kept the cupboard charged.

"What'd you want to do?"

"I don't know. I was never able to find out. I was stuck with what he made me do. I vowed that I would never be that way with my own son. I'd let him do anything he wanted. It was easy then, because it was the new way of thinking. Permissiveness, they called it. Children should be allowed to develop their own personalities, all by themselves; it was right down my alley. That turned out to be a big mistake—I probably went too far, to an extreme. I ended up with a son that hated me. What was offered as permissiveness was taken as indifference."

"Dad always said you never cared about him much. But I don't think he hates you."

"Whatever the word, the result's the same. He never visits. He doesn't care. He didn't even go to his mother's funeral."

"That's not his fault. He didn't know about it."

"I sent a note."

"I know, but—"

"It doesn't matter. I dug myself into my work, such as it was, even if I despised it. The only thing that kept me going was the Lafitte case. Even there, I have to credit my father."

"I thought he died before the case started."

Edward nodded. "He did. Maybe that's a good thing, because if he'd been around, I probably never would have started it. What I mean about his keeping me going—I always felt he was watching over my shoulder, telling me I never finished anything I started. That's what kept me going, even though I wanted to give it up, many times.

"It took too long. Sometimes I felt like a man who starts to build a house all by himself without realizing how big a job it is. He gets sick and tired of it halfway through, and wishes he'd never started. Whenever that happened to me, I'd think of Father, standing at my shoulder and telling me I never finished anything. I didn't know that I'd become an old man before I got finished."

"You're not so old."

Edward tapped the face of the watch. "I'm just about at the end of my rope. I need somebody to take over for me." He grinned straight at Mickey. His hands covered the watch, as if that would stop the running of time.

Mickey shifted his lean body, creaking the chair. He looked away, obviously uncomfortable. "Why me?"

Edward felt his strength return, the second wind that lawyers get, even old lawyers. "Because you're my grandson. And I owe you for what I did to your father." *And for what your father's doing to you.*

"You don't owe me—"

Edward held up his hand. "And because I think you need something. Everybody does. Something to shoot for, a higher goal. Something to lift him above the mud— And ... because I think you can do it. I think you've got the guts and the courage to stand up to the Stratmeyers of the world for what you think is right."

There. It was said. After the long labor of his life, just when the final solution was at last placed in his hands by a benevolent God, this was the ultimate sacrifice he would make. But there was no finer reason. And no finer person.

Mickey sat with his hands on his knees, feet flat on the floor. "You think I can ... hack it?"

Edward relaxed. "I have every confidence." He reached for the telephone. "Shall I call them now? Tell them you'll do it?"

"How much time's left?"

Edward scanned the watch. "About two hours. I have to call before six."

"Why six?"

"That's when the Society adjourns."

"They'll kick you out if you don't call?"

"Probably. But I think they just might give me another chance if I tell them about the new evidence."

"What new evidence?"

"Your solution to the riddle."

"But I don't have a solution."

"Get on with it then," Edward said in a sing-song tease.

"Well." Mickey slapped both hands on his knees. "Can't hurt much to be any later than I already am. But what if I don't figure out where it is?"

"You'll figure it out." Edward pulled himself closer to the desk and flipped the folder open in delight.

CHAPTER 12
The Lafitte Society
Saint Louis, Missouri
February 6, 1934

The meeting gaveled to order with the pronouncement that Edward expected.

"I'm sorry," Chairman Rossiter said to Edward. "The Society has elected to hear you out at this session. However, as our letter to you indicated, you are on notice that this is to be your final appearance."

"Why?" In spite of his preparation for the moment, and in spite of his prepared statement, it was the best that Edward could falter out.

"The motion, adopted at our last meeting, reads that our credibility has been stretched to the breaking point."

"Is that all the motion says?"

"The motion itself is privileged information. We are under no obligation either to spell it out to you or to give you further consideration. We will, however, hear your presentation today. You must understand that this will be your final audience."

Edward reeled. What would Clarence Darrow have done? In Darrow's instance, at any rate, the court would have been required by law to hear him through until the very end, no matter how long it might take. Unless, of course, the court had seen fit to dismiss the case before its conclusion. For what reason? Lack of evidence, perhaps.

Could the much-esteemed barrister have accomplished the verdict in less time? The answer was unquestionably negative, for the evidence was too disparate, too spread around the globe. New information, uncovered by others, was not published in a single instant. Unfortunately, Edward could not have accomplished the task as some might think Clarence Darrow would have.

In any event, he was no Clarence Darrow. And this was no court of law. Edward gathered himself for his final performance and looked about the room. There was one new member, on his immediate left, a Dr. Engelbreit, who had replaced the little man with the name never known to Edward. The doctor wore a full gray beard which he constantly stroked, even when he was speaking.

"Have I not," Edward began nervously, "submitted a body of evidence—"

"What evidence is that?" Stratmeyer asked.

"Did I not submit a roster of the crew of *BonHomme Richard*, for example?"

"You did." Rossiter rushed in to fulfill his role as chairman.

"And, on the roster, was included a powder boy named Mark Paul. However, that doesn't prove—"

"I realize, Mr. Chairman, that single items such as the roster do not provide proof. However, I plead that you judge the case on its merit in its entirety; a binding together of provable facts to create the whole—"

"You submitted no evidence about the Acadians." Stratmeyer was not to be left out.

Edward whirled to him. "I would not think," he said, leaning over the polished table, "that it would be necessary to submit to you established, accepted history. If that be the case, I submit the entire contents of the St. Louis Public Library as evidence."

"Mr. Livingston," Rossiter said in a strong voice, "it isn't necessary to submit evidence for accepted facts. I believe Mr. Stratmeyer was referring not to the history of the Acadians, but the fact that William Paul might have—cohabited—with one of them."

Edward drew himself up, away from the group. He strode to the window overlooking the river, his thumb in his vest. "If I might," he said to the icy pane, "ask you what you would consider proof?"

Stratmeyer tapped his pencil on the table. "There are," he said, as if explaining a process to a very small boy, "such things as birth records even for bastards. And it was pointed out to you that the fire was a remarkable coincidence. Whatever the reason, that evidence is lacking."

Rossiter gripped his gavel. "If we assume," he said slowly, as if collecting his thoughts, "that the fact of the illegitimate birth is correct, and that this Jean Paul was conveyed to France by his mother, we are also asked to assume that he somehow landed on board *BonHomme Richard*."

"I thought I explained that."

"Not, obviously, to the Society's satisfaction."

"I related the difficulties John Paul Jones had in collecting a crew."

"But that does not prove that he took on board an illegitimate nephew—"

"There was the affidavit from the English judge."

"We have taken that into account. But nothing is said about the breech-loading cannon. Or even the relevance of the battle with *Serapis*."

"That relevance will be demonstrated later in my dissertation."

"Mr. Livingston," Rossiter said, tightening his hold on the gavel. "You've made some compelling arguments. But you've been lacking in proof—"

"I've submitted proofs." Edward was grasping, clutching at straws. "Does the affidavit mean nothing?"

"The affidavit has been filed. However, it must be considered as the railings of a common English sailor, probably much overblown—"

"Why would he make reference to a nephew if there was no nephew on board?"

"Well taken, Mr. Livingston. You must agree, however, that the evidence is slight, and that the story itself verges on the incredulous."

"I've told you that the case must be built on circumstantial evidence."

"Circumstantial, yes. But it's the evidence we're lacking. Much is the purest of speculations—"

"I beg of you to hear the case in its entirety."

"We've agreed to hear you out today. Are you prepared to conclude?"

"Conclusion today is impossible."

"The Society has determined that it wishes to hear nothing further after today. Please proceed." Rossiter tapped his gavel on its block and leaned back in his chair.

Edward was shattered. The case had run aground before it cleared the harbor. There was nothing to do except to run the engines full. He nodded to the chairman.

"There is adequate documentation, I believe," he said in his most sonorous tone, "that, in fact, there once existed a real person named Jean Lafitte. For that, there should is no need for further proof. History also tells us that this Lafitte person was either a pirate or a privateer, whichever you prefer, however slight the difference between them may be. History also relates that Jean Lafitte had a family, of which two brothers are definitely known. One was named Pierre, whom we shall hear more of later. The other brother was named Alexander.

"Although there were considerable differences in the appearances and manners of the three brothers, they were often confused, one with the other, even in accepted historical accounts. Early in their careers, they were admonished by a captain they served under to 'never give true names.' It was good advice. Accordingly, Alexander changed his name to Dominique Youx. There were several spellings, which further confused the historians. Nevertheless, the historians do agree that, in the year eighteen oh one, brother Alexander journeyed to France to fight with Napoleon's army. A war had erupted, which we now refer to as The French Revolution.

"Let's take stock of the situation. Jean Lafitte and his brothers Pierre and Alexander were privateering, or whatever, in the Caribbean. John Paul Jones was dead. Jean Paul was employed by a shipping firm at L'Orient. Alexander, for whatever reason, volunteered to serve in Napoleon's artillery."

"The newspaper article says it was Jean who was the artilleryman," Stratmeyer said, refuting his assertion that the Society paid no attention to newspaper articles.

"The article was incorrect. We must sift the wheat from the chaff. As I have said, the brothers were often confused for each other. What matters is that Alexander journeyed to France. There, he met Jean Paul."

Steinbach chimed in with his thin voice and thick glasses. "Why didn't you get the artillery rosters?"

Edward nodded at him. "I tried that. Few of the rosters exist, and I was unable to find any that included either name. Remember, the year was eighteen oh one. Revolutionary France was no more concerned with rosters of men than they were guest lists at funerals. In any case, Jean Paul was definitely not interested in warfare. He had already had his fill of that horror at Flamborough Head. In all probability, if he had persuaded himself to fight, it is unlikely he would have entered into a combat of the French against the French. His real hatred was for the English. It was the English who had chased his mother from her homeland, it was the English who had fought the terrible battle with *BonHomme Richard*. Jean Paul had a higher purpose. His goal was to return the body of his uncle John Paul Jones to America, yes, to the America that had forsaken their most courageous hero. In March, eighteen oh four, Jean Paul arrived in New Orleans with his illustrious baggage."

He paused to allow the statement to sink in, waiting.

Stratmeyer wriggled in his chair. "Mr. Livingston," he said in a loud voice, "am I correct in assuming that the illustrious baggage you refer to might be the remains of one John Paul Jones?"

Edward nodded, allowing his face to register horror, as if he had overlooked something. "It was."

"And—for a period of twelve years—the body of John Paul Jones mouldered in its coffin?"

The reply was irresistible. "It had no other choice."

Stratmeyer shook his head. "I don't believe that such a thing as cold storage existed in those days."

"It did not."

"Then how did Jean Paul manage to preserve his illustrious baggage for twelve years?"

"The body was interred in a leaden coffin, packed with hay and straw, filled with alcohol."

"I thought he was buried on the cheap."

"He would have been, had the American minister had his way. But Commissaire Pierre-Francois Simonneau of Paris was indignant that such a distinguished person should be given a pauper's burial. He paid for the funeral expenses himself. It was one of the things that so upset Jean Paul, that the Americans should slight him so and allow the funeral expenses to be paid by the French."

"Was this—lead coffin, alcohol thing—was that the usual way for the French to bury their dead?" Steinbach asked.

"Not usual," Edward replied. "It was uncommon, but not usual. Only the more wealthy could afford it. We owe our thanks to M. Simonneau. He hoped that burial in this fashion might preserve the body so that, one day when the Americans came to their senses, they might transport the body to its proper location."

"Very good," Stratmeyer said. "You explained how the body was preserved for twelve years. But you haven't explained why Jean Paul waited twelve years. You said he worked for a shipping company. It would not appear that passage should be such a problem. Why was it?"

Edward was disarmed by Stratmeyer's almost affable manner. "It wasn't a problem for Jean Paul. The problem was the coffin."

"Why?"

"In those days, there was a great superstition that a body on board ship asked for great calamity. It was almost as bad," Edward smiled, "as having a woman on board."

"But Alexander didn't care?"

"Upon Alexander's arrival in L'Orient, he encountered Jean Paul. He was struck by the uncanny resemblance to his own brother. Not only were the facial features similar, but the hair, as well. The way he moved, the way he walked. Even the accent was much alike. On the first sighting, Alexander might have thought that Jean Paul actually was his brother, come to join him in France. Of course, Alexander told Jean Paul about the similarity."

"I didn't realize we know so precisely what any of them looked like," Stratmeyer said.

"Oh, but we do," Edward exulted. "Jean Lafitte is described as tall, poised, with a gentlemanly demeanor. Alexander was short, dark, with a chest like a bull. For brothers, they were very dissimilar in appearance. Furthermore—"

Rossiter interrupted. "We will note the cited descriptions, Mr. Livingston. Please proceed." He glanced at his watch.

"The similarity in features was coincidental; however, it is generally accepted that every person has, somewhere in the world, a double that is remarkably like himself in appearance and mannerism. There was also the similarity in accent. But you will recall that Jean Paul was raised by his mother, a transplanted Acadian, an *emigré* from France. His dialect was almost certainly different from that of the typical Frenchman as a result of her years in the New World."

"Sounds like fantasy," Stratmeyer said.

"Current history indicates," Edward said politely, "that Jean Lafitte came from France. Is that correct?"

Stratmeyer nodded.

"Is it fair to state that, at this point, this Society has also accepted that ... presumed ... fact? That Jean Lafitte came from France?"

"We have accepted it."

"And what was the name of the ship your Jean Lafitte crossed the Atlantic on?"

Stratmeyer sat with mouth agape.

"What was the date?"

Rossiter tapped his gavel. "I'm afraid, Mr. Livingston, that we've run out of time."

"Mr. Chairman," Stratmeyer said quietly, toying with his pencil, "Mr. Livingston had raised some very good points, however fantastic his story might be. We have no proof that Jean Lafitte was born in France, although we have gone on record as accepting it. But we have no proof. Out of all the various birthplaces that historians have suggested, we have settled on France because it appeared to us to be the most logical. We call ourselves The Lafitte Society. Our purpose is to study the life of Jean Lafitte. Yet, we don't even know where he was born. We have suggested to Mr. Livingston that he provide a birth certificate. How can we ask that, in all good conscience, when we can't even provide one ourselves?"

Edward was stunned. He felt as if his feet had lifted from the floor.

CHAPTER 13
New Orleans, Louisiana
February 6, 1993, 3:35 PM

"Sounds like Stratmeyer was coming around. Too bad thay'd already voted to kick you out." Mickey's voice seemed disembodied in the half-light.

The day grew dark because of the heavy clouds, and the lamp created only a circle of light around the desk. Over the fireplace, the gold medal shimmered like a small Chinese gong.

Edward tipped back in the soft chair. "Stratmeyer's attitude was too good to be true. But he recovered at the next meeting, became nasty again."

"So they voted you back in?"

"What?"

"They voted you back in? At the next meeting?"

Edward drifted from The Society and its meetings, back to the central problem: of what to do about Mickey. "Why don't you stay here? I'm all alone in this big old house, now. You could go to school."

"No college." Mickey pushed himself up from the armchair and scuffed out of the circle of light, nearer the medal.

"You could get a job, if you want. It's easier to find work in New Orleans, I should think."

"Dad'd kill me."

"Why?"

"He don't want me messing around here."

"Why not?"

"He just ... don't."

Edward heard a clink, as if Mickey had rolled the model cannon against the arsenic bottle.

"Does he give a reason?"

"Sometimes."

"What reason?"

"He's got lots of them."

"Tell me one."

Mickey abandoned the cannon. Edward saw his shadow turn and move closer to the desk. His lower legs appeared in the light. "That night in jail's a big one."

"I didn't put him in jail. He stole some cigarettes from a liquor store."

"You didn't get him out, either. He says that started everything."

Blaming everything on the night in jail made about as much sense as blaming the assassination of Archduke Ferdinand for World War I. "I did get him out."

"Not until the next day, though."

"Did he tell you why I didn't get get him out until the next day?"

"You wanted to come down on him."

"Did he ever," Edward said, rearranging himself on the chair, rocking forward to fold his hands on the desk, "mention that I wasn't home the night he got put in jail?"

"No."

"He didn't mention that I was out on the bayous that night?"

"No."

"And that I rushed downtown to get him out as soon as I heard?"

"He never said nothing about that. Just that you made him stay in jail."

It was exasperating. Not only that Charleton would tell

Mickey such a tale, but that he would even make it up in the first place. The trouble was, he probably believed it himself.

"Do you believe it?"

"I don't know what to believe anymore."

Nothing was to be gained by putting Mickey on the spot. It was well to let the matter drop. "Let's just let it ride."

"Okay by me." Mickey fell back into the armchair.

Edward tapped his fingers on the file folder. "Where were we?"

"Talking about the next meeting. That they voted you back in."

"Oh, yes." At least Mickey seemed to be maintaining his continuity about the case. Better than his grandfather was doing, in fact. "Apparently, Stratmeyer realized that the Society couldn't prove everything, either."

"But you made up a lot of stuff."

"I didn't make anything up. I merely tried to piece together the unexplained. Like the English affidavit that said a nephew was on board; the roster, that showed there was a powder boy on board named Mark Paul; the real reason Pearson gave up, when he had actually won the battle. Questions that respected historians simply avoided. For example, I had Jean Paul in France, and I had to get him to America. It would have been a lot easier to just say that he sailed there, and let it go at that. That's how Stratmeyer got his Jean Lafitte to Louisiana from France."

"That would've been a cop out."

"Exactly. But I found other bits of history that wouldn't dovetail together. I just glued the ill-fitting parts together, then filled in the cracks."

"You made stuff up."

"I made nothing up. I reconstructed the events. That's

what *a priori* is, a way of employing cause and effect. A way to answer the unanswered questions."

"How'd you get back with them? The Society?"

"I waited a few months, then wrote a letter. Asked them to grant me another audience."

"And they said okay."

"It took them three years, but yes, they allowed me to appear again, in nineteen thirty-seven. By a narrow vote, so they informed me, I was granted one additional audience. When I reappeared, I continued where I had left off, just as if nothing had happened."

"About getting Jean Paul to America?"

Edward nodded. "There weren't many ships sailing at that time from France to America, because it was after the Louisiana Purchase. Jean Paul was seasick most of the way—"

Mickey laughed.

"You don't believe that?"

"How'd you know that he was seasick?"

"There are lots of historical references that said Jean Lafitte got seasick. They say he couldn't even ride in a rowboat without getting sick. It didn't add up with the swashbuckling pirate image most people have of Jean Lafitte. But it reinforced my theory about his being two people. Not even schizophrenics can turn seasickness on and off."

"Okay. So they pulled into New Orleans—"

"You're getting ahead of my story. You're as bad as Stratmeyer. There was a long sea voyage, which was important. Alexander and Jean had a chance to talk."

"To get him ready to meet the real Jean Lafitte."

"You're getting ahead of my story again."

CHAPTER 14
New Orleans, Louisiana
January 15, 1805

PRES. BY Edw. Livingston, Esq.
FEBRUARY 6, 1937

"Alexander," the man said, introducing himself. "Lafitte," he added after a moment. His French was accented, sounding strangely foreign, even on the docks at L'Orient. A sing-song lilt reminded Jean Paul of his mother. The man had been hanging around the docks for weeks, closely watching Jean's every move, always at a discreet distance. He appeared to be a derelict, of which there were many about the docks. His heavily bandaged face marked him as a wounded soldier, no doubt seeking surreptitious passage out of war-wracked France.

"Talk to Captain Dubois," Jean instructed the man, nodding toward the tall figure then descending the gangplank. This ox-like man was a nuisance, keeping him away from his business. Jean returned his attention to a mass of bills of lading bundled on the head of a cask of gunpowder. *Bonheur*, a large brig of Holland Dutch construction, was in the final stage of loading. Mostly gunpowder and shot, a few cannon. It wasn't unusual, for a considerable amount of war matériel had been shipped from L'Orient to Egypt and Italy. Now that Napoleon had been crowned emperor, it was said he would conquer the world.

"I want to talk to you," Lafitte said. The one eye glittered. Captain Dubois stepped to the dock and strode quickly past, deferentially saluting as he went. Not to Jean Paul. To the ox-like man with the bandage.

"What did you say your name was?" Jean asked.

"Lafitte."

It was not an uncommon name in France. The Lafittes were, after all, an important banking family. But this man didn't talk much like a banker. Another family of Lafittes made cannons, but this Lafitte didn't look like a foundry worker, either.

"What can I do for you?"

"It's what I can do for you."

"What—"

"I hear you want passage to America," Lafitte said in a voice so low that it could hardly be heard over the screeching of the gulls. "This ship is going to New Orleans." He nodded at *Bonheur.*

"Maybe you don't understand."

"Maybe you could explain it to me."

"I have a problem."

"Just one?"

"One big one."

"So let's have a big glass of ale." Lafitte glanced at *Bonheur.* "You've about finished loading my ship, anyhow."

His ship? Jean Paul scurried after him in wonder, clutching the bills of lading. They pushed their way into a crowded *brasserie* a short walk from the pier.

"How did you know I wanted passage to America, Mr. Lafitte?"

"I asked around. And you can call me Alexander." He banged the flat of his hand on the bar for service.

"Why?"

"Because I want you to work for me. In America. And you want to go to America." Alexander ordered ales. The biggest tankards.

"Work? Doing what?"

"Same thing you're doing here, only in New Orleans. I been watching you. Like the way you work. And you got good English, good French. Some other languages, too, that I don't know."

"Lots of nationalities come into L'Orient. Some of the languages rub off." Jean Paul's mind raced because of the unexpected good fortune.

"We got lots of nationalities, too. Lots of captains, lots of ships. We need somebody like you, somebody to run things ashore. An *un marchand*, same thing you're doing here." Alexander glanced at Jean. "And you want to go to America."

"But I'm not *un—*"

"You'll do." Alexander thrust a cloudy mug of ale at him. "What's your problem?"

"I have baggage."

Alexander laughed. "There's lots of room. *Bonheur* is nearly empty. You should know that, you're loading her."

"This is special baggage."

"A woman?"

"A coffin."

"A—coffin?" Jean nodded. "Occupied?" Again, Jean Paul nodded. The generous offer would be withdrawn. No captain had yet consented to sail with a body aboard. Bodies, they explained, were buried at sea.

"Where is it?"

"In the warehouse. On the dock."

"Is it ... is it—"

"Well preserved. There's no—you'd never know a body's inside."

"You want to take ... a coffin ... to America?"

Jean nodded.

"What for?"

Jean gulped a large swallow of ale. "If I go," he said through foamy lips, "my baggage has to go."

"She'll sink the damn ship," Alexander muttered.

He stood beside Jean watching ten men stagger up the gangplank with the heavy coffin.

"You should have been there to see us get it out of the grave."

"You dug it up?"

"In the middle of the night. We had to find a farmer with a tripod big enough to lift it, one they used for moving heavy stones. Even then, it took a team of horses. We hired an artillery caisson for the trip to L'Orient."

The one black eye glittered with appreciation.

Bonheur lurched in the first of the swells after rounding the shelter of Isle de Groix. Jean Paul gripped the rail tightly, sagging his chin to his chest. Already, the roll of the sea had brought on the familiar queasiness. He turned to the sound of a snort behind him.

"You're no sailor, I reckon." Alexander approached the rail, not requiring its touch for support.

He seemed to have a good nature, not unusual for short people. His broad shoulders and huge chest made him appear inordinately strong. The swarthy face, what could be seen of it from under the bandages, warned the beholder to beware, affable nature or not.

"I never pretended to be a sailor."

Gulls coasted over the wake of the ship, no longer screeching, perhaps saving their breath for the return flight to the receding coast of France. The coastline had already closed in with the turning of the ship. The large bay filled with clusters of masts like intertangled tree branches was no longer visible and might never have existed.

Jean Paul wondered about his decision. At the same time, he exulted in the daring of it.

The Isle de Groix moved past on the port side of *Bonheur.* The ship's sails were taut and full, rolling her more perceptively. Jean gripped the rail tightly.

"You're sure like my brother. Except for the sailing." Alexander laughed. Jean Paul peered at him. "He doesn't look anything like me, if that's what you're thinking," Alexander said hastily. "He's tall and slim, like you. Fancy dresser, too." He eyed Jean Paul up and down.

Jean was proud of the calf-length coat he had bought especially for the trip, the Wellington boots that reached above his knees, the new weskit with its shiny brass buttons. The sailors on board treated him with respect.

One talented mouse of a man had even done a quick sketch on a scrap of foolscap. Jean Paul treasured the sketch, for no one had ever done such a thing before. It was well done, even if the artist had drawn a sword in his hand. "Looked like it ought to be there," the gnome explained before he scrambled up a rat-line.

"He even has the same name," Alexander continued.

"Jean?" Jean Paul asked, struggling with the heeling of the ship.

"Aye. Jean Lafitte. You'll like each other, I think."

"I'm looking forward to meeting him." Jean turned to hide his face. His stomach had become uncontrollable.

The ship reached the extreme of her northerly tack and heeled about, her sails shuddering as they spilled their wind. With the new heeling, Jean Paul lurched against Alexander, who stood as solidly as if his boots were nailed to the deck.

"Ever been to sea before?" Alexander didn't flinch when a spray of water doused them.

"Twice," Jean Paul gulped. "The first time, I was too little to remember."

"Where'd you sail from?"

"New Orleans."

The one eye opened wider. "You from New Orleans?"

Jean Paul nodded. "I'm a Yankee now. Napoleon sold Louisiana to America, remember," he said proudly.

"Yankee?" Alexander shook his head. "Back when you was born, New Orleans was Spanish, weren't it? Or French?"

"My father was from Virginia."

"And your mother?"

"Cajun."

"That makes you half-French, then."

"I'm a Yankee," Jean repeated adamantly.

"A good thing, to be a Yankee. Yankees helps to keep the damn Britishers out."

Jean lost all interest in the conversation. He yearned to retreat below, to ride out the rolling of the sea from the relative comfort of his hammock.

"What was the second time you sailed?"

"*BonHomme Richard.*" Jean gulped, feeling the nausea arise from deep within.

"Captain Jones?" Alexander asked, his face incredulous. "Is that who—"

Jean Paul nodded and raced for the ladder before he embarrassed himself further.

***

On the fifteenth day at sea, *Bonheur* reached a period of sunny calm, unusual for mid-winter in the Atlantic. Below, Jean Paul noted that his hammock no longer swung with the motion of the ship. He felt well again for the first time since they had rounded the Isle de Groix. Pleased, he tore away the blanket that had covered him for so long and clambered up the ladder into the sunshine.

He flinched when he burst onto deck, shocked by the red-scarred face of Alexander without the bandage.

Alexander grinned. "Welcome aboard."

The entire left side of Alexander's face was seared a deep red color, especially above his left eye. That eye, as black and glittering as the other, must have been preserved by the eyelid, for the lid was red whenever Alexander blinked.

"What happened to your face?"

"Muzzle blast. Swabber didn't get all the sparks out of the bore. When they dumped in the powder, she blew."

"Where was that?"

"Damn Britishers." Alexander, apparently, blamed every mishap on the British.

"Why was it," Jean asked slowly, "that you left your ships? And went to fight in France?"

Alexander stared at the horizon, crisp and blue in the calm sunshine. "We was lookin' for help."

"Help?"

"To chase the damn Britishers out of the Caribbean." He eyed Jean closely. "And to keep the Yankees out of Louisiana. There's a lot of good folks there that wanted to keep Louisiana French."

"The British I can understand. Why the Yankees?"

"They don't like the way we do business. But I was too late. It's Yankee, now. Like you said."

"How were you going to keep them out?"

"Don't know. It was a stupid idea."

"Were you going to try to talk Napoleon into it? Into keeping Louisiana for France?"

"Like I said, it was a stupid idea. I thought I'd walk right up to him, tell him what I had to say. Nobody'd even tell me where he was. They probably didn't know."

"But you stayed in France to fight?"

"Some soldier said they needed artillerymen. I'm good with cannon. I thought it might be a good chance to show how good I was, make Napoleon notice. Maybe I could talk to him then. It was all I had."

"Did you ever get a chance to talk to him?"

"Naw. Seen him once, though. Not to talk to. Then the damn cannon blew up in my face. When I come to, he was gone." Alexander folded his arms on the rail. "So tell me about your second time at sea. About *BonHomme Richard*."

"Don't know much about it," Jean said. "I was just a powder boy. Sixteen years old."

"You can grow up fast in a fight like that." Alexander shook his head. "Nobody could ever figure out how Jones won."

"It was the breech-loader," Jean said, anxious to show this cannoneer that he knew about guns.

Alexander turned his head and rested his chin on his shoulder. The red eyelid blinked. "The what?"

"The breech-loader. After we splintered the Englishman's mast—"

"I didn't know Jones had a breech-loader."

"Most people don't. I'm not sure the Captain did, even, until right at the end."

"Nobody uses breech-loaders. They blow up in your face."

"This one didn't." He waved at Alexander's burned face. "Doesn't look like muzzle-loaders are much better."

"It's the first time," Alexander said, "that I ever heard of a breech-loader that was any good."

A cool breeze wavered in from the north. *Bonheur*'s sails flapped and the ship began to move. Jean Paul felt the deck come alive under his feet.

"Do you know the name of the foundry?" Alexander stood stiffly, now clutching the rail.

"The foundry?"

"What made the gun."

"Lafitte, as I remember. Does that make sense?"

Alexander nodded. "It makes sense. There are Lafittes in France who make cannon. No relation, though."

***

On the thirty-fourth day at sea, the weather again fell calm, permitting Jean Paul another of his rare forays onto the deck. He was perplexed to find the deep blue color of the sea had turned to a muddy brown as far as he could see in every direction. *Bonheur* was hove to.

"It's because of The River." Alexander hung over the rail and peered down at the chocolate water.

"The Mississippi?" Jean Paul felt joyous exultation that he was now so close to his homeland to be in the very dirt washing from its shores, although, strain as he might, he couldn't see land.

He started suddenly with surprise, for there, not more than a half-mile over the starboard quarter, a full-masted ship bore down on them in the light breeze.

"What ship is that?"

"*Success*." Alexander watched closely as the ship came about behind *Bonheur*, then approached slowly from the starboard, dropping away sails. She came even, then all her sails were gone but the tops and she steered closer. At last, the hulls bumped slightly, and Alexander leaped easily across the gap created by the tumble-homes. Jean Paul watched him joyously embrace a figure on the deck, then the pair disappeared below, clasped in each other's arms.

"It's one of Alexander's ships." Captain Dubois stood at Jean Paul's elbow.

"How many ships does he have?"

"Not sure. Six, I think."

Jean Paul was impressed, happy that he had the good fortune to encounter such a powerful mentor. Although he had been aware that Alexander had a number of ships, he had not known how many. Such an entrepreneur could be very useful in this new land.

"How long to New Orleans?"

"A day, maybe." Dubois peered to the lowering sun. "We'll lay out here this night, go up the river in the morning."

Success drew slowly away, until she lay a half-mile off the starboard quarter.

After the brown sea and the brilliant day had turned a deep tropical black, *Success* sidled closer. Just before they bumped, Alexander leaped back. At once, she hoisted full sail and pulled away.

Alexander climbed to the quarterdeck, and after a few moments *Bonheur* hoisted her sails and they sailed away in the wake of *Success*.

Alexander rejoined Jean Paul. "We won't be going to New Orleans."

Jean Paul felt the familiar sinking in his delicate stomach. "There's trouble there," Alexander said.

In the morning, the first sight of his homeland, longed for for so many years, was but a flat line on the horizon. The sight was a disappointment.

"Grande Terre." Alexander jerked his head at the green strip of land.

Jean Paul was stunned. Was this the fabled America?

"When," he asked, "will we go to New Orleans?"

"I told you. We won't be going to New Orleans. We'll unload at Grande Terre."

"Tell me what the trouble is in New Orleans."

"Customs. That's the trouble. Yankee customs."

Jean Paul stood motionless, torn with inner conflict about his homeland, his pilgrimage.

The land slowly grew larger with their approach, and he could discern the masts of a ship that appeared to be rooted in the land itself.

"That'll be *Success*." Perhaps Alexander understood his apprehension. "In the bay behind the island."

They stood in silence, watching the land approach, until at last, *Bonheur*'s bow turned toward a narrow inlet.

"Barataria Pass," Alexander said.

A sharp order from *Bonheur*'s sailmaster caused all sails to be furled except the tops. The ship slowly coasted through the pass, which opened into a large bay, obviously deep enough to accommodate blue-water ships.

Once through the pass and into Barataria Bay, *Bonheur* warped slowly eastward until she lay some two hundred yards southerly of *Success*. To the south, Grande Terre Island lay low, barely rising above the water. A small cluster of fishermen's huts, sheltered by a jungle-like growth of palmetto, stood beyond a poor pier that extended into the bay across a narrow beach. In a cleared area beside the huts, an old sail draped from poles set into the ground, probably a rain water catchment, for a large wooden barrel stood at its low end. The sound of shouts drew his attention to *Success*. Two men in a small boat set off in their direction even as *Bonheur*'s anchor rattled and she swung about.

It appeared that the anchoring signalled a halt to the sea-breeze over the island. An oppressive heat kneaded a biting humidity into his every pore. It's January, Jean Paul considered. What must it be like in July? He was thankful for the flowing sailor's shirt and the loose trousers. He wondered if he might ever wear his coat and weskit again.

In spite of their location in the bay, some hundreds of yards from land, clouds of mosquitoes appeared from every direction at once, zinging about the moisture of his eyes and ears and every other inch of his perspiring body.

What a miserable, miserable end-of-the-earth. The boat approached swiftly across the still water, disturbed only by the touch of tens of thousands of invisible insects. One of the boat's occupants expertly handled the oars without even a splash while the other sat in her sternsheets, his eyes on *Bonheur*.

"It's Pierre," Alexander said. "Come to take us ashore."

Realization plummeted into the pit of Jean Paul's touchy stomach like a cannon ball. He had been deceived. He was in the very lair of the pirates.

RESP. SUB., G. Choteau, Sec.
FEBRUARY 6, 1937

CHAPTER 15
New Orleans, Louisiana
February 6, 1993, 3:49 PM

"How much of that was true? How much did you make up?" Mickey's voice from the shadows sounded skeptical.

Edward closed the file. "It was all true." He looked at the watch, disturbed to find it blurred. He blinked rapidly, but that didn't help. He looked at the telephone dial and found that the numbers blurred as well. Perhaps it was because of the long reading, perhaps because of the trying events of the long day.

"You could prove it?" Mickey folded his arms over his chest in the traditional signal of disbelief.

Edward felt he was losing his audience. It was taking too long. "I had the proofs for what needed to be proved."

"And you filled in the cracks with your—"

"*A priori.*"

"But what parts could you actually prove?"

"Accepted history records," Edward began, "that a person known as Jean Lafitte arrived in Louisiana from France in early eighteen oh five. Accepted history also states that Alexander Lafitte returned from his first tour of duty with Napoleon at the same time. No historian, however, mentions the coincidence of the date. No historian has ever put the two together, speculated that they might have sailed on the same ship. Yet, it is entirely probable that they sailed together. There were few ships sailing between France and Louisiana at that time, remember. The conclusion's entirely logical."

"But you couldn't actually prove it."

"What could I possibly offer to prove it? The ship's log? I provided Stratmeyer with an attested affidavit about Jones' nephew on the *BonHomme Richard*, and he didn't want to believe even that! But the fact that they did or did not sail on the same ship has no effect whatsoever on the eventual outcome. It is unimportant, however logical. Are there," he asked Mickey, moving his head from side to side in a cat-like motion to improve his vision, "other specifics that bother you?"

"Sure. Lots."

"Namely?"

"The whole story."

Edward pressed his hands weakly against the blotter to stop their shuddering. "Specifics," he said, willing himself to continue. "Any story, any case, is made up of specifics. If you—"

"How about the coffin?"

"What?"

"The coffin. You said it was so heavy it took ten men to carry it."

Edward nodded slowly, as if to indicate that the question had been a good one. "John Paul Jones," he said, "was originally buried in a leaden coffin, filled with alcohol, inside an outer wooden coffin. I merely calculated the gross weight and determined that it would've required ten strong men to carry it."

"You can prove that? About the lead and the alcohol?"

"Prove it? It's one of your accepted facts. Check the history books."

Mickey fell silent, except for the tapping of his foot on the floor.

"Anything else?" Edward asked.

"You told me before," Mickey said, "that the two Jeans never met. That when Jean Paul arrived, Jean Lafitte was in prison."

"Jean Lafitte was captured after a fight with a Spanish

ship and thrown into a Cuban prison. Some accounts state that he was released shortly thereafter, but that hardly seems logical. The imprisonment made a big difference to his outlook for the remainder of his life. It's inconceivable that he was in prison for only a short time."

"Did that old newspaper article say anything about his being in prison?"

"Nothing whatsoever."

"Sounds like you cheat. You use the stuff you like. Throw out the stuff you don't."

Edward smiled. Stratmeyer had said the same thing, in nearly the same words. Edward attempted the same argument with Mickey that had proven successful with Stratmeyer. "Do you read the newspapers?" he asked Mickey, spouting out the question as if it had only just occurred to him.

"Sometimes."

"Do you believe everything you read in them?"

"Hardly any of it."

"Yet you believe some of it."

"Yeah."

"You find that newspaper stories are usually prejudiced?"

"They sure are."

"Depending on the slant the reporter intends to convey?"

Mickey looked as if he realized that he was falling into a trap.

"Some parts are fiction?" Edward pressed.

"Yeah, but—sometimes—like in this story, it sounds like the whole thing's fiction."

"You mean there never was a John Paul Jones? A *BonHomme Richard*? There was no battle at Flamborough Head?"

Mickey didn't answer. He wriggled, discomfort lining his face.

"The defense rests," Edward said.

Mickey didn't speak for a very long time. Edward waited.

"So," the boy said finally in a low tone. "They loaded John Paul Jones into a pirogue and rowed him up the bayou to—"

"It took two pirogues. The coffin was very heavy, remember."

"I guess you have proof of that? About the two pirogues?" Mickey was picking on everything.

Edward shook his head. "No proof. Simple mathematics. I calculated the weight of the coffin, as I have said, the lead, the alcohol. I checked the load-carrying capacity of pirogues. The weight of the coffin was roughly twice that. It follows that two pirogues were required. Simple deduction. You don't need *a priori*. Yet—I suppose you might label it as a fiction."

Edward turned the lamp to shine on the wall of maps. "They went northwesterly through Barataria Bay to the outflow of Bayou St. Denis. Up St. Denis through Bayou Cutler to Bayou Barataria. The first high ground suitable for a cemetery lies at the southeast corner of the intersection with Bayou des Oises."

"You figured all that out."

Edward pointed to the wall. "You see the route marked on the maps. I paddled it myself, many times."

"What difference does it make about the route?"

Edward shook his head. "Not much, maybe. No more important than the fact that Jean Paul arrived on the same ship as Alexander. But it was important to me. I wanted to verify every detail it was possible for me to verify. I wanted to present an unassailable case."

Mickey looked up sharply. "Do you think it is?"

"Is what?"

"Unassailable?" Mickey had trouble with the word.

Edward spoke carefully. "There are still," he said, "some aspects which must be clarified."

"So. You're not done with it yet."

"Very nearly. It's a case of monumental proportions, and I've been working single-handedly. It isn't complete, and I have no knowledge when it will be, or, indeed, if it will ever be. Nevertheless, I believe that when you've heard all the evidence, you'll agree that the case is formidable."

"But I guess," Mickey said, "the Society doesn't think so."

"I really don't know what they think. But they have, at least, been listening."

"Jean Paul didn't sound like much of a pirate."

"He wasn't. It is perhaps why he didn't become one. He was a merchant, you will recall. He was finished with fighting. The battle at Flamborough Head had given him enough of that. But he was stuck with his covenant with Alexander, which was something like an indenture to him."

"And you figure he looked like Jean Lafitte."

"He did. Close enough, anyway, that those who had not seen Jean very often wouldn't argue about it."

"When did the real Jean Lafitte get out of prison?"

"You're getting ahead of my story again."

"There must have been hell to pay when the real Jean Lafitte got back and found an accountant running the show. Taking his place."

"I told you. The two Jeans never met."

"Oh, yeah." He grinned. "But it would've made a better story."

"I wasn't looking for a 'better story,' I was looking for the truth."

"You know," Mickey said, his face fixed in thought, "the whole thing would be easy to prove."

"How?"

"By probing," Mickey said, straightening himself in his chair. "Out at the cemetery. Poke a long rod in the ground. If the story's true, there should be a lead coffin out there somewhere."

Edward released his lungful of air. False alarm. He chose his words carefully, unwilling to diminish Mickey's spurt of interest. "And if you should strike something," he said, "it would only prove that something is buried there. Not terribly conclusive evidence in a cemetery. I often considered probing," Edward continued. "I have sat for many long hours out at the cemetery, contemplating that very possibility."

"Why didn't you ever try it?"

"If I struck an object with the probe, it would prove nothing. If I did not strike anything, it would merely mean that I had probed in the wrong place, or not deeply enough. If I used a sampling probe, I might be able, even, to prove that a leaden coffin was buried there. But even that wouldn't prove that the coffin was that of John Paul Jones."

"Yeah, but—"

Edward ignored the interruption and tried to lead him on a little. "The only positive proof would be exhumation. Even then, considering the long period of burial and the high water table in the area, exhumation might be inconclusive."

"But you said the body was preserved in alcohol—"

"It would be unrealistic to suppose that the alcohol could have remained for two hundred years. Even the tiniest of leaks in the coffin would—"

"Still." Mickey looked excited. "I think you should do it."

"The graves have been covered over with a thick concrete slab. The probing would be difficult."

"Then just dig them up."

Edward shook his head. "I have many reasons not to. In the first place, there are laws regulating exhumation in Louisiana. There would have to be very good cause, and my case isn't yet ready. I'd need to get a court order, assuming even that the order were obtainable, I'm not ready. If the exhumation were performed and nothing was found, I would be labeled as a fool."

"But it'd be settled. Once and for all."

"Not necessarily." Edward shook his head. "We would have no certain knowledge that we had exhumed the right grave. Or even, for that matter, that we had dug in the right cemetery."

"I thought you said you checked that out."

"I said that I checked the routes, and found that this particular cemetery lay on the first high ground north of Barataria Bay. It was the logical site. However, it's possible that Jean Paul carried out the actual burial in another location entirely, knowing that people would assume the ground at Bayou des Oises to be the right one. After all, the body was precious to Jean Paul. And the act wouldn't have been without precedent. The Pharaohs of Egypt did that very thing as a matter of course in order to thwart grave robbers."

Mickey opened his mouth to speak, but Edward cut him off. "Furthermore, if I had actually found him, my case would have been destroyed."

It was not something he wanted to say to the Society.

Mickey stared, not understanding. "That one you got to explain."

"If I did succeed in discovering the body, and was successful in the identification, I would merely have raised historical questions. Small satisfaction in that. I wouldn't have been considered a sleuth, which was my goal in the first place.

And, as I have said, if I failed, I'd be labeled a fool. My aim was to convince the doubters that I was right, not to prove it to them. Following that, the proof would be conclusive. The evidence I submitted was probative."

Mickey didn't care about the legal mumbo-jumbo. "I still think you ought to dig 'em up."

Would that be your solution? "Most people," Edward replied, "would arrive at that conclusion. At my very next audience before The Society," he continued, "I presented some definitive evidence. It did not yet prove where John Paul Jones was buried, but it definitely proved that he is not entombed at the Naval Academy Chapel in Annapolis."

Mickey waited.

"It was a little hard for the Society to swallow," Edward said slowly, "that for all these many years, the United States was paying homage to an unknown Frenchman instead of a Revolutionary War hero."

CHAPTER 16
The Lafitte Society
Saint Louis, Missouri
February 6, 1938

Edward's voice rang loud in the panelled quiet of the meeting room. "Gentlemen." After a proper rhetorical pause to ensure that he had the attention of all, he continued. "I will absolutely prove to you that John Paul Jones is not—I repeat, *not*—interred at the Naval Academy at Annapolis." He stood straight. "As is commonly accepted."

The marble bust of John Paul Jones stared benignly from

the center of the table, his upturned nose showing no interest whatsoever in the proceedings. The eyes of the Society members shifted continuously and uncertainly from Edward to the bust, as if they were embarrassed that the Admiral's ears should hear this preposterous charge.

After the stunning opening statement, for Edward had learned from Darrow that a story must start with the conflagration rather than the striking of a match, the Society waited to see what lunacy might remain, waited to see how Livingston would hang himself today. But he waited too, waited so long that the members looked to him as if they wondered if he were still in the room or had simply been struck dumb.

Stratmeyer saved the day, as Edward was confident he would. "Mr. Livingston, I feel that it's fair to warn you that I have here," and his head inclined slightly toward a brown folder on the table, "a report by one General Horace Porter, dated May nineteenth, nineteen oh five." He looked sharply up at Edward. "You are familiar with it, I presume?"

Edward nodded. "I am," he said unevenly, biting his lip as if he rather preferred not to be familiar with it.

Stratmeyer watched Edward as he spoke. "General Porter," he explained to his colleagues from the side of his mouth, "was a very distinguished American. He graduated third in his class at West Point. He served commendably under General Grant in the Civil War. He was awarded the Congressional Medal of Honor. He was appointed Ambassador to France by President William McKinley." Stratmeyer paused. He shifted in his seat and ignored Edward entirely. "In eighteen ninety-nine, while General Porter was Ambassador to France," he continued, his voice rising, "he began a search for the body of John Paul Jones." The butcher Stratmeyer was at it with his meat cleaver. "He was successful, and his search culminated in nineteen oh five when a squadron of cruisers escorted the body to Annapolis under the order of President Theodore Roosevelt. The remains were then entombed, with due pomp and circumstance, in a place of supreme honor, a special crypt at the United States Naval Academy."

Stratmeyer's voice became increasingly quiet with authority as he neared the end of his dissertation. He turned his head, boring his eyes into Edward as if that individual had trampled the American flag into the Mississippi River mud.

Outwardly, Edward registered shock, horror. His face flamed red. He took a step backward, as if he anticipated physical as well as verbal assault.

Sucked you right in, didn't I?

Stratmeyer wasn't finished. He slammed the flat of his hand sharply on the brown folder, then rose to his feet, nearly upsetting his chair. "I move," he proclaimed in a greatly raised voice, sweeping his gaze about at his fellow Society members, "that we terminate this discussion entirely."

Rossiter quietly took command. "Mr. Stratmeyer," he said calmly, fingering his gavel, "will you take your seat, please."

"A motion's on the floor." Stratmeyer's face was redder than Edward's.

"Mr. Stratmeyer. Please."

Stratmeyer looked about at the shocked members of the group, then dropped indignantly in the direction of his chair. Pushed backward by his precipitous rise, the chair wasn't exactly where he thought it was, and the butcher's buttocks caught only the front edge. Frantically, he clutched the edge of the table to keep from sliding to the floor.

"There's a motion on the floor," Stratmeyer repeated after he had recovered his composure.

You nearly were, too.

"I believe," Rossiter said in a calm voice, greatly contrasting with Stratmeyer's outburst, "that you are out of order. Mr. Livingston is here at our invitation to make a presentation. We must listen to—"

"A motion's on the floor!" Stratmeyer didn't give up easily.

Rossiter sighed. He looked slowly about the table, locking on the eyes of each member before he moved on to the next. When he had finished his scrutiny, he asked in the softest of voices, "Is there a second?"

No one seconded the motion. Each member sat rigidly in his chair, not daring to look at either Stratmeyer or Edward. The unfortunate new member, Lionel Croft, glanced repeatedly from face to face as if he were unsure what he had gotten himself into.

Rossiter banged his gavel. "Motion dies for lack of a second." The chairman turned to Edward, who had remained throughout with his thumbs in his vest and one foot pointedly forward. "Will you proceed, Mr. Livingston?"

Edward held the pose for a critical moment longer. He directed a question at Stratmeyer but inspected the wall just over that individual's head. "Mr. Stratmeyer," he said. "How tall am I?"

Stratmeyer snorted. He tapped his fingers on the brown folder.

Rossiter began cautiously, "Mr. Stratmeyer—"

"I have no desire to further these foolish games," Stratmeyer said with great heat, tapping his folder with increased fury.

Edward reconstituted his pose, shifting so that his left foot was forward and his left knee bent.

"Humor me, please." Stratmeyer continued tapping. Edward let the question rest for the moment. "I agree," Edward said then, rolling lightly on the balls of his feet as he strolled about the room, his thumbs still in the armholes of his vest, "that General Porter was a very distinguished soldier. He was appointed Ambassador to France, and I am sure that he served that position most capably, although it is generally accepted that such appointments are largely bestowed for reasons of honor rather than merit. But, gentlemen," he said, wheeling on his slick soles to face the group, "General Porter was not a forensic pathologist. Furthermore, he had no authority to search for the body of John Paul Jones. His search was made on his own time. He spent his own money, since none had been authorized for the purpose by the United States. He spent some thirty-five thousand dollars on the search, which was no small sum at the beginning of the twentieth century.

"Why did he do it? Well, he states himself that he 'had a deep sense of humiliation as an American citizen that our first and most fascinating naval hero had been lying for more than a century in an unknown and forgotten grave and that no serious attempt had ever been made to recover his remains and give them appropriate sepulchre in the land upon whose history he had shed so much luster.' That's a direct quote from page forty-nine," he said to Stratmeyer, who was at the moment leafing through the report.

The members of the Society shifted in their seats.

"It is likely," Edward continued pontifically, "that his patriotic stirrings must have been similar to those of our Jean Paul, who had pre-empted the general by more than a hundred years."

Edward allowed his last statement to settle into the silence of the room before he continued.

"Porter began an exhaustive search for the cemetery, although there could have been only one resting place for foreign Protestants at the time of the death of John Paul Jones. He found it, of course, on a street formerly called L'Hopital Saint Louis, at the corner of Grange aux-Belles. Right where it always was. He found that sacred site covered with buildings 'of an inferior class,' he says." Edward nodded to Stratmeyer. "Page fifty-six. The old cemetery had been filled over, made into a garbage dump before the constructions. This statement, incidentally, is inconsistent elsewhere within Porter's report, for he had said that 'the French have a profound respect for the dead and the sacredness of places of burial.' The page for that reference," he said to Stratmeyer, "escapes me at the moment."

Edward straightened, as if strengthening himself for the horrors that would follow. "'They used this sacred place as a market garden. The moldering bodies of the dead fertilized its vegetables. Later, the garden was used as a common dump, where dogs and horses had been buried. The soil was soaked with polluted waters from undrained laundries. As a culmination of degradation, it was occupied by a contractor for removing night soil.'"

Edward allowed his voice to catch at the last. He hesitated before continuing. "Page fifty-eight," he said to Stratmeyer, who now pushed the report vehemently aside. "Porter received permission to mine underneath the existing buildings. He obtained the services of a French mining engineer named Paul Weiss to direct the work. He hired a crew of men to sink various shafts in open areas and to mine galleries under the buildings. Porter had obtained a copy of a letter from a Mrs. Janet Taylor, who was the oldest sister of John Paul Jones. In it, she stated that the body had been placed in a leaden coffin. The knowledge of the leaden coffin greatly simplified the work, for the diggers were now able to ignore remains not so contained. Soundings were made from along the lengths of each gallery so that the location of any leaden coffins could not possibly be missed. Porter found his first leaden coffin on February twenty-second, nineteen oh five. Its copper inscription plate had fallen off, and was at first illegible. Upon cleaning, however, he made it out to read *'M.E. Anglois, Twenty de May, Seventeen Ninety.'* He paid no further attention to that coffin."

Stratmeyer could contain himself no longer. "That information," he said, his face distorted with yellow wrinkles, "is all in this report." He tapped the brown folder on the table before him. "There's no need to—"

"Mr. Stratmeyer!" Edward pretended great anger. He felt his face flush red as before. "These facts," he said in a rushed voice, "are very critical to my position."

He stood back and smiled, as if he had already forgiven the old butcher. "I will prove to you," he continued in a voice so soft that it hardly carried across the table, "that General Porter dug up the wrong man."

Rossiter gently tapped his gavel. "Sounds like this might be a difficult session," he said to Edward with a smile. "Let's take a ten minute break."

The Society rose as one, all except Stratmeyer, who remained adamantly in his chair and fingered the Porter Report.

CHAPTER 17
The Lafitte Society
Saint Louis, Missouri
February 6, 1938

Rossiter called the meeting back to order.

"Mr. Livingston," he said after the members had resumed their seats, "this all sounds most fascinating, and I am very impressed by your obvious intimate knowledge and verbatim recollection of the report. However, I doubt that it is necessary to go into such detail. Mr. Stratmeyer has a copy of the report. If necessary, we can review it at our leisure."

Edward nodded, making a deferential bow to the chairman. "Sorry. I'll try to speed things up."

He strolled to the window and effected a more conversational tone. "Porter's men found five leaden coffins in the cemetery, all told. He dismissed four of them for various reasons. But one had no nameplate at all. It was the one he ordered to be opened. Upon the opening, they encountered a strong odor of alcohol and a body wrapped in a winding sheet nestled in a bed of straw."

In spite of the recrimination by Rossiter, Edward could not contain himself. The moment was too ripe. He slowly turned from the window, bent himself slightly from the waist, and quoted directly from the report in a low, ghostly tone: "'Half a dozen candles were placed near the head of the coffin, and the winding sheet was removed from the head and chest, exposing the face. To our intense surprise, the body was marvelously well preserved, all the flesh remaining intact'—"

"Mr. Livingston," Rossiter reminded.

Edward straightened. "Sorry," he said. "But there is one

additional matter of significance that must be spoken to." He looked to Rossiter as if for permission to proceed, and received a nod in return.

"The nose had been badly bent over toward the right side and pressed down, probably distorted because of its close proximity to the lid of the coffin. That fact was most unfortunate, for, as you will see from my exhibits, the nose becomes very important. Porter had with him a duplicate of a Congressional Medal awarded to Jones in seventeen eighty-seven, struck by the noted medalist Augustin Dupré, which showed his face in profile. The observers were in agreement that the profile on the medal matched the one in the coffin in spite of the disfigured nose."

Edward resumed his lively pacing about the room. He noted that all eyes followed him as he moved, even those of Stratmeyer, who had completely abandoned his study of the report.

"The body was not in uniform. There were no momentos in the coffin. There was nothing to indicate that this body was their quarry, with the exception of the similarity to the medal. They measured the length of the body, and found it to be roughly the same as the height of John Paul Jones." Edward halted and held his right index finger high. "A point to be remembered, gentlemen." He continued his pacing. "The body, lead coffin and all, was removed to the Paris School of Medicine for further study. Oddly, Porter made no mention of the weight, or the difficulty the men must have had in carrying it along that narrow, low-ceilinged passage.

"The examination took six days and was carried out by a team of experts assembled by Porter." Edward paused. Again he held his finger high. "And most of the information on Jones was provided to the experts by Porter himself. In the harsh light of the examining room, the Congressional Medal was no longer relied upon, perhaps because it was too small and lacking in detail. Instead, two busts were appropriated, both by Jean-Antoine Houdon. One, in marble, was life-sized, and represented Jones in the uniform of an admiral. The bust on the table before you is an exact duplicate of the Houdon bust."

Edward paused while everyone studied the sculpture. He hoped they appreciated the effort, for the packing and shipping to St. Louis had cost a pretty penny.

"The other bust," he continued after a moment, "in terracotta, was three-quarter size, in court dress."

Edward had completed a slow circuit of the room, still keenly aware that all eyes followed him as he progressed. He returned to his place at the end of the table before his stack of papers. He paused once more, pretending to contemplate his next words, although he knew precisely what they were to be. Edward unbuttoned his coat to reveal a red ribbon around his neck and a gleaming gold medal.

Stratmeyer moved right in, as if on cue. "Mr. Chairman," Stratmeyer said, addressing himself to Rossiter. "I object again. Mr. Livingston has gone on too long with his attempts to discredit this report."

In response, Edward lifted the ribbon from the back of his neck. Stratmeyer and the others were glued to his every movement.

"Porter makes it clear," Stratmeyer continued, slapping his hand on the folder, "that Jones was easy to identify because of the preservation of his facial features. Mr. Livingston has submitted no real evidence, only his own conjectures—"

He halted in desperation when Edward dropped the heavy medal beside the folder with a loud clang.

"The Congressional Medal," Edward said slowly, drawing

out his words dramatically, "struck by Augustin Dupré in seventeen eighty-eight." He gazed ruefully at the gleaming gold. "This," he added, "is not the real medal. This one was made from the original dies, has been gold-plated, and is guaranteed to exactly duplicate the original." He smiled at Stratmeyer. "I can furnish authenticating documents that attest to its accuracy. It is a facsimile," he continued with a mysterious voice as if he were whispering in a crypt, "of the reproduction that Porter compared, by candlelight, with the figure in the coffin. Please take special note of the nose. Prominent, wouldn't you say? Turned up on the end?"

Stratmeyer studied the medal without comment.

"Compare the profile on the medal with the bust before you," Edward declared in a loud voice. "The bust, I might add, is likewise an exact duplicate of the original. I can provide papers on that, as well. But," he continued, hooking a thumb into the armhole of his vest, "study the two for a moment. Very similar, aren't they? Especially note the nose."

Stratmeyer remained still and silent as if he were becoming more cautious of traps.

"They should be similar," Edward went on. "Dupré used the bust as a model when he made the medal. Why, do you suppose," he asked Stratmeyer directly, "that when Dupré made the medal, he used the bust? Why didn't he use the real live man as a model, the man who had personally ordered the medal to be struck, at the direction of Congress?"

Stratmeyer didn't move a whisker.

"It might be," Edward continued, knowing he would get no response, "that Dupré was aware that Jones was pleased with the bust. You will recall that the Admiral was a very vain man. He had already fired one renowned medalist, Jean-Martin Renaud. Why? Was it because he was displeased with

Renaud's sketches? We'll never know the answer. The secret is buried with him."

Edward walked slowly to his end of the table. He fumbled in his papers, then extracted a large glossy photograph, which he sailed through the air to land beside the medal.

"A photograph of Renaud's study, currently at the Boston Public Library. This is the design that was rejected. You will note considerable differences. In the Renaud, the face is full. Heavy lines around the mouth, under the ear. A double chin. Bumps on the forehead. The differences are significant. The angle and relative difference in size of the ear. The change in hair style. In Renaud, curls are obvious over the temple. But please note. The most significant difference is in the shape of the nose. And, most significant of all, in the Renaud photograph, the nose is straight. There is no pronounced upturn at the end." Edward pointed to the bust. "Note that on Houdon's bust the hair is drawn straight back. No curls. The face does not appear as one would expect of a commander. Rather, it is inquisitive, almost boyish. Pay particular attention to the nose. It bulges noticeably at the end. Upturned, you might say." He sailed another photograph across the table. "A silhouette by one Jean Millette," Edward said. "Seventeen seventy-six. The Franklin Roosevelt Library. Note the upturned nose." Another photograph. "A Miniature by Lowendal. Naval Academy museum." Edward struck a questioning pose, grasping his chin between thumb and forefinger. "In this engraving you will note a difference in the man entirely. In fact, you must even take my word for it—at the moment—that it is actually intended to represent John Paul Jones. Here, he has a roll of curls that nearly hide his ears. He has an extraordinarily high forehead—not at all like any of the others. In spite of his naval uniform, he could almost be a Methodist minister."

The members of the Society chuckled, all except Stratmeyer.

"In fact," Edward continued, waggling a finger in Stratmeyer's direction, "this miniature is not unlike an occupant of this very room!"

The Society chuckled audibly. The photograph did indeed resemble Stratmeyer.

"Oh," Edward continued as he selected yet another photograph. "I forgot to mention—that in the Lowendal—the nose is straight. Here," he said, sliding a new photograph across the table, "is a portrait by Charles Wilson Peale, done in seventeen eighty-one. It hangs in Independence Hall, Philadelphia. Jones is in uniform, but appears distinctly un-admiral-like. I should add that Lieutenant Dale, who you will recall was Jones' First Officer aboard *BonHomme Richard*, thought the Peale portrait to be an excellent likeness. However, Thomas Jefferson, who saw much of Jones in later years, said that the portrait looked to be of a different person entirely."

"Mr. Livingston," Rossiter intervened like a judge, "where does this all lead?"

"I'm trying to prove, Mr. Chairman," Edward replied, "that many respected images of John Paul Jones exist, and did exist at the time of Porter's exhumation. Each is very dissimilar from the other, so much so that none can be said to serve a useful purpose in the identification. Especially when such a very prominent feature as the nose appears in so many various forms. And especially when the actual nose of the man himself was so severely distorted by the lid of the coffin. The representations are so varied that, if one were to pick and choose, one might easily match *any* of these with almost any corpse that might be found. Here, for example," he said, sliding out yet another photograph, "is a painting which hangs at the Naval Academy. Admittedly, it was done almost one hundred years after his death, but I show it to you for your amusement. In it, he looks like a pugilist, ready to do battle with the great prizefighter Joe Louis—"

"You have amused us enough, Mr. Livingston," Stratmeyer said. "We don't require further amusement. The fact remains that a panel of experts identified the body at the time, using a bust—"

"And exactly which bust did they use, Mr. Stratmeyer?" Edward asked. "I refer you to the notes by Dr. Papillault, who at the time was the assistant director of anthropology in the School for Advanced Studies at the Paris Institute. Porter states that this esteemed doctor was a scientist of rare experience in the examination and identification of human bodies. Dr. Papillault notes considerable differences, especially in the two busts, both by Houdon, that were used for the identification. The one in terra-cotta, then owned by the Marquis de Biron, which I have unfortunately not been able to photograph, states that one has a thinner, more emaciated figure than the other. The modeling and the study are different, he explains. One has an energetic face, even dominating. In the other, the rough sailor has become a man of the court. 'Houdon attenuated the energy of his features, he diminished the robustness of the face, effaced the bumps of his forehead.' Papillault borrowed features from the two of them and combined them to make his comparison.

"The terra-cotta bust was executed later in life. By that time, Jones had become a man of the court, and wore curls about his ears. We know that features change as one ages, especially if one suffers physically from illness as Jones did late in life. Yet, the principal identification was made from the earlier bust, when he was active, robust. In his prime. There were many representations available at the time, as I have shown you. It was, I submit, a game of 'choose a likeness to confirm the identity of the body we have found. Combine the features of several, if it suits you.' Yet Porter states, and I quote his exact words, they 'enabled one to verify the perfect resemblance existing between the reproduction of the features of the Admiral and the corpse.'"

Edward paused. He slid his wallet from an inside coat pocket and methodically withdrew a dollar bill, which he held high. "A dollar bill," he proclaimed. "And on it—a picture from another of our Revolutionary War heroes—the esteemed George Washington."

He handed it grandly to Lionel Croft, who inspected the bill briefly and passed it to his right.

"Study the drawing carefully," Edward said, watching the travel of the bill about the table. "It is based on a portrait by Gilbert Stuart done in seventeen ninety-six. Alas, although the Stuart portrait represents every schoolboy's image of the features of our first president, it is said that it does not much look like him. Note the wide jaw, the broad nose, the puffy cheeks. Not very flattering at all."

Edward groped in his trouser pocket. He exposed a coin, which he dropped on the table before Croft, who immediately picked it up and inspected it. "A quarter," Edward said, watching Croft's face. "Also with a likeness of Washington, in profile."

Edward abandoned Croft's face and strode around the room exuding confidence, his head held high. "Note that the head has an oval shape. A narrow jaw. A thin nose. A small mouth. Aristocratic, perhaps. In direct contrast to the dollar bill, which makes Washington look rather like a tired washerwoman. The profile on the quarter," Edward continued, "is based on a bust by one Jean Antoine Houdon." He whirled to face Stratmeyer. "The very same sculptor who created the bust of John Paul Jones. If you were exhuming the body of George Washington," he asked sharply, leaning slightly toward Stratmeyer, "which image would you use? That of the dollar bill? Or that of the quarter?"

Stratmeyer was undeterred. "There were other tests as well. The identification was not based solely on the likeness. There was the autopsy."

"Ah, yes," Edward answered. He resumed his pacing about the room, hands clasped behind his back. "The autopsy."

CHAPTER 18
The Lafitte Society
Saint Louis, Missouri
February 6, 1938

Edward repeated his earlier question to Stratmeyer. "How tall am I?"

Stratmeyer looked away.

"Would you say that I am short?"

"What does this have to do with Porter's report?"

"It has everything to do with it."

"Then I don't care to discuss it."

"The report is above reproach?"

"In my opinion."

"In every regard?"

"In all the important ones. Lawyers like you," Stratmeyer said scornfully, "can find something wrong with everything."

"So you're saying—there might be something wrong with the report? It isn't above reproach?"

"On all the major points, it is."

"I'm talking about one of the major points. In fact, *the* most major point."

"Get on with it, then."

"I'm trying to. How tall am I?"

"I don't see how your height has anything to do with the report."

"It has everything to do with it. How tall am I?" Edward straightened.

Stratmeyer looked him up and down. "Five foot ten," he said at last.

"Exactly right, Mr. Stratmeyer. Extraordinary."

Rossiter intervened. "Mr. Livingston, I think—"

Edward ignored the chairman and closed in on his prey. "Would you say," he asked Stratmeyer, "that my height is about average?"

Stratmeyer's head pulled back on his neck. He tucked his chin into his chest. "Average."

Edward showed relief. "How tall would I have to be if I were considered a 'short man?'"

"Mr. Livingston." Rossiter pointed his gavel, but Stratmeyer held up his hand.

"Let him finish his little game." The butcher pursed his lips as if giving the question considerable thought. "Five foot seven."

"Do you recall, in Porter's report," Edward continued, glancing at the brown folder on the table, "how tall he indicated John Paul Jones was?"

Stratmeyer shook his head, his lips still pursed. "Why don't you tell me?"

"Five foot seven."

"Extraordinary." Stratmeyer deliberately mimicked Edward.

"Isn't it, though? Is that why, you suppose, that Jones was considered to be a short man? Indeed, a small man?"

"I never thought about it."

"Perhaps you should." Edward stepped to the table and extracted a sheet of paper from his pile. "This," he said, sliding the paper down the table to Stratmeyer, "is a copy of a reference to Jones by Abigail Adams, wife of John Adams. She had met Jones several times. You will note that she refers to him as a 'little man.'"

Stratmeyer looked at the paper and nodded. "She does."

"And here," Edward continued, extracting a second sheet, "is a reference to Jones by John Hancock. Does he not also refer to Jones as a 'little man?'"

Again, a glance, a nod. "He does."

Another sheet of paper. "A reference by one Nathanial Fanning. Does he not say that Jones is of 'low stature'?"

A nod.

"Another by the Marquis de Lafayette—"

"Mr. Livingston." Rossiter asked, "what are you trying to prove?"

Edward glanced at Rossiter with gratitude. "I am trying to prove, Mr. Chairman, that John Paul Jones was considered by his peers to be a short man."

"You proved it." Stratmeyer tossed the papers back to Edward. He grinned and folded his hands atop Porter's report. "Everybody agrees that Jones was short. I agree. Porter did. The body he found was five foot seven. That's short. It checks out."

The grin faded when Edward sorted through his papers and extracted, with an exaggerated flourish, yet another sheet. Edward drummed his fingers against his chin as he studied the paper. "It is well known," he said, "that the heights of men have increased considerably in the past several hundred years. Due to improved diet, so the experts say. It is only necessary to observe suits of armor from earlier periods to note how the height of man increased." He looked directly at Stratmeyer. "I have toured many museums, both in England, and on the Continent. I have measured the size of suits of armor. I have visited museums of vintage fashion and measured the clothing. My own investigation has revealed that the *average* height of European men in the eighteenth century—which was the period of time that John Paul Jones walked on this earth—was five feet, four inches."

Edward dropped the paper before Stratmeyer. "If John Paul Jones were indeed five foot seven as Porter indicates, he would have been three inches taller than the average. He would not have been considered," Edward said, looking straight at Stratmeyer, "a small man. Rather, he would have been referred to as a *tall* man."

Stratmeyer was unmoved. "You tabulate this data yourself?" he asked, his eyes fixed on Edward's sheet.

"I did."

"Well, then—"

Edward picked a delicate newspaper clipping from his briefcase. "I realize," he said thoughtfully, scanning the thin paper, "that you are suspicious of newspaper articles." He cupped the hand under his chin again. "However, a report was very recently carried out by Japan's Ministry of Health and Welfare, and the contents are so coincidentally pertinent that it bears introduction at this point. That report states that the average height of a twenty-year-old Japanese man today is five feet, eight and a quarter inches. That's four inches taller than the same age group thirty years ago."

Stratmeyer rocked in his chair. "What does that have to do with—"

"According to an American study," Edward continued, "the average height of a twenty-year-old American male has increased one inch in the past twenty years." He allowed his spectacles to slip lower and peered at Stratmeyer over the top.

"So?" Stratmeyer said. "That's today! We're talking about two hundred years ago!"

As cool as Clarence Darrow, Edward allowed the clipping to flutter to the table. Still watching Stratmeyer, he extracted yet another sheet from the pile. "A report," he said, holding the paper out to Stratmeyer, "showing comparative profiles of growth, as recorded from enlistment rosters in the British Royal Marines for the eighteenth century. The average height at that time," he intoned with the heaviest resonance he could muster, "was five feet, four inches."

Stratmeyer fell silent, either because he had become wise or convinced.

"Mr. Livingston," Rossiter said gently.

"Yes?"

"Where," the chairman asked, "did Porter get the information that Jones was five foot seven?"

Thank you, Mr. Rossiter. Edward studiously and deliberately selected two books from his briefcase. He held the books high for all around the table to see. "A two-volume biography," he announced, "entitled *Paul Jones*, by one Augustus C. Buell." He lay the books on the table. "This biography was published in nineteen hundred. Of course, as we have noted, Porter began his investigations into the location of the remains of John Paul Jones in June, eighteen ninety-nine. His search culminated on April fourteenth, nineteen oh five, at the completion of the autopsy.

"Porter served as Ambassador to France from the time of his appointment in March, eighteen ninety-seven until his resignation March fourth, nineteen oh four. His term as Ambassador would have coincided with the period of Buell's research for the biography. Buell may have consulted with the Ambassador, which may have spurred Porter into his search for the body of Jones. Porter does make references to Buell in his report, so we may be assured that he relied on it. Perhaps they even become friends. In any case," Edward continued heavily, "the biography by Buell was considered—at that time— as the ultimate authority on John Paul Jones. Certainly, it was the most current."

"I take it, Mr. Livingston," Rossiter asked, "the reference to the height came from Buell?"

Edward nodded. "It almost certainly did. Porter baldly states that Jones was five feet seven inches, without giving reference to the source of his information." He turned to Stratmeyer. "Page sixty-six. I have read Buell, quite thoroughly. On two occasions, he states the exact height of John Paul Jones as five feet, seven inches, although he cites no source. On several occasions, he refers to Jones as 'a small man.'" Edward drew back from the table and folded his arms. "Buell has subsequently been termed by some as 'the father of lies' about John Paul Jones. His volumes contain so many untruths that historians consider his writing to be a work of fiction. It is unfortunate that Porter relied so heavily on Buell's citation of the height of John Paul Jones."

The members of the Society remained silent.

Edward straightened, tightening his folded arms. "Gentlemen," he said in a low voice, "there is no scientific evidence that would suggest it is possible for any man to grow three inches in his grave."

CHAPTER 19
New Orleans, Louisiana
February 6, 1993, 4:09 PM

"Did they buy it?" Coming from the shadows, Mickey's voice sounded disembodied, like the voice of a ghost on Halloween.

Edward slid away his glasses and lay them atop the file folder. He rocked back in the soft chair and grinned, arched his eyebrows, and paused for dramatic effect before answering, one slowly articulated word at a time. "Hook. Line. And sinker."

"Fantastic!" Mickey sprang from the chair, as delighted as Edward. "How did you know? Did they vote on it?"

"By a show of hands."

"Because of the height thing?"

"The proof of the height was, as Rossiter put it, 'an unequivocal fact.' I had made my point. It would not have been surer if Porter had dug up a black man with three arms and one eye."

"So you won!"

"I won that round. Even Stratmeyer agreed. The vote was unanimous. After the vote, I went into the rest of the autopsy, but I needn't have bothered. The remainder was academic, but I recited it anyway, because I thought it might be important. And it further substantiated my argument: The doctors found a small spot on one of his lungs, which indicated he might have had pneumonia. Remember, the alcohol had preserved the parts pretty well."

"Is that what he was supposed to have died of? Pneumonia?" Mickey's body was all in motion, moving in and out of

the circle of light. Edward groped his glasses back, not wanting to miss his excitement.

"No. Not pneumonia. Jones was very ill at one time of his
life, and they conjectured that he might have had pneumonia
then. It was only conjecture, but it was one of the identifica-
tions that Porter seized upon, however."

"What *did* he die of?"

"The death certificate cited 'dropsy of the chest.'"

"Sounds awful."

"Does, doesn't it? You see, Jones suffered with severe swell-
ing in the latter part of his life, especially in the lower regions.
Doctors called it 'dropsy' in those days, an accumulation of
fluid."

"Did they find out anything about dropsy in the autopsy?"

"There were evidences of nephritus in the liver. Nephritus,
simply another word for 'disease,' could cause symptoms of
dropsy. Porter seized on that, as well."

"But you said Porter was such a responsible guy. A Civil
War general, and all that. How come he was in such a hurry?"

"He was spending his own money. He had hired people to
dig up half the cemetery. He found a body without a nameplate on the coffin, and the body had certain similarities to
John Paul Jones. And Porter was at the moment unemployed,
anxious to return home."

"You mean—who's ever going to know, anyway?"

"Perhaps something like that. It's hard to blame him. But
there were other things, too. Other inconsistencies."

Mickey had almost disappeared in the gloom. Edward found
him standing close to the mantel, peering up at the medal.

"The coffin was virtually empty, except for the body, of
course. Wrapped in a winding sheet. No uniform. He wore a

small cap on his head like a skull cap, with some indistinct markings that they thought might represent the letters JP. There were no mementos to indicate that this man was such a re-vered hero. Not one."

The rain drummed down outside, so heavily that it was audible even in the quiet study. The street lights had flickered on along St. Charles Avenue, streaking their amber light through the rain and glistening on wet cars splashing through the puddles in low places where the drains were clogged or inadequate.

"Not even," Edward continued, "his sword."

Mickey reached up to touch the medal, making it swing gently, shimmering a muted golden light.

"What happened," Mickey asked without turning, "when they announced their vote?"

"Oh, they didn't release their findings."

"Why not? That was big stuff!" Mickey abandoned the medal.

"It wasn't an official vote, just a show of hands. Nothing was entered in the minutes. I could understand their position. They could hardly make an announcement at that point that the wrong man was entombed at Annapolis. They still re-quired solid, definitive proof."

"Did you ever give them the proof?"

"We're getting to that. But the identification of John Paul Jones' body was outside their purview, anyway. They were The Lafitte Society, remember, not the John Paul Jones Society."

"Yeah, but if you proved—"

"That was only half the battle, at least as far as John Paul Jones was concerned. They agreed that Porter had erred. They hadn't committed themselves on his transport to Louisiana by Jean Paul. And when they agreed to that, if they did, I still had to show good reason for his body to be buried in Barataria. I put a lot of miles on my pirogue to prove that."

"I thought you already knew where the cemetery was."

"Oh, I knew about the cemetery, all right. But I didn't know how the colony was set up, how it worked, or the locations of the warehouses."

"You needed that to prove where John Paul Jones was buried?"

"Among other things; I also needed to locate all the trade routes and mark them." Edward swung his hand at the wall of maps, the multi-colored lines up the bayous.

"Did you find anything? In all that digging around?"

"I didn't find any gold coins, or pieces of eight. But I figured out how the system worked. I knew it wouldn't be good enough to simply say to the Society that Jean Paul buried John Paul Jones in the cemetery beside the Bayou des Oises. I had to take them back, lead them by the hand through the swamps."

"*A priori* again?"

"It settled Porter's hash, didn't it?"

CHAPTER 20
Grande Terre Island, Barataria
January 16, 1805

PRES. BY Edw. Livingston, Esq.
FEBRUARY 6, 1940

The black bodies glistened naked in the morning sun. They poised momentarily on the waist of *Success*, then plunged into the turgid waters of Barataria Bay. Some leaped willingly, others hesitatingly. Some balked until sailors prodded them over the side with belaying pins.

Jean Paul watched from the island, seated in the shade of a palmetto overhang that extended from the front wall of a fisherman's shack. Alexander sat close beside him on a rough wooden bench. They watched a naked female, bony thin but for a bulbous pregnancy, who shrieked when prodded and shrieked again when she splashed into the water, belly first.

"First bath they's had in months," Nez Coupé said. He had a bench all to himself on which he sprawled, leaning his back against the splintery boards of the shack. "And God knows they needs it." He watched Jean Paul closely. He snorted a laugh, a lisping burst like a winch wanting grease.

Nez Coupé. Cut Lip. One of the more unsavory-appearing members of Lafitte's band, his face was disfigured by a red lumpy scar from the lower part of his nose to his mouth. The flesh, apparently severed by the slashing of a knife, had not been properly matched before the healing began, which resulted in an upper lip not in its original alinement. A single brown tooth revealed itself even when the whiskery mouth was closed.

"Longer'n that," Pierre said. "You should smell the ship."

Alexander's brother Pierre sat on an intricately carved chair that might have graced a palace in its glory days. Reduced to three legs, the chair inched into the sand with each of Pierre's heavy movements. He looked nothing at all like his older brother. Pierre was tall, nearly as tall as Jean, but was vastly overweight, like a full spread of dirty sail, giving him the appearance of laziness and devotion to drink. His small eyes, squinted nearly closed from the glare of the sun on the water, were disarmingly crossed.

They gathered on the front porch of the fisherman's shack,

if the overhang could be called a porch at all. There was no
floor underfoot, only the fine sand of Grande Terre Island.
But the overhang provided shade from a sun biting hot, even
in January.

"Should have put them darks farther away," Nez Coupé
said. More of the brown tooth showed when he wriggled his
nose. "I smells them."

There was quite an odor. But Jean Paul was unsure if it
came from the slaves or from the rotting vegetation on the
island. Or spoils from the Gulf, washed up on the seaward side
of the island. Or from Nez Coupé himself, for whom a dip in
the bay might have been as beneficial as for the slaves.

"Jean. What's with Jean?" Nez Coupé folded his arms over
his belly. His lip twitched.

Jean Paul started at the sound of his name. But it was to
Jean Lafitte that Nez Coupé referred. Jean Paul relaxed slightly
and watched a half-dozen pirogues converge on *Success*, cluster-
ing about like skittering water insects.

"Only know what he told me," Alexander said, gesturing
at Pierre, who now sat with his chin sagged into his huge
rounded chest. "Jean was in *Dorado*. Pierre sailed in *Success*.
When they couldn't get in at Mobile to unload, they went to
New Orleans. Same there. The Customs boat come out before
they had even lost wind. They turned right around without
anchoring and sailed back down the river." Alexander touched
a finger to the scars above his eye.

Nez Coupé grunted. "Fed'rals. Yankee Customs. It ain't
the same as 'twas before you went away. It's all 'Merican now."

"Then they came here, to Grande Terre," Alexander continued. "Turned the darks over to a fisherman, Pierre told me."

"That's the fisherman." Nez Coupé pointed to a straw-hatted figure warping a pirogue alonside the finger dock. His muscular arms curled the paddle so deftly that hardly a ripple showed in the water. "His name's Manual Perrin. This's his shack."

"After the unloading," Alexander said, watching the fisherman leap onto the dock, "they sailed back to Port-au-Prince. Jean pulled ahead, In *Dorado*. Pierre was maybe a mile behind." He paused when the first pirogues from *Success*, loaded with goods, began to touch the beach.

"*Dorado* must have caught a good breeze. She pulled away over the horizon, which she should never have done. *Success* heard cannon, so she piled on canvas. When she pulled over the horizon, she saw *Dorado* surrounded by Spaniards. Then *Success* lost her wind altogether. She sat becalmed and watched the Spaniards sail away to Cuba, taking *Dorado* with them."

"Bastards," Nez Coupé muttered.

They fell silent and watched the unloading. Jean Paul looked back to the deserted *Bonheur*, wondering just how he was going to manage the disposition of the coffin.

"There ain't much hope, then," Nez Coupé grunted.

"Not after Jean cut up the Spaniards on *Atrevida*. They would've been pretty mad."

Alexander's face strained. "Could be," he said. "But I'm going after him, anyway."

"To Morro Castle?" Nez Coupé scoffed. "You'd never get under the guns."

"Maybe we'll need better cannon."

Nez Coupé squinted one eye closed, pulling his lip up even farther. "Thought you brung some back from France."

"Some. But I need to go again."

"Why?" Nez Coupé exploded. "You just come from there. Best be here, to figger out how to handle the Fed'rals."

"I brought you a man to do that." Alexander looked at Jean Paul.

"Heh?" Nez Coupé's eye flung open. He leaned forward, startling Jean Paul, who drew back as if he were about to be attacked. "Him?" He stared at Jean Paul. At his billowy white silk shirt, fresh out of the trunk that morning. At his shining shoes with the glittering buckles, specially cleaned for the first sojourn into the New World.

Jean Paul stirred. He felt alien, unsure, and he wanted no part of this nest of pirates and smugglers, if that's what they were. He gathered himself to object, but was uncertain. It would be easy to be laughed at or worse, in this coarse place.

"He's *un marchand*."

"*Un marchand*, is he?"

Before Jean Paul could protest, Alexander tapped him on the knee. Like a warning. "Let's take a walk," he said, in a low voice.

He rose swiftly, nearly upsetting the narrow bench, and headed along the beach toward the unloading. Jean Paul shot a quick glance at the leering Nez Coupé before hastening to follow his benefactor.

"We had an agreement," Jean Paul said when he caught up with Alexander.

"Still do." They skirted the growing pile of merchandise unloaded from *Success*, thrown willy-nilly on the dirty sand. Bolts of cloth, partially unwound; ornately framed mirrors in an open packing case; another open box containing hatchets and knives spotted with rust; burlap sacks flung on the damp sand, sugar spilling from a ruptured bag.

"I lived up to my part of the agreement," Alexander said. "Now you need to do yours."

"We were supposed to go to New Orleans."

"Not my fault," Alexander flung over his shoulder. "You heard what happened there: New Orleans is closed."

"I didn't hear that it was closed."

"It's closed to us."

As they passed the pen that was the *barracoon*, the slaves stood watching with sullen eyes from behind the fence. The pregnant female sat on the wet sand, apparently unharmed by her fall into the water and swim to shore.

Alexander drew up where a palmetto overhung the beach, touching the tips of its fronds into the water.

"Maybe it's closed to you," Jean said, standing close.

Alexander scrutinized him. He touched a tentative finger to the burn mark above his eye. "Meaning?"

"I mean," Jean stammered, "not for legitimate—"

"What's legitimate?"

"Well." Jean cautioned himself. His position was, after all, tenuous. "What," he asked, "are you going to do with that?" He gestured toward the merchandise heaped on the beach. Another pirogue had arrived. The pile was growing.

"We'll run it in from here." Alexander bent to pick up a stick from the sand.

"Run it to where?"

"To New Orleans."

"How?"

"By pirogue."

Jean Paul was exasperated. He looked about at the enclosed bay, the two anchored ships. The laden pirogues paddling to the little island. "Just where in hell," he asked with deliberation, "*is* New Orleans?"

Alexander crunched down on his heels. He drew an erratic north-south line in the sand with the twig. "Mississippi River," he said. He jabbed a hole with the twig alongside the line that represented the river. "New Orleans." The twig returned to the mouth of the river, then drew a crooked line westward. Another jab. "Grande Terre." He looked up to see if Jean Paul was watching.

From the hole that was Grande Terre, the twig wobbled northward and curved east to New Orleans. "Bayous," Alexander said. "Where the river used to run. Still does, sometimes. When it floods."

"So you go up the bayous? In pirogues?"

"Fishermen do. All the time. That's what Manuel Perrin does."

"How long have *you* been doing this?"

"Never did it before. We used to sail right up The River. Like Nez Coupé said, it's different now. The Americans are here. Customs."

Jean Paul was puzzled. "But you've been away, in France. With Bonaparte. How do you know—"

"Pierre explained it all to me last night."

"It sounds like smuggling."

"You could call it that. It's what's got to be, I reckon."

"How do the darks get there? Swim?"

"They goes in the pirogues, too."

A light rain began to fall. A bolt of bright red silk began to darken from the wet.

"You didn't tell me there would be smuggling."

"Didn't know, before. Weren't smuggling, before."

They could smell the stench of the slaves, the fouling of the crowded *barracoon*.

"The darks get smuggled, too?"

"Guess they have to be." Alexander nodded, his eyes studying the map in the sand.

"Are the slaves illegal?"

"Naw. Slaves ain't illegal. Not so far, anyhow."

"But the smuggling of them is."

"Reckon."

"I don't like that."

"Don't like what?"

"Any part of it. The smuggling. I don't like the slavery, either."

"Nobody likes it much. But they got to be. They's just goods, like anything else. They slaves before, anyhow."

"What?"

"We didn't make them slaves. They was, already. When Pierre took them from the Spaniard."

Jean Paul pondered this peculiar rationalizing. "You'll sell them? In New Orleans?"

"Your job. That's your half of the agreement."

Jean felt rain patter on his shoulders. The agreement had nothing to do with smuggling. Or pirating. Or slaves. He shook his head. "That's not our agreement. We agreed that I would run your shipping business. In return for your—"

"Nothing's changed."

"Smuggling's changed. You didn't say anything about smuggling."

"Smuggling don't matter. Nobody cares, in New Orleans, whether things is smuggled or not. Ports is closing everywhere. Between the Americans and the English ..." Alexander's voice trailed off. "The English are moving in on Martinique, Guadaloupe. This'll be the only place left."

"This?"

"Barataria."

Jean shook his head violently, flinging the raindrops from his hair. "Barataria isn't New Orleans."

"It's as close as we can get."

"How long will it take to get the stuff up the bayous by pirogue?"

"Three days, Pierre says. That's a problem; one of the problems. It's too long. Three days up, three days back, plus the time for selling. Captains don't want to wait that long."

"Why don't you go someplace else, then?"

"Told you. There ain't no place else. And this's the best market. New Orleans. The German coast, upstream on the river, lots of new plantations; they need the darks to work the land."

"Why not just take them into New Orleans? Pay the customs?"

Alexander shook his head. "Too expensive. Couldn't sell anything. Have to charge seven hundred dollars a head. Farmers can't afford that. If we take them up the bayous, we can sell them for two hundred."

"I won't do it. It's not our agreement, whatever you say."

"All right," Alexander said, tapping the stick against his thigh. "So what'll you do, then?"

Jean thought quickly. "I'll take the coffin to New Orleans. By pirogue."

"Then what?"

"Buy a wagon. Haul ... him ... to Washington City."

"Then what? Go knocking on the door to the President's house? Say, 'I've got John Paul Jones, out here in a box? Where should I put him?' They'll laugh you right out of town, if they don't lock you up."

Jean felt a tightening in his stomach. Alexander was right. It did sound absurd. The opportunity at L'Orient for transport to the New World had all happened too quickly. There hadn't been time to think it out. And they hadn't gone to New Orleans, after all. Instead, to some stinking fishing village—

"Best way might be to live up to our agreement." Alexander was still tapping the twig against his trousers. "That hasn't changed. You still owe me. If it hadn't been for me, you'd still be at L'Orient with your Cap'n."

Jean Paul wished he were.

"After a time," Alexander went on, "you'll be rich. Your chance will come. Then you haul Jones to Washington City. Maybe in a coach and four. All dressed up, fancy as you please. The President might even believe you."

The rain fell harder. Jean felt his shirt stick to his back from the wet. The bolt of silk had turned completely dark. The spill of sugar was no longer white; it blended with the sandy beach.

"You better get a warehouse built here," Jean Paul said. "Before everything's—"

He started at the dull boom of a cannon, muffled in the rain. At the west end of the island, the high yards of a ship glided above the palmetto scrub, making her way through the pass.

Alexander threw the twig into the water and raced through the rain back to the fishing village and the approaching ship.

RESP. SUB., G. Choteau, Sec.

FEBRUARY 6, 1940

CHAPTER 21
New Orleans, Louisiana
February 6, 1993, 4:26 PM

Mickey paced back and forth between the wall of maps and the fireplace, hands behind his back as if deep in thought. From time to time, reflected illumination from the desk lamp caught reddish highlights in his hair. Edward rotated the watch to the right-side-up position. Only an hour and a half remained.

"Say it." Edward could contain himself no longer.

Mickey halted before the fireplace. "Say what?"

"Whatever's bothering you."

His T-shirt had now pulled fully from the waistband of his jeans, exposing a lighter-colored, cleaner band around the bottom. "Just thinking about what you said, that's all. About those guys on Grande Terre."

"*A priori?*"

"Not sure I know how to do that yet."

"I spent a lot of time on that island. Picturing how it must have been."

"I guess you must've."

"What they said. What they did."

"Yeah."

Mickey seemed to have lost some of the enthusiasm gained after the flurry of excitement about Porter's digging up the wrong body.

"You don't believe it," Edward said, watching him closely.

"If I was a judge, I'd probably throw out your testimony. For lack of evidence."

Edward smiled. "You watch a lot of television?"

"Some." Mickey turned down the corners of his mouth and vigorously nodded in agreement. "Not much else to do."

In this modern world, even the darkest of hovels had a television set. Even the dark hovels of Carrollton. No telephone, perhaps, but always a television, the cheapest form of entertainment.

"You watch Ben Matlock? Perry Mason?"

"Never miss 'em." Mickey grinned broadly, his lips tight together. "I like lawyers."

Television provided narrow glimpses into courtrooms, however idealistic and rudimentary those glimpses might be. Legal dramas neatly fit into required time slots, including commercials, no matter how complex. Not quite like the real world, but the regular viewer did learn something about the justice system.

"Then you know about circumstantial evidence?"

"Sure. But I never heard about *a priori* before. Not until today, anyway."

"But there's always circumstantial evidence, isn't there?"

"Not always. Most of the time, there're *just* witnesses."

"You mean, for example, like a witness that saw somebody shoot somebody?"

"Like that."

"Does the witness see the bullet fly from the gun?"

"What?"

"The witness sees the gun in the suspect's hand. He hears the explosion. Sees the victim fall. Does the witness see the bullet fly?"

"Naw. He can't."

"Because the bullet flies too fast, right? Therefore, the flight of the bullet is assumed. The fact that it traveled to the victim is circumstantial."

Mickey clapped his hands on his thighs. "Did you just make that up?"

"It's an old example of circumstantial evidence. Every case deals with circumstantial evidence, whether it's called that or not. Whether it's even mentioned or not."

"But your story is all circumstantial."

If you think that, you haven't been listening. "I brought Jean Paul to America from France. Like the path of the bullet. Except I showed the bullet, too. After the bullet arrives at the victim, certain things begin to happen. We know that without being told. A blood vessel bursts. A bone breaks. A heart is stopped. We don't mention those things, usually. They're taken for granted. We only say that the perpetrator shot the victim and the victim died. So, what's wrong with my conjecturing certain things that happened to Jean Paul after he arrived? Or certain things he did?"

"But you don't really know what he did."

"I know he had to eat. He had to sleep. He had to go to the bathroom."

"Those are regular things. Not the things you said he did."

"But they're all circumstantial events. I merely went beyond those normal activities. He didn't just stand still and hold his breath for a hundred years, did he? What's wrong with projecting other things he might have done? To prove events that actually occurred?"

Mickey slapped his hands together in resignation.

"Tell me one of the events," Edward said, "that bothers you."

"Okay." Mickey's face brightened. "The thing about Alexander. You said he turned right around after he got to Barataria and sailed back to France. To get a breech-loading cannon, you said."

"History records," Edward said evenly, "that, in eighteen oh five, Alexander did just that. History says he returned to

France to fight with Napoleon again. Why would he do that? He had just come from France. History has no comment on that. However, history does say as soon as he got to France, he turned right around again and returned to Barataria. Why, for heaven's sake, would he do all that?"

"Maybe he just changed his mind a lot."

"It doesn't make good sense, does it? Don't you think that my story has more of a ring of truth?"

"But ... you're making up things. Twisting history."

"Am I? Something like the old story about the *Filles aux Cassettes?*"

"The what?"

"Back in eighteen twenty-one, when the Mississippi Company sent prostitutes from France to their employees in New Orleans. They were called Correction Girls, because the Company recruited them from the prison at Saltpétrière. The prostitutes didn't work out too well. The men wanted wives, not whores. So the Company tried again. This time, they advertised among good middle-class families for unmarried daughters who needed husbands. There were plenty of applicants, and the Company could be choosy. The girls were given little chests, or caskets, to carry their personal things in. So they were called *Filles aux Cassettes.*

"Years later, an odd thing occurred. It seems that none of the whores had children, but the *Filles* had plenty, because no one wanted to claim descendancy from the whores. One historian wrote that by some queer physiological mischance, none of the Correction Girls ever bore a child. The *Filles aux Cassettes*, on the other hand, must have been extremely fertile, each becoming the mother of at least a hundred children. Many of the finest families in New Orleans claim to have descended from the *Filles aux Cassettes*. None claim the Correction Girls. People believe what they want to believe. Now, *that's* twisting history."

Mickey laughed. "But that story isn't accepted history."

"Just ask those people that claim to have descended from the *Filles* about whether it's accepted or not. The Porter Report was accepted history too, you know. Still is, by most people."

Mickey bowed to him. One hand fore and one aft, just as he had greeted the busts of Napoleon and John Paul Jones.

"You make a good case."

"I am a lawyer, you know."

Mickey swung around and settled back in his chair, apparently satisfied. In spite of the outward appearance of a teenager, and in spite of the severe generation gap, Edward was beginning to regard him as a responsible adult.

"It was Alexander's idea?" Mickey asked. "To set up the smuggling thing and travel up the bayous? I always heard that Jean Lafitte thought all that up."

"Alexander didn't get credit for many of the things he did. And there were some big things, later. He was one of the unsung heroes of history. Perhaps it was because he was short, disfigured; ugly, even. He didn't look the type. Jean, on the other hand, was tall and handsome. Jean got all the credit."

"Distorted history."

"The history books are full of it."

"Yeah." They laughed together at the unintended pun. Edward liked this feeling of the growing bond with his grandson.

"But Jean Paul deserves plenty of credit, too. Alexander may have dreamed up the idea, but Jean made it work. Remember that Grande Terre was three days from New Orleans. When the captains sailed into the bay with their goods, ill-gotten or otherwise, they didn't want to wait around to collect their money. The captains wanted to get going, so Jean formed an association. He kept books on each ship. He itemized their goods, saw that they were moved to warehouses nearer New Orleans so buyers could make the trip out and back in the same day. He had to borrow money to pay off the captains, set up the warehouses and stores, hold the merchandise until it sold."

Mickey sniggered. "Doesn't sound much like a pirating operation."

"It wasn't; it was a business. Jean borrowed the money, just like any other businessman."

"Where would a pirate go to borrow money?"

"Remember: *he* wasn't a pirate. Mostly, he borrowed the money from a New Orleans banker named Joseph Sauvinet." Edward waited to see how that was received. "Okay?" he asked.

"Okay."

"There were many ships involved," Edward continued. "He called them his ships, although they weren't his ships. He called the men his men, although they weren't his men. He built a clapboard house on the highest part of the island, had it painted white and built a veranda all the way around so he could watch the activity both in the Gulf and in the bay. He dressed like a pirate and acted like a pirate. He played that part to the hilt, swashbuckling right along with the best of them. No one knew that he shrank from fighting and got sick in a rowboat. No one knew that he was an accountant in a pirate's costume. He was everybody's favorite pirate. New Orleans loved it.

"But he was making the Customs service look foolish when most of the supplies to New Orleans came up the bayous without paying duty. Governor Claiborne posted a reward for his arrest, and Jean posted an even bigger one for Claiborne's. New Orleans loved that, too, for everybody hated Claiborne. Business was great. Until one day in eighteen fourteen. A British ship appeared in the Gulf, and nothing would ever be the same again."

CHAPTER 22
Grande Terre Island, Barataria
September 3, 1814
PRES. BY Edw. Livingston, Esg.
FEBRUARY 6, 1946

Jean Paul stood on the wide veranda and watched the brig make a slow approach from the Gulf. Sunlight glinted intermittently on polished brass surfaces as she rolled in the slight chop. He unlimbered a long telescope and focused on the brig's somnolent Union Jack ballooning from her stern post, too heavy and ponderous to fully swell.

"What the hell—" he muttered aloud.

A white flag of truce waved from her top in a sudden burst of breeze. Mid-ships, a knot of white-clad sailors lowered a small gig over the side of the ship. Two sailors scrambled down a rope ladder, then reached up to assist a pair of resplendent officers who clambered down and stiffly took seats in the stern.

No British ship had ever come so audaciously close to the southern American coast. "What mischief could they be up to?" he asked aloud as the sailors rowed vigorously for shore, stirring a second white flag in the bow of the gig.

Jean Paul lowered the telescope when his Baratarians began to crash through the undergrowth on the gulfward side of the island. They lined up along the narrow beach, pushing and shoving, shouting provocative taunts at the English ship riding at anchor a comfortable distance beyond cannon range.

The gig neared the shore, expertly propelled by the English sailors in their dazzling white uniforms. It was within range of small arms now, and the Baratarians on the beach became increasingly noisy and raucous. Jean Paul lay aside the telescope and tore from the veranda and down the little-used path to the beach.

"Let them pass," he ordered.

The gig spun about and bumped stern first into the sand to allow the officers to disembark. Their job done for the moment, the seamen sat at stiff attention, oars properly vertical.

The brilliant ceremonial uniforms of the officers contrasted sharply with the slovenly loose clothing of the Baratarians, who were now reduced, under the glaring eye of their "Bos," to a subdued snorting and joking.

Jean Paul hesitated. Of late he had become increasingly concerned about the piracy and the smuggling and the slavery, to which he had devoted himself in order to accomplish a higher purpose. But this was hardly the time to falter. He marched along the narrow strip of sand like the pirate he pretended to be. He drew up before the taller and more resplendent of the two despised British officers. "Jean Lafitte," he said boldly enough that all along the beach might hear.

"Captain Lockyer. Royal Navy. Commanding His Majesty's brig *Sophia*." The voice was affected, aristocratic. The captain's face and neck were burned bright red right down to his stiff collar.

"Captain McWilliams, His Majesty's Marines." The other officer was affected in a different fashion, like a sergeant uncomfortably fitted into an officer's uniform. The marine held an oilcloth packet under one arm.

The Baratarians rustled their muskets. They shuffled bare feet in the sand and pressed in closer, adding to the obvious discomfiture of the officers, who darted their eyes about sharply and continuously.

"Might we speak?" Captain Lockyer's rapidly shifting eyes implored the need for privacy.

Jean Paul nodded. "This way, gentlemen, if you please." He struck off along the narrow path to the house, not bothering to check if the British were following. He smiled at the louder clatter of muskets which indicated that they would be sure to.

The officers scrambled along the path, dodging palmetto fans reaching out to brush their fine uniforms. They gazed with wonder at the fine house. Constructed of smooth milled clapboards painted white, it stood incongruously above the palmetto-roofed warehouses and workers' cottages grouped along the island's leeward side.

Inside, they looked about with even greater wonder, for the interior was not nearly so imposing as the exterior. Furnished only with mismatched chairs and high accounting tables, it would not be their notion of the lair of a Pirate King.

A highly polished harpsichord stood before a window. Captain McWilliams strode at once to the instrument, his sword slapping against his thigh. Delicately, he chose a leather plectrum and brushed it softly against the strings.

"We have come on business." Captain Lockyer quickly terminated the marine's venture into the arts. The soldier lay down the plectrum at once.

Jean Paul bowed slightly in spite of himself. He gestured to a pair of chairs and retreated to a corner cupboard. "Will you have wine?"

"If you please." Lockyer settled into a chair, careful to keep the hem of his coat from the floor. He peered about the cluttered room with disdain.

"You have very fine glaziers," he said when Jean handed him a long-stemmed goblet, "here in the Colonies."

Jean bit back a retort, stung by the insufferable arrogance of the man, and was tempted to remind him that Louisiana had never been a colony of Britain.

"The best." He handed a matching goblet to McWilliams. Irish crystal.

"Weavers, as well," said Lockyer, eyeing Jean Paul's fine coat from France.

"And weavers."

"Fine boots."

"Good wine." Not to be left out, McWilliams chimed in with his parade-ground voice. He held his goblet high to peer into it from beneath.

Jean Paul sat facing the two. "Alas. We don't have the climate for wine in Louisiana. The wine is imported."

"I wasn't aware," Lockyer said in his affected accent, "that the French spoke such admirable English."

"Many do."

"Do you read English as well as you speak it?"

"I read."

Locker placed his wine glass on the floor, then nodded to McWilliams, who handed across the oilskin packet.

"I have here," Lockyer said, tapping delicate fingers on the oilskin, "various offers from His Majesty's government."

Jean Paul sipped his wine.

"The first," Lockyer continued, untying the packet, "is from Lieutenant Colonel Edward Nicholls, commander of

His Britannic Majesty's Forces in the Floridas." He handed a
paper to Jean.

It was a letter addressed to Monsieur Lafitte or the Commandant at Barataria: *I call on you with your brave followers to
enter into the service of Great Britain in which you shall have the
rank of Captain. Lands will be given to you all in proportion to
your respective ranks. Your ships and vessels will be placed under the
orders of the commanding officer of this station. We have a powerful
reenforcement on its way here.*

Jean Paul deliberately lay the letter on his knee and
smoothed it to conceal his agitation.

"We understand," Lockyer said, "that your brother Pierre
is at this moment in prison in New Orleans."

"You are well informed."

"He will be set free."

Jean gulped a swallow of wine.

"There are other letters."

One was signed by Captain the Hon. William Henry Percy,
of H.M.S. *Hermes.* Addressed to Lockyer, it authorized him to
make this visit and the accompanying offer to the Baratarians.
The other, addressed to "The Commandant of Barataria," threatened in veiled terms that the community was certain to be
destroyed if the alternate offer should be found unacceptable.

"You leave me little choice," Jean Paul said after he had
studied all three of the letters, slowly, to allow time for his
mind to work.

McWilliams aroused himself. "There is also," he announced
in a gruff voice, "an additional offer of thirty thousand pounds
sterling, to be paid directly to you." He coughed, glancing
toward Lockyer for confirmation, who sat unmoving. "That
offer, as you can understand, is to be kept confidential."

"I will need time."

Lockyer's eyebrows lifted. "For what purpose?"

"I have many ships, many men. Most are, at this moment, at sea. They must be informed. Otherwise, when they return to Barataria—"

"I see your point." Lockyer drained his wine glass.

"How much time will you require?"

Jean hesitated. It was obvious that the British planned to invade New Orleans along the routes through the swamps. But first, it would be necessary to placate the pirates—especially their "Bos," but it could be the very opportunity that Jean had so long sought. "Two weeks."

Lockyer rose to his feet, McWilliams with him, as if the pair were attached by invisible wires.

"We shall return, then, in a fortnight."

Jean Paul began the drafting of his own letters even before the British officers had reached their gig. The first was complete by the time they set foot on the deck of *Sophia*.

Addressed to Edward Livingston, the lawyer who was then seeking Pierre's release, the letter asked that gentleman to deliver the remaining two letters to Jean Blanque, a member of Louisiana's House of Representatives. One of the remaining letters was addressed to Blanque himself, which requested him to deliver the other to Governor Claiborne.

The third warned the Governor that the British were coming.

Jean lay down his pen and gazed through the window at the empty sea. He could soon expect to hear from Claiborne. Or Lockyer.

RESP. SUB., G. Choteau, Sec.

FEBRUARY 6, 1946

CHAPTER 23
New Orleans, Louisiana
February 6, 1993, 4:43 PM

"So who answered first?" Mickey asked from deep in his armchair. "The Americans or the British?"

Edward looked through the glare of the desk lamp on the file folder. "The Americans. Claiborne sent a fleet of gunboats and the Forty-Fourth Infantry."

"The infantry? To fight British ships?"

"The infantry attacked the Baratarians. Not the British."

"Doesn't make sense."

"Look it up."

"Claiborne must have been an idiot."

"That's what Jean Paul thought."

"You're telling me," Mickey said from the corner of his mouth, "that the British navy sailed in to cut a deal with a gang of pirates, because they wanted help with a war against the United States. Then the United States marches in and takes on the pirates?"

"That's the way it happened."

"Why would the British want to make a deal with a gang of pirates in the first place?"

Edward tugged off his glasses and smoothed his eyebrows. "You know about the War of Eighteen Twelve?"

"Some."

"It was like a continuation of the Revolutionary War. The British wanted their colony back. They planned three major thrusts: one from Canada, attacking Detroit and Buffalo; another through Chesapeake Bay, toward Washington, which was when they burned the White House; and the third from the south, up the Mississippi. And that meant New Orleans.

"New Orleans was tough because it was a hundred miles from the Gulf. To attack, the British ships would have to sail against the river current and pass under the guns of Fort St. Leon. They considered two approaches; one was from the east, through the swamps and Lake Borgne; the other through Barataria. The way from the east was very difficult. So was the one from Barataria, but it was better than the other. All they had to do was buy out Jean Lafitte and his men."

"Still hard to believe that the British navy would try to make a deal with pirates."

"The letters are on file. Historians disagree on the manner of approach by the British officers. Which side of the island Lockyer landed on, for example. Whether it was morning or evening. Whether or not Lafitte could speak English, even. The result is the same."

"You talked about a lawyer named Edward Livingston. I didn't know you were that old."

"I told you early on that a man named Edward Livingston was Lafitte's lawyer in New Orleans."

"Oh, yeah."

Edward grinned. He replaced his glasses and rubbed the top of his head. "He was no relation, but he did me a big favor."

"What?"

"I think the Society gave me my first hearing because they thought I was a descendant."

"But you're not, are you?"

"None whatsoever."

"Maybe you're the same person."

"You'll never know what the historians will dig up next."

Mickey contemplated his grandfather as if considering

the possibility. "I still don't understand why the Americans didn't attack the British instead of the Baratarians."

Edward slowly shook his head. "The Americans weren't ready to take on the British. They had only two ships on The River: *Caroline* and *Louisiana*. Besides, the British weren't at the gates yet. And Claiborne was fed up with the Baratarians. The letter was the last straw; he thought Lafitte was trying to make a fool of him again. He called a Council of War to review the letters. He probably pointed out that the British might, just might, employ the pirates and come to the city through the delta. So he ordered the army and the navy in to wipe them out. Commodore Patterson and Colonel Ross were instructed to finish them off once and for all."

"I guess there must have been a heck of a fight."

"No fight at all. The Baratarians fled without firing a shot."

Mickey gazed steadily at his grandfather. "Why?"

"Why what?"

"Why wasn't there a fight? I thought these guys were supposed to be tough."

Edward laughed. "They were, without a doubt, the toughest collection of hooligans anywhere in the world at the time."

"But they just cut and ran?"

"It was what their 'Bos' told them to do. He forbade them to fire on the American flag."

Mickey snorted.

"Historical fact," Edward said. "The Baratarians set fire to their ships in the bay and scattered. When the Americans arrived, they took what they wanted and burned everything else."

"Why would he—the Bos—have told his men not to fire on the American flag? After all their troubles with the Americans?"

"Historians have never questioned Jean's motive. They simply say that Lafitte was a great American patriot."

"But everybody thought he was French. That's what you said."

"Everyone thought that. Of course, he might have been French and still be an American patriot. That's not the important point. Remember that Jean Paul's sole aim was to deliver his uncle's body to the President of the United States. Scrapping with American troops was no way to get into the President's good graces."

"Sounds pretty far-fetched."

"Not as far-fetched as the accepted story. That's the one that doesn't make sense."

Mickey nodded, his lips tight. "Maybe so," he said. "What happened to Jean Paul? He ran away too, I guess?"

"He did. He holed up with some friends on the Bayou Lafourche. Jean had a lot of friends."

"But he lost everything."

"He didn't lose his men. Not most of them, anyway. And he didn't lose all his goods. Just the stuff that was on Grande Terre when the attack came."

"What about the rest of it?"

Edward waved again at the wall of topographic maps. "All in the warehouses. The principal warehouse was at a place called Big Temple, near the intersection of Bayou Barataria and Bayou des Families, the closest one to New Orleans."

"And the army didn't get any of that stuff?"

Edward shook his head. "No. There was also Petit Temple, down at the Bayou Rigolettes. But the important one was at Lake Salvador. That was where he stored his guns. It was the most difficult one for me to find."

"You mean you've actually gone out and found these places?"

"I've told you. I found every one of them. Not much left

anymore; just a few rotting timbers. Even cypress doesn't last forever."

Mickey wasn't thinking about warehouses. "You said Jean Paul looked just like Jean Lafitte."

"I didn't say he looked *just* like Lafitte. The two of them were very similar in appearance. Remember that the privateers didn't see each other a great deal. They were at sea most of the time."

"The guy with the cut lip knew he wasn't Lafitte."

"But why would it matter? Maybe some of the others knew, as well. But why rock the boat? This ... fellow ... imposter or not, got their business going. Without him, they'd have been out of work. And, in any case, many of them changed their names frequently. Nothing new in that at all."

"All right," Mickey said. "After being shot up by the army and the navy, after running to the swamps, everybody gets back together again—"

"No. They didn't. Not to continue the privateering, at any rate. General Andrew Jackson asked them to fight the British."

"Right after the army went in to shoot 'em up?"

"That was Claiborne's idea. Not Jackson's."

"Claiborne was the Governor, wasn't he? Seems like he would have the say-so."

"Jackson over-rode the Governor by declaring martial law."

"Didn't Jackson care about what the Governor thought? That the pirates were just a band of crooks?"

"Jackson thought so, too. But that was no longer so important to him. He had no trained army, and a war to fight with about two thousand men, mostly backwoodsmen from Kentucky and Tennessee who grumbled a lot and couldn't understand why they were in Louisiana in the first place. There were some militia as well, Creoles with dueling pistols and hunting rifles. But the Baratarians, he knew, were fighters. They'd been fighting all their lives. They had plenty of cannon, and storehouses full of gunpowder and flint. Jackson knew when he had the short end of the stick. What would you do if you were facing the cream of the British army? The mightiest military force in the world?"

Mickey nodded. "I'd take whatever I could get. But I don't see why the pirates—privateers—agreed to it."

Edward nodded his head so hard the glasses slipped to the end of his nose. "It makes no sense at all, the way accepted histories tell it. It only makes sense if you remember that Jean Lafitte was really Jean Paul. And Jean Paul had a very good reason—the very good reason that I've been talking about all afternoon: he needed to get his uncle buried."

"If I remember right," Mickey said, "Lafitte didn't fight at the Battle of New Orleans. He was a scout, or something."

Edward slid away his glasses and waved them over the desk. "The historians say that Jean Lafitte wasn't in the battle. And they were right: *he* wasn't—Jean Paul was."

"I wonder why they never mentioned that?"

Edward ignored the sarcasm. "Jean Paul was a hero but no one noticed. Andrew Jackson got the credit for saving the nation. He went on to become the seventh president of the United States."

"So Jean Paul made a president, too."

"The Society had a hard time with that."

CHAPTER 24
Chalmette Plantation, Louisiana
January 8, 1815

PRES. BY Edw. Livingston, Esg.
FEBRUARY 6, 1953

The bugles sounded early that morning, even before the sun brought the fearsome day.

"Somebody's up," Manuel Perrin's voice grunted from deep within his layer of sacking. He heaved himself upright to a sitting position on the floor of the wagon.

Manuel was so wrapped in multiple layers of sacking against the cold and the wet that only his nose and lips protruded from the protective layers. A puff of white breath glimmered in the weak light and floated away on the still air.

"That'll be the Brits." Jean Paul's voice was uncommonly weak and scratchy. Like the rest of him, his throat was constricted from shivering through the long wet night.

The bed of the wagon was too hard and unyielding for sleep. While the night was yet quiet and the stars still glittered overhead and before the fog had risen from the river, he gave up entirely on the prospect and scooted himself forward to dangle his frigid legs in space. He crinkled his cold nose at the smell of old fish and wondered just where Manuel had found the rotten sacking.

He crept one hand from under to touch the long telescope by his side, useless until the sun rose and burned away the mist. The Mississippi rolled somewhere before him, unseen still in the weak light and under its blanket of fog, but the sound of the river was there, the lapping of wavelets that slurped and splashed their protest at sticks or roots protruding from the riverbank.

Jean strained to listen, but after the bugle, no sound could be heard from across the river. Nevertheless, he knew that the British would be rousing themselves, rattling sabers and muskets, noises dampened by fog and distance.

Light flared a hundred yards downriver, illuminating the mist into a red balloon like the rising of the sun.

"Patterson's got a fire." Manuel yawned. He found his big straw hat, from somewhere, and strapped it on his head.

"So the Brits can get the range, I guess."

The fire had blazed intermittently all the long night from Patterson's position, serving as a beacon to the British howitzers on the plain. Although Patterson's emplacement was beyond the range of most of the British artillery, the mortars on the east bank of the river could easily reach him.

"He'll wish he'd stayed cold," Jean said, "when they get the range."

Patterson's men had thundered their three 24-pounders and six 12-pounders for a week, harassing the British across the river. The guns were salvaged from the sinking *Caroline* after she had been devastated by British fire, the same schooner that had led the attack on Grande Terre. And now, only four months later, Patterson was fighting alongside the very same Baratarians with the very same guns. Jean Paul shook his head. The ironies of war were almost beyond belief. He sat on the tailboard of the wagon and watched the mist brighten in the east.

He felt the touch of a breeze on his cheek. The fog began to dissipate along the riverbank. Already, he could see the edge of the water appearing here and there. Then, almost as if whooshed away by a giant fan, the air cleared and the east bank came into view, followed by the plain itself. Suddenly, a rocket fired from the British camp, to lose its spitting, blazing self in the gray clouds that remained over the clearing fog. Cannon boomed almost simultaneously, first from the British downriver, then from Jackson's line on the Rodriguez Canal. On his right, Patterson's battery replied, then a salvo from the sloop *Louisiana*, anchored near the west bank on his left.

Jean slid from the tailgate to the ground. "Time to get to work," he said to Manuel.

The mist quickly lifted, almost as if the booming cannon had chased it away. Jean Paul looked to the plain and gasped. He reached for his telescope.

It was a glorious sight that greeted him on the field across the river, the splendid might of Britain on parade. Long orderly columns of British advanced across the cane stubble, red tunics latticed with white cross belts. He focussed the telescope on them, saw the grim determination on their faces, saw the bayoneted rifles carried in the port arms position.

In the center of the field, a Royal regiment advanced, haughty and proud in their red coats with blue facings. The fog had cleared so that he could easily see the pennant snapping at their forefront: a rose centered on a blue ground, a white horse in each of the corners.

Beyond them, another column, this one wearing white facings on their coats and carrying black knapsacks, proud buglers hooting the advance.

The steady beat of drums could be heard even across the river, strangely delayed from the marching feet in his telescope. It was a stirring display, a glorious picture, proud, colorful. Behind them, the British cannon showed rainbow flashes in the lingering mist.

An additional columned movement caught his attention. He shifted the long telescope slightly. A file headed by tall bagpipers shrieked the song of war. Dressed in dark green tartan trousers, black gaiters and forage caps, this was a large group. They would, he guessed, number some thousand men.

He lowered the glass. These were Scots, his kinsmen. Again, the ironies of war.

A few horsemen, obviously officers, dashed about alongside the columns, waving swords, shouting exhortations to their men. "Fools," Jean Paul muttered. "Their officers set themselves up on horses to make better targets."

A weak roll of drums came from the left. Jean swung the telescope around to Jackson's line along the Rodriguez Canal. There came the indistinct sound of a few chords from "Yankee Doodle." Behind Jackson's line, the municipal band of New Orleans had formed themselves up, bright in their Napoleonic uniforms. The Place d'Armes, they called themselves. Jean Paul grinned.

Jackson's line stretched almost a mile along the canal, from the river to the swamp. At the near end, atop the low levee, a redoubt had been constructed forward of the line itself, its two 6-pounders providing enfilade fire. The redoubt, he saw, was manned by the 44th US Infantry.

The same infantry that had so recently destroyed Grande Terre.

He shifted the glass upward, following Jackson's line of defense, flitting past a pair of brass 12-pounders and a small howitzer.

"There's Alexander!" he blurted aloud. In the third battery, the bushy-bearded Alexander squatted beside the carriage of a 24-pounder. He was eating while chatting with his men, and paid no attention whatsoever to the advancing armies. Jean Paul chuckled.

"He's having his breakfast," Jean said to Manuel.

"Cornbread and whiskey, I'd guess. The British can damn well wait 'til he's finished!"

Just beyond Alexander's cannon was a second 24-pounder, also served by Baratarians, commanded by another of the Baratarians: René Beluche. As Jean watched, Rene's cannon fired, momentarily obliterating the remainder of the line with a cloud of dark smoke.

He lowered the telescope. Manuel stood close beside him, peering across the river with bulging eyes. "They're lost."

"Eh?" Jean's hands shook. He tightened his fingers around the telescope.

"They're lost. Look at that." Manuel waved at the field.

It did look absurd. On the right, a proud army thousands strong, advanced—the finest army in all the world—swirled their bagpipes, rolled their drums, blared their bugles, snapped their pennants. On the left, a muddy rampart before a canal, manned by only a handful of regulars, frightened militia, a few buccaneers. A dozen cannon, give or take a few. Jean didn't answer. He raised his telescope.

Beyond the 24-pounders manned by Alexander and René was the only big gun on the line: a 32-pounder manned by portions of the crew from the sunken *Caroline*.

Jackson had placed his heaviest armament in the center of the line. Right and left, the cannon tapered to six-pounders. The weakness on his right, however, could be supported by Patterson's battery and the *Louisiana*. On his left was the swamp. And a six-inch howitzer.

Even Jean, with so little experience in such matters, spotted the weakness that veterans like Alexander and Jackson himself had overlooked. He had mentioned it to Jackson, but by that time, all of the cannon were already emplaced, and he dispatched only a line of riflemen to defend the haphazard rampart at the edge of the swamp.

"Not to worry," Jean reassured Manuel. "Alexander's the best there is." He snapped the glass shut. "But we'd better give him a hand, anyway."

"Do you think," Manuel said, eyeing the little swivel gun mounted in the wagon, "we can do any good?"

"I don't know." Jean heaved himself over the tailgate. "But we can give it a try." He reached a hand down to help Manuel aboard.

"With this little gun?" Manuel lay a hand on the cold breech, beaded with moisture from the damp.

"This little gun," Jean replied, "beat the British before. We'll see if it can do it again."

"This same gun?"

"Well, one like it."

This was the gun Alexander had brought back from France but had never employed. Originally mounted on the railing of *Bonheur*, it had been discarded because of the crack that appeared on one of the arms that held the removable breech in place. Alexander had become very cautious with gunpowder ever since the blast in the face while he served with Napoleon.

The gun had lain forgotten at Big Temple until it was mistakenly transported to the powder magazine just across the river from New Orleans, where Jean Paul found it sinking into the mud. Distraught over the weakness of Jackson's line of defense, he enlisted Manuel, who found a wagon and with his strong arms helped windlass the rusty swivel aboard.

They bored a hole through the heavy planked floor of the wagon and dropped the little gun into place, then loaded all the cases of cartridges they could find at the powder magazine.

"Get some of those cases open." Jean concentrated his attention on the gun itself. The gun was indeed a twin to the one employed in the battle aboard *BonHomme Richard*. He touched his finger to the wet rust and the gun swiveled about easily, perfectly balanced.

It was not his intent to engage in any fighting himself, for the battle long ago at Flamborough Head had sickened him enough. That was why he had volunteered to provide reconnaissance service for Jackson, and why he had seen to it that he was across the river at the time that the British attack was expected. But the weakness of Jackson's line at the swamp bothered him immensely, for the general's promise of a pardon would be to no avail if the British were victorious.

The gun was well supplied with cases of canisters, conveyed to the powder magazine and abandoned in the mud with the gun. Gray now with age, some of the wooden boxes had been opened and discarded along with the gun, for they would serve no other weapon.

Manuel handed him one of the canisters. Formed of a dull brass, green now with age, it was shaped like a cylinder with one pointed end. A short fuse protruded from the other.

Jean tapped out the wedges from the arms behind the breech to loosen the peterara, which held the canister in place for firing. He lifted the peterara, then slid the canister into the breech, noting how perfectly it fit, careful to feed the fuse through the hole provided.

He was tapping back the wedges to cinch the peterara before he thought to inspect the crack that had so alarmed Alexander and caused him to abandon the gun. But the imperfection did not seem so substantial. Hardly an inch long, it would have gone completely unnoticed through the rust had he not known precisely where to look. He ran his finger over it, wondering if such a minor fault posed any real danger.

"Ready?" Manuel stood behind him, a slow match sputtering in one hand.

"A moment." Jean bent slightly behind the breech and swung the gun to line up on a column of red advancing through the middle of the field.

"Mile and a half, would you say?" he uttered from the side of his mouth to Manuel.

"Good a guess as any."

Jean elevated the gun so that the muzzle obscured his view of the advancing redcoats. "Fire," he said to Manuel.

The bang of the gun was surprisingly small, not at all like the booming cannon just downriver at Patterson's position. There was very little recoil. He felt only a slight jolt in his hands. He straightened to watch, to see if he could determine the hit. He glanced at Manuel.

They shook their heads together.

"It didn't fall in the river," Jean said. "We would have seen it."

Again they loaded, and again they fired, Jean careful to provide a greater elevation to the gun because of the distance. He quickly straightened and attempted to follow the flight of the flying cone.

This time they saw it. The missile exploded in the shadowy moss-hung swamp across the battlefield. For a moment, the woods were brightly lit by the flash of the exploding canister. Apparently, a second fuse had sprayed grape-shot near its point of impact.

The shot had, unbelievably, passed completely over the heads of the enemy!

"Another, Manuel! We're firing too high." They grinned at each other. The little gun's trajectory was surprisingly flat.

The next shot was nearly a direct hit. They saw the explosion at the head of an advancing column that was closely skirting the edge of the swamp. Redcoats fell in disarray. Their fellows behind halted, mystified by the explosion that had suddenly appeared from nowhere, for they were yet too far from Jackson's line to be affected by his cannon.

"Another, Manuel. We've got it now."

The red and green-suited columns began to swerve away, angling farther from the river, perhaps because their officers thought that the fire had come from Patterson's batteries.

Again the little gun coughed, and an instant later they saw the explosion, partially obscured this time by the growing clouds of smoke from the batteries on the field. A barrage of rifle fire sparked through the smoke from Jackson's line, followed by tremendous flashes of cannon. And more smoke.

"Another, Manuel. That rifle fire won't reach."

The little gun was heating up from the continued fire. Even the long aiming cascabel had grown warm to the touch. Jean paused to allow the metal to cool. He inspected the crack, forgotten during the excitement of the firing, but it seemed not to have changed.

The long column of tall Highlanders swerved rapidly away from the river, still too far from the Americans to be concerned with the enemy's rifles.

Jean could not resist the temptation, kinsmen or not.

"Another, Manuel," he said, nursing the hot cannon lower with his fingertips. He aimed just slightly over the heads of the forefront of the column where the stalwart bagpipers were shrilling away as if they were on parade.

"Fire!"

The shot whipped apart the proud soldiers like a giant scythe. The entire forward portion of the column were flung to the mud, their bagpipes stilled. For a moment, the column halted as if dismayed, then they advanced again, stepping over the bodies of their fallen comrades.

"Another, Manuel."

And on that final shot, when the field across the river was blanketed with scarlet and Sutherland Green, when the remaining Highlanders finally wavered and halted, the hot, fatigued metal gave way.

The crack separated the wedge arm completely from its mount. The peterara flew high into the sky. The blast struck Jean full in the chest.

The explosion hit like the hot breath of a monster dragon. It lifted him from his feet and flung him to the bed of the wagon, where he lay sprawled like a clutter of discarded rags.

When he fell, the back of his head struck an unseen object with such cruel force that he heard the crushing of bone and his eyes filled with involuntary tears and red mist.

Manuel Perrin's distorted face hovered close, blood running from an open cut in his cheek. The straw hat had gone, blown away. The fisherman stumbled over something, his own foot perhaps, and bent close. His lips moved, but if he spoke, Jean heard no words.

There was only the booming of cannon, until Jean Paul's eyelids grated down the darkness. The reverberations moved slowly away until finally he was hardly able to hear them at all and he wondered why it had become dark so soon after the dawn.

Faintly, he heard music, but most faintly, when The Place d'Armes struck up "Hail Columbia."

RESP. SUB., G. Choteau, Sec.
FEBRUARY 6, 1953

CHAPTER 25
New Orleans, Louisiana
February 6, 1993, 5:00 PM

"Aren't you getting hungry?" Edward suddenly realized he hadn't eaten since a bowl of corn flakes at breakfast.

"Sure."

"How about a pizza?"

"Sure."

"You could call. Ask them to deliver."

"Sure. I know a good place."

Edward drew himself to his feet while Mickey dialed a number, apparently from memory. "You know the number by heart?"

"Sure." Mickey placed the order. Extra large, of course. "What do you want on it?" Mickey asked.

"You choose."

"Everything," Mickey said into the phone, and hung up.

"Let's go see," Edward said, longing for a break after his exhausting description of the battle, "if the car's still in the garage, while we're waiting."

"Sure."

"Follow me." Edward pointed the cane like a lance and bounded through the door, but not as dramatically as he had earlier.

The corridor was black dark. Edward fumbled for the light

switch and they both flinched when the overhead bulb blazed. He led the way along to the kitchen and felt inside for a second switch. A relic from the original wiring, it was a rotating knob that still miraculously worked after so many years.

Mickey whistled. "Wow. That your medicine?"

It was Agnes' medicine. Bottles of various sizes and configurations stood in deep ranks on a countertop like a small pharmacy.

"Your grandmother's." Edward led the way through the kitchen to the outside door, carefully circumventing the round oak table in the center of the room and as carefully avoiding a look at the multi-colored bottles.

She had been methodical and well-organized with her medication. She carried around a little calendar book, graciously provided by the pharmacy, in which she noted for each date the various medicines she took in accordance with a complicated system of scheduling, although she was so attuned to the timing that the notations hardly seemed necessary.

"Dad said she took a lot of pills. You could always hear her coming."

It was true. One could detect her approach long before she appeared because of the rattling of the pills in the bottles she carried in her purse. The purse was never out of her grasp, even at home. On the rare occasions that she set it down, the purse clattered like a sack of nails.

"I don't think you should keep on living here," Mickey said, stumbling against a chair drawn up to the round table, "in this big old house all by yourself."

Edward snapped on a switch by the outside door, flooding the back yard with light. "Plenty of room for you to live here with me, if you want." Edward turned to face his grandson. Mickey's face was blank. "Let's go," Edward said, abruptly striding through the door and along the covered breezeway through the back yard.

"Wow!" Mickey exclaimed when the light flashed on in the garage.

The top of the car stood higher than either of them and was draped with a brown cloth cover that hung to the floor. The garage walls were lined with sheet rock and painted white. In one corner, an electric dehumidifier hummed away, a small red light showing that it worked. A small pipe at the bottom of the dehumidifier dripped slowly into the grate of a floor drain.

Mickey lifted one corner of the cloth cover and stooped to peer under.

"Take it all the way off."

The cover slithered to the floor and the car stood in all its gleaming magnificence.

"Wow!" Mickey exclaimed again, his eyes round with awe. "She's a virgin!"

Edward watched Mickey walk around and around the Pierce-Arrow, reaching out his hand to touch from time to time, reverently pulling his fingers away just before contact.

The car was a deception. He had never told Agnes that it came from his father's insurance money. Neither had he told her that he bought it because of a belief that it would spawn a flood of clients.

It was a foolish, youthful pipe dream. The clients had never appeared, but he'd kept the car as an investment, and now had come the time for the investment to pay off.

"Can I sit in it?" Mickey was vibrant with anticipation.

Edward watched Mickey cautiously open the driver's door and slide inside. After an ecclesiastic moment he gripped the big steering wheel with both hands.

Charleton had sat there like that once, holding the steering wheel with the very same expression on his face. In those days, when Charleton was small, they delighted in their trips to the bayous to catch crawdads on lard can lids lowered into the water on long strings.

"How much of it's original?" Mickey was peering under the mammoth dashboard.

"Every bit. Right down to the spark plugs." Edward strutted to the driver's side without the assistance of the cane.

"She's priceless." Mickey's voice had taken on a deep respect.

She *was* priceless. There was no speck of rust anywhere on her. Each week, Edward went over the car and through it, whisking any dirt that might have the temerity to enter the sealed garage. He lightly coated with oil any parts subject to corrosion. Even the tires were still original. Wooden blocks under the axles supported the weight and the surfaces themselves were regularly polished with Wall-Black.

"Can I look under the hood?"

Mickey had already scrambled out and was at the spring-loaded fasteners on the side before Edward could draw in his breath for a reply.

The fire smelled pungent, good, not unlike the earthy aroma of the swamps where the cypress logs once grew. Edward settled into a wing-backed chair before the fireplace, relishing the warmth on his cheeks.

"A little cool, out in the garage," he said.

"Not damp, though." Mickey tossed a small log into the fire, unleashing a shower of sparks. He was vibrant, cheerful. *Should have taken him out to the garage before.*

Firelight flickered on the black and white checkerboard floor of the parlor, on the rows of Father's leather-bound lawbooks along one wall.

"Whatever happened to Jean Paul's father?" Mickey asked. The tour in the garage had been a good idea; his enthusiasm had grown.

"William Paul. He separated from his wife. Theirs was not an amicable relationship. He died in Virginia. Afterward, his wife wouldn't have anything to do with the estate. John Paul Jones served as executor."

"What about Jean Paul's mother?"

"I wasn't able to trace her, but I must admit I didn't try very hard. There was no reason to."

Mickey gazed over the fireplace at a painting of a ship under full sail. "So Jean Paul was killed when the cannon exploded? And they buried him beside John Paul Jones?"

"By the Bayou des Oises. Manuel Perrin took the body there. It was Manuel who had helped Jean Paul bury his uncle in that cemetery."

"So that's how come the newspaper said Jean Lafitte was buried there? Everybody thought Jean Paul was Jean Lafitte."

"You're getting it."

"I'd like to see the cemetery."

Things were most certainly looking up.

"I'll go out there with you. In the Pierce-Arrow. As soon as you get her running."

It was another master stroke. Mickey grinned hard enough to break his face.

"Is it a public cemetery?"

"The Perrins took title to the land. Mary Perrin still lived nearby when I first started my research. She's the great-great-granddaughter of Manuel."

"Did you talk to her?"

"Many times. And at great length."

"Did her story check out?"

Edward smiled with his recollection of the old lady. "Some parts of it," he said. "Much of what she said had to be discounted as over-romanticizing, to make her ancestor more glamorous than he was. The newspaper story did that, too. In fact, I suspect that's where the reporter got the story. But some parts simply wouldn't bear up to the facts." He turned to the fire. He felt exhausted, and allowed his head to dangle forward.

"Do you want to finish the story some other time, Grandpa?"

Edward snapped his head upright. "No. I'm all right. Just need the pizza, I guess." *There must be less than an hour remaining.*

"There was a meeting today, wasn't there?"

"Yes. Unfortunately. I have to call them before six."

"In St. Louis?" Mickey dropped into a wing-backed chair, the twin to Edward's.

"Always in St. Louis."

"How come? Jean Lafitte lived in New Orleans."

"There's a school of thought," Edward said, "that Jean Lafitte lived out his last days in St. Louis."

"The real Jean Lafitte?"

"The real Jean Lafitte."

"Did he?"

"Who knows? I haven't checked that far."

"You said you could prove anything, if you wanted to."

Edward smiled. "So where's the medal?"

"Am I supposed to have it figured out by now?"

"Maybe."

"Did you know, when you were at this stage? After the battle?"

"No. But when I was at this stage, I didn't know that I could have known."

"And you don't think it just got lost in the shuffle."

"Not likely, is it? All of Jones' other personal effects turned up. Even the ceremonial sword that Catherine of Russia gave him."

"Maybe it's like you said about the cracks—maybe it fell through one. Or maybe it got lost in—"

"The mists of history. No. It was too important to simply get lost."

"So what happened to it, then?"

"That's the riddle, isn't it? The final, absolute proof of the case hangs on the whereabouts of that medal."

"Well," Mickey said. "I haven't figured it out yet."

"When you find the medal, you will have found the man."

"Is that a clue?"

"Yes."

"It doesn't make sense."

"Well. Maybe because you haven't been thinking about it for as long as I have."

"But you haven't finished with the story yet."

"Not quite. There are some clues left. Looks like you'll need them."

"You could just tell me the clues now." Mickey was teasing.

"They wouldn't mean anything by themselves. You must hear the rest of the case."

"Okay. Tell me the rest."

"I need the file. It's on my desk."

"I'll get it."

Mickey heaved himself up from the chair and started for the door of the study.

"The next meeting," Edward muttered in a low tone as if speaking to himself, "was a very long one. At that meeting, I was faced with two unexpected happenings."

Mickey hovered in the doorway.

"The first was that I found myself facing a revitalized Stratmeyer. The second was that this new Stratmeyer produced evidence that threatened to demolish me completely."

"What evidence?"

"Bring me the file."

Chapter 26
The Lafitte Society
Saint Louis, Missouri
February 6, 1959, Morning

Edward entered the meeting room with a roll of maps under his right arm and a cardboard box under his left, a yardstick in his right hand and a look of eager anticipation on his face.

The look of anticipation turned to astonishment when he saw Stratmeyer.

Although the familiar butcher sat in his customary place and wore his customary facetious grin, he was young again.

Edward nearly dropped the box, the roll of maps, and the yardstick.

"Mr. Livingston." Steinbach stood at the head of the table in the chairman's position. "Allow me to introduce Henry Stratmeyer, Junior."

Henry Stratmeyer, Junior, bounded to his feet at once and extended his hand.

"Dad retired," he said. "I'm his son."

Edward fumbled the yardstick to his left hand. He feebly held out his right hand, elbow tight against the maps to keep them from falling.

Stratmeyer, Junior, had the same bald head as his father, round and knobby. The same rough fingernails. The hand was every bit as gnarly as the original Stratmeyer's.

Edward was totally disarmed. His hopes were dashed that he might eventually outlive his arch enemy and prevail before the Society. Now he was faced with the old butcher's reincarnation. He resolved to forever refer to this Stratmeyer offspring simply as "Junior."

"I know all about your case," Junior said. "Dad went over everything with me. The minutes from all the meetings. Maybe that's why they appointed me. To maintain the continuity." He smiled at Steinbach. Junior resumed his seat. His father's seat. "He was very impressed by your rendition of the battle at Flamborough Head," Junior added.

Was he? Edward was staggered.

"You're going to prove your version of the Battle of New Orleans today? That's what Dad said." Junior indicated a package on the table before him. "I must warn you that new evidence has come to light." He even sounded like his father.

Edward had difficulty finding his voice. "New evidence is always coming to light." He looked at the package, wrapped in plain brown wrapping paper like a pornographic magazine.

Junior splayed out his hands over the parcel, as if a little ashamed of it. "If you're ready," he said, pre-empting the chairman just like his father used to do, "we'll hear your presentation first."

"Right." Edward fumbled the maps onto the table.

"But I must warn you. I read up on the battle."

"Right," Edward repeated. He looked down the length of the cluttered table. "I'll need room," he said, stooping to place the cardboard box on the floor under the table.

The Society members gazed at him without comprehension until he lay down the yardstick and began to unroll the map. It nearly covered the table top, requiring the quick withdrawal of paper pads, pencils and glasses of water. And Junior's mysterious package.

They all studiously assisted with the unrolling and solicitously placed pads of paper and glasses of water to flatten the drawing. Edward took up the yardstick like a pointer.

"This map of Chalmette Plain," he began, "was prepared for me by an engineer. It's the site of the Battle of New Orleans. It's based on modern topographical maps, altered to show the configuration in eighteen fifteen."

"I suppose," Junior said smoothly, "you'll explain how you got the eighteen fifteen configuration."

It was a good point, and Edward was glad that Junior made it. "I accumulated all the old maps I could find. Some were by Major Lacarriere Latour, Andrew Jackson's engineer. I also found sketches in the Royal Artillery Museum in London. Maps from the Public Works Department in New Orleans. The Corps of Engineers." He looked at Junior. "Okay?"

"Okay." He seemed more congenial than his father, at least.

"I should make it clear that not one of the old maps matched any of the others. My engineer worked hard on this, piecing it together. It represents his best effort from all the material available."

"Looks good," Junior said.

Edward began to think of him as a friendly witness. "You

will note that the course of the Mississippi River is signifi-
cantly different than today," he said, tracing the end of the
yardstick along the wide path colored blue on the map. "The
present course is ghosted in for reference purposes," he explained. "The Mississippi was much wider at the time of the
battle. It was more curvilinear. The Corps straightened it with
their levees, for better or for worse."

He ran the yardstick along a narrower blue line near the
upper edge of the map. "The Rodriquez Canal." Another blue
line near the lower edge. "The Raguet Canal." He tapped on
various black squares. "The Macarte house, Jackson's headquarters. The Villare house. British headquarters. Jackson's main
line of defense was along the Rodriguez Canal. He sent General
David Morgan of the Louisiana Militia across the river to continue that same defensive line, should the British cross over.
But General Morgan didn't like the lay of land in that position,
so he moved downriver to the Raguet Canal."

Edward slapped the yardstick repeatedly against his thigh.
"General Morgan was hardly a great general, and Jackson doubt-
lessly recognized that. He probably sent him across the river
to get him out of the way. General Morgan had only one
claim to fame: when some of the British did cross over and
attack his line, Morgan drew his saber, spurred his horse, and
shouted 'Follow Me!' But no one followed. The good General
Morgan found himself alone on the field. Nevertheless, that
slogan was so good it was adopted as the official motto of the
United States Army Infantry in nineteen twenty-two."

He looked around the room, but no one smiled. Only
Junior appeared to show any interest.

"Commodore Daniel Patterson," Edward continued, "the
very same Commodore Patterson that laid waste to Barataria,

established batteries on the west bank just above Morgan's position."

Edward stooped to the box. He straightened, several toy cannons in his hand, one of which he placed on a marked position at the west bank of the river. "Relics from my childhood." He grinned. "I thought they might make the battle more realistic."

Again, no one smiled.

"Historians vary on the size of Patterson's guns. Some say he had a number of six-pounders, but it didn't matter if he did. Six-pounders had a range of only fifteen hundred feet, and the river was almost a mile wide, so their balls would never have reached the battlefield. He had a half-dozen twelve-pounders, too—twelve-pounders had an effective range of five thousand eight hundred feet—they would have reached."

Edward took a pen from his inside coat pocket. He lay the yardstick on the table atop the map and carefully described an arc by holding a finger atop one end to act as a pivot. The felt tip pen squeaked across the paper, leaving behind a bright red line. He stood back to admire his handiwork, then bent again to roughly shade in the transcribed area.

"Mr. Livingston." Steinbach fingered his gavel. "How long is this going to take?"

"I'd like to show the gun emplacements, Mr. Chairman. Their range of fire is critical. You can see that Patterson's guns could only cover a very small part of the battlefield—"

"Let him go. This looks interesting." Edward was not surprised to find that Junior could command as much respect as his father.

"Remember," Edward continued after a quick glance at Steinbach, "that the red line shows extreme range. To reach that distance, cannon balls must be fired high into the air. They would fall from a great height. They would most certainly destroy anything they hit directly, but they wouldn't skip. Chalmette Plain was very muddy that day. Most of the balls from Patterson's battery would have simply buried themselves in the mud."

Edward stooped to the box and came up with more toy cannon, which he placed along Jackson's line at the Rodriguez Canal.

"Jackson's line," he said, "was about a half-mile long. He had only fourteen guns. In some places," he continued in an abstracted fashion as he searched on the map for the previously marked locations, "the guns were spaced as much as seven hundred feet apart. His biggest gun was a thirty-two pounder, which he placed here, near the center of the line. He also had twenty four-pounders, one eighteen, three twelves, three sixes, and two six-inch howitzers." Edward straightened. "A total of fourteen cannon."

The members appeared to be bemused at the toy battlefield being created before their eyes while Edward worked to create arcs from each gun to show their fields of fire.

"Down here by the swamp," he said when he had finished, "you will recall that Jean Paul pointed out to Jackson a weakness in the line. There are no cannon, for Jackson had run out, except for the six-inch howitzers." He took a handful of toy soldiers from the box, which he placed along the line at the edge of the swamp. "Riflemen. It was all he had left." Edward slashed a red line, using the yardstick as a straightedge, to show the maximum field of fire from the riflemen. "You can see," he continued, waving the yardstick across the map, "that about one-third of the plain could not be covered by his guns. It was out of range of everything."

Edward tapped the yardstick thoughtfully against his cheek. "One additional item to be considered. Time of fire." He began to pace slowly around the table. "A good crew could fire a twelve-pounder at the rate of one round per minute. A twenty-four pounder, each one- and-a-half minutes." He paused and rocked up on his toes. "Remember: I said a *good* crew. Jackson didn't have any good crews, except for Alexander. The rest of his gun crews were farmers, backwoodsmen. Not artillerymen. Inexperienced crews such as these could require four times as much time between firings. Say, one round each four to six minutes. Now," he said, pausing for gravity, "the battle—the real battle—lasted for only two hours. In that period of time, Jackson's men could have fired, at the calculated rate of one round each five minutes, say a maximum of three hundred and thirty-six rounds."

"You didn't count Patterson's guns," Junior said.

"Quite right. I didn't. He made too small a contribution to the battle. As soon as the British began to advance, they moved out of Patterson's range entirely."

"Okay."

"As I was saying," Edward continued, resting the yardstick on his shoulder like a rifle, "Jackson could have thrown a maximum of three hundred and thirty-six rounds. Actually, that's a high number. He probably fired far fewer than that. You must consider that the men would tire, and their rate would slow. Two hours is a long time to heft twelve-pound balls around and they were working in that deep mud. The guns weighed four thousand pounds apiece. Re-aiming would require moving that great weight, in the same heavy mud."

He paused to await dead silence in the room. "And yet," he said in a loud voice, "in that two-hour battle, the British suffered two thousand, thirty-six casualties." He looked around himself, pretending amazement. "That would mean, assuming that a ball struck its target with each firing, each shot claimed six men. Simple mathematics. That wouldn't allow for misses, and the inexperienced gunners must have missed a great deal. Bear in mind, too, what I said about extreme range, and the heavy mud, which prevented skipping."

He bent again to the cardboard box, and straightened with a handful of toy soldiers, painted red. "Now," he said, "imagine that you're the British. The battlefield lies before you. What would be the avenue of attack?"

No Society member dared to move. At last, Junior sacrificed himself, bless his soul. He leaned forward and placed his finger on the map. "In this open space," he said. "Where the guns can't reach. Simple logic, isn't it?" Edward placed a red soldier near the line of the swamp. "Lieutenant-Colonel Timothy Jones and his Fifth West India." Another soldier, slightly farther from the swamp. "Major-General Samuel Gibbs, Fifty-Ninth Regiment of Foot." Another soldier: "Major-General John Keane, Ninety-Third Highlanders. But not Rennie. Poor Colonel Rennie and his Light Companies attacked nearer the river, inside the range of the westernmost guns. He didn't make it." Edward lay that red soldier on its side. "It would have been foolish to charge through the places torn up by cannon balls, wouldn't it? Ask Colonel Rennie. The majority swept around to the right, toward the area near the swamp, where the cannon couldn't reach."

"But Jackson put riflemen there, you said." Steinbach was paying attention.

"Very few of the British ever got close to the riflemen. General Coffee had excellent marksmen down there, but the majority of the enemy never got within range. The battalions of Plauche, Daquin, and LaCosta didn't fire a shot. Neither did three-fourths of the Forty-Fourth Infantry. Look it up in your history books, gentlemen."

"You forgot something," Junior said.

"Did I?"

"The *Louisiana*."

"Ah. Quite right. Thank you," Edward said heartily. "My mistake." He took a ship's model from the box and placed it in the river near the west bank, opposite the end of Jackson's line. "Unfortunately, the river was too wide. The *Louisiana* was too far away to be effective. It would have been better if she had anchored on the east side."

Junior nodded. "That's what I read."

Edward folded his arms and looked down at the younger Stratmeyer. "You say you've studied up on the battle. Do you see anything here that I've done wrong?"

"Not so far. But I didn't think about the ranges of the guns and their firing times."

"Oddly enough, you're not alone. I haven't found a historian who did consider it. But there was one other thing," Edward said, cupping his chin with one hand. "Do you recall what the British ascribed the loss of the battle to?"

Junior shook his head.

"Do you recall something about the 'withering fire from across the river?'"

"I didn't read the British account. Only the American."

"Perhaps you should. But some American historians refer to it as well. 'Cut down by a giant scythe,' they said. Where did that 'withering fire' come from? Patterson didn't have the range. *Louisiana* couldn't reach across the river."

Edward paused, giving Junior time. But he wouldn't bite.

Edward stooped to the box one more time. He straightened with one additional toy cannon, which he grandly placed
on the west bank of the river, slightly south of the extension
of Jackson's line.

"Jean Paul's breech-loader," he said dramatically.

He bent to draw an arc on the map, pivoting from the
new gun. "Estimated range of fire: in excess of eight thousand
feet. More than enough to cover the battlefield." He lay the
pen on the map. You must remember," he added, "that the
Americans were a vastly inferior force facing the finest army
that existed in the world at that time. Just as John Paul Jones
once faced the finest navy in the world. The British, led by
Major-General Sir Edward Packenham, fielded some seven
thousand seasoned troops fresh from their victory over Napoleon. The Americans assembled less than half that number, all
untried on the field of battle. It is foolish to assume they won
simply because we think they were in the right. Or that they
were especially brave. Brave men, even those especially brave,
are not immune to cannonballs.

"A single gun tipped the balance." With the end of the
yardstick, Edward tipped over Lieutenant-Colonel Timothy
Jones. "A gun capable of extremely rapid fire, perhaps three
times each minute." Major-General Samuel Gibbs bit the dust.
"A gun with a prodigious barrage, although that in itself might
not have sufficed. We know that guns alone do not win wars.
A far greater weapon is morale, psychology, the fear of the
unknown. A psychological effect that the very same enemy
felt thirty-five years earlier off Flamborough Head." Major-
General John Keane fell.

"You think that one gun could make all the difference."
Junior had his hands folded atop his package.

"Sometimes it takes very little to turn the tide of battle."

"Why, do you suppose, the historians never mentioned it?"

"There's new evidence all the time." Edward smiled. "But the historians didn't realize the gun existed. The British and American soldiers obviously didn't. The gun didn't have the roar that Patterson's twelve-pounders did. Or their own cannon, a mile closer. So it would be easy to say that 'the withering fire from across the river' came from Patterson's batteries."

"And nobody thought to check the range."

"Until now," Edward repeated. He arched his heavy eyebrows. "Without that gun, New Orleans would almost certainly have fallen. The Mississippi River would have become a British canal. General Packenham had in his pocket a royal commission designating him governor of the entire Louisiana Territory. He had instructions to ignore ratification of the peace treaty at Ghent. He was promised an earldom. All he had to do was to capture New Orleans. Our own St. Louis," he said, waving his hand at the window, "would have become the capital of Missouri Province, Commonwealth of America."

Drained, Edward paused. In the pause, Steinbach's gavel tapped softly on the table.

The Society rose as one man. Edward looked around, dumbfounded.

"We go to lunch now," Steinbach announced in a weedy voice.

We're talking about losing the war here, and you want to go to lunch?

"You may accompany us if you like."

"Perhaps," Edward said with a gasp, "we could continue. At lunch."

Steinbach shook his head. "We don't discuss business at lunch. Mr. Choteau can't keep notes and eat at the same time."

They trooped out of the room like a file of soldiers. Junior first. Edward last.

Junior's mysterious package remained behind, on the edge of the battlefield next to Patterson's battery.

Chapter 27
The Lafitte Society
Saint Louis, Missouri
February 6, 1959, Afternoon

Lunch was a nightmare.

They marched down Olive Street two abreast like a troop of soldiers on their way to service for firing squad duty.

A block from the river, they turned into a dark restaurant, reforming into single file. They threaded familiarly to a round table in a bay window from which one could see nothing, for the window was heavily glazed with stained glass and lead.

The table was already set with stacks of spareribs heaped high on platters and slathered with a heavy red sauce. Beside each platter stood enormous bowls of cabbage and ceramic pitchers of beer. Edward loathed spareribs more than anything in the world. Except cabbage.

Only a sufficient number of chairs surrounded the table to accommodate the members of the Society and they quickly sat, leaving Edward to foolishly stand bereft and alone until a Germanic waiter arrived with a deep scowl and an additional chair.

The members shuffled begrudgingly, leaving him a narrow space into which the hostile waiter dropped a plate and a cloth napkin curled around a set of silverware. After some moments, a glass appeared for his beer. Disgusted by the food, Edward dug into it nevertheless, serving himself a minute portion of the evil-smelling cabbage and the smallest sparerib he could find.

If his compatriots noticed his discomfort, they ignored it. They launched themselves into the ribs and the cabbage and the beer with gusto and silence, not speaking a single word while they cleared the platters and emptied the bowls and drained the beer pitchers.

Upon completion, they rose as one by silent signal and dolorously filed from the restaurant to the street, where they re-formed into double ranks and marched back to the meeting room. They resumed their places around the table as if they had never been gone.

The toy cannon still guarded the battlefield.

The British soldiers still lay where they had fallen.

The mysterious brown package still ticked away.

Steinbach tapped the gavel. "You may proceed, Mr. Livingston."

Edward nodded and wiped his lips, uncomfortably certain that vestiges of his single miserable sparerib remained redly about his mouth.

"The battle," he began, waving his hand at the map, "may not even be the significant question which should be addressed. There remain questions that have never been raised in any history I been able to find: Why did the Baratarians fight in the battle at all? And why, for heaven's sake, did they fight on the side of the Americans?"

Edward swept his hands behind his back and paced to the window overlooking the river, and the eyes followed him. He stood some moments to build rhetorical emphasis, then spun about to face his audience.

"Let's start with Jackson. How did it happen that he asked for the help of the Baratarians? Jackson had, after all, earlier referred to them as 'hellish *banditti.*' Such a request for assistance would be the equivalent today of General MacArthur's asking the Mafia to fight the Japanese.

"Historians tell us that Jackson feared the British, and well he might have. He feared them so greatly, they say, he stooped to enlist ruffians and outlaws. Other historians tell us that Jackson needed cannon and powder. Still others indicate that he had ample cannon and powder. Who is to be believed? It is my opinion that he invited the Baratarians out of spite for Governor Claiborne, who he considered an ass. Which he probably was. There would be no better way to show contempt for the Governor than to recruit the very bandits that Claiborne had so recently gone in to annihilate.

"At any rate, we know the Baratarians did fight on the side of the Americans. It's the single aspect on which all historians agree. But why did they? 'Because of their patriotic fervor,' the historians say." Edward sagged his jaw. "The Baratarians?" he all but shouted. "Patriotic to whom? To the Yankees, who made so much trouble with their despised Customs Service? These Baratarians weren't even Americans, for the most part. Their leader Jean Lafitte, was a *French*man, they tell us." He mellowed his tone. "Of course, that isn't to say that Frenchmen couldn't be American patriots simply because they were Frenchmen. After all: without them, our Revolutionary War might have turned out quite differently. We owe a great deal of gratitude to the French. But we're not talking about Frenchmen here. We're talking about a band of buccaneers labeled 'pirates' by the governor and 'hellish *banditti*' by the general. Some historians claim another reason: 'Because Jean Lafitte wanted a pardon,' they say. A pardon? For what purpose? What did he need a pardon for? We know that the Baratarians were indeed granted a pardon by President Madison because of their services in the battle. We also know what they did afterward: they didn't go fishing. They didn't farm or blacksmith or bake bread or make candles or whatever legal pursuit they might have followed after a thankful government issued them a pardon for all past sins, whatever they might be." Edward dropped his tone so low that some of the members leaned forward to hear. "They started buccaneering again." He raised his voice to its normal level and swept around the room waving his hands. "They started buccaneering again! As if the pardon had never happened."

He paced to the window and cupped his hand around his chin. "There is logic only if it is considered that Jean Lafitte was not Jean Lafitte at all. The pardon—even the desire for the pardon—would only make sense if this man was not Jean Lafitte at all. Only if he were really Jean Paul would the pardon make sense. It was Jean Paul who wanted the pardon because he wanted to be on the right side of the law and because he wanted to travel to Washington and hand over the body of his famous uncle to the President."

Edward turned slowly to face the group. "Gentlemen," he said. "Consider that."

The defense rests.

Everyone in the room remained as quiet as the fallen British soldiers.

At last, Junior stirred. "But Jean Paul failed," he said.

"Only because of his untimely death."

"And was buried beside his famous uncle."

Edward could only nod.

"Mr. Livingston." Junior drew himself to his feet and approached. A flagrant violation of Society protocol, it was the first time Edward had known any member to speak when he was not sitting at the table.

"I, for one, am impressed," Junior said. "As impressed as my father was at your recitation of the battle off Flamborough Head. You've made a number of telling arguments today, too."

Junior seemed to realize that he should be addressing the Society. His eyes flicked to the floor, then back to Edward's face before he turned and approached the table.

"Mr. Livingston," he said to the members, "has raised some very good points that, to my knowledge, have never been raised before. I'm referring, for one, to the Battle of New Orleans and the ranges of the cannon. I'll look into that, although I don't doubt for a minute that Mr. Livingston has given a most accurate interpretation of the battle. But the bigger question is that of the pardon, which is of prime importance to the Society. So important that the Society has even established the date of its annual meeting to celebrate the anniversary. Why did Jean Lafitte want the pardon? Why did he throw it away after he got it? Even assuming he would have fought a battle at the side of his enemy to get it. This question requires a considerable amount of investigation." Junior turned to face Edward. "Still," he said. "Something is missing."

Edward waited.

"I don't know what it is. The presentation—all of the presentations by Mr. Livingston, actually—have the ring of truth. There's reason here that's just beginning to surface. But something is lacking. A single, definitive proof, perhaps. If we could be provided with at least one piece of substantive proof—anything at all—the entire argument could come together. Jean Paul, the battle with *Serapis*, the Battle of New Orleans, everything. With one solid truism, the other doubts would vanish."

"I've been looking for that for quite a long time," Edward said.

"I know," Junior replied. "But you've given us postulates.
We need an axiom. Just one will do, probably. If it's good
enough."

"You don't talk like a butcher," Edward blurted. He could
think of nothing else to say.

"I'm not." Junior grinned at him. "Couldn't stand the
smell of baloney. I'm a professor of American History at St.
Louis University."

Edward was taken aback, not only by the unexpected ges-
ture of support, but by the sudden knowledge of Junior's esteemed academic status.

Before he could recover, Steinbach interrupted with a tap
of his gavel. "Gentlemen," Steinbach said, as if returning a
proper order to the meeting. "I must remind you that we have
other items on the agenda today."

"Sorry, Mr. Chairman." Junior resumed his seat.

Edward decided that he should hereafter think of Junior
as Professor Junior.

"There is also the matter of our new information,"
Steinbach said, pointing the handle of his gavel at the mysterious brown package.

Junior picked up the package and turned in his seat to
hand it to Edward. "A journal," he said. "Just released. Written by the man himself."

Edward tore open the parcel with quivering hands. Inside
he found a slim hard-cover book entitled *The Journal of Jean
Lafitte*.

"I'll be interested to see how you handle it." Junior's smile
had all but evaporated.

CHAPTER 28
New Orleans, Louisiana
February 6, 1993, 5:21 PM

"Grandpa." The indefinable tone in Mickey's voice made Edward's heart sink.

"Yes?" He knew what was coming.

Mickey stood before the fireplace, his face turned away, his feet twitching to the beat of that infernal distant drum. "I got to go home."

Edward found his cane. He toyed with it to calm his shaking hands. "Worried about your father?" No response. Just the twitching knees. "He knows where you are."

"Yeah. But he'll still be mad."

"What about the pizza? I can't eat it all by myself."

"Oh, yeah. Soon as that comes, I better go."

Originally, the car held his interest, but that hadn't lasted. And the riddle, to involve him, then that too had failed. Now, there only remained a pizza to glue a tenuous hold.

Mickey busied himself with the poker, jabbing at the coals. For a lovely moment, Edward felt himself drifting off into sleep, into a quiet world without frustrations like sons and grandsons.

"Maybe you ought to get some rest now."

Edward snapped his eyes open. Mickey hovered close before his chair. The poker was back in its holder. The fire blazed brightly with a new log. "I've *been* resting." Edward massaged the back of his neck to relieve a growing stiffness. "Where was I?" He asked, hoping to draw Mickey back into the case, to postpone the subject of his need to return to Charleton.

Mickey backed dubiously into his chair. "You just got

through fighting the Battle of New Orleans, and explaining why Jean Paul had to be the one who wanted the pardon. And that you got Lafitte's journal dumped on you."

"Ah, yes."

"Sounds like they were just putting you on."

"How's that?"

"They knew about the journal. You didn't. But they let you go all through your big play with the cannons. Then they told you."

"Maybe. I don't think they put me on, though. I was scheduled to give my presentation at that meeting. The journal was something new. If they'd given it to me first, I probably wouldn't have been able to fight the battle as I did."

"When Jean Paul won the battle all by himself."

"I never said that Jean Paul won the battle all by himself."

"But—"

"Who can say how the battle might have come out if he hadn't been there with the breech-loading cannon?" Edward paused to collect himself. "Who can say how anything may have worked out—if this or that hadn't happened?"

"Can't argue with that."

"It was the shot," Edward said dramatically, "never heard 'round the world." He settled back into the chair. Perhaps his case hung only on the thread of a pizza, at the moment. But it wasn't lost yet. Father couldn't accuse him of giving up.

"But how could Jean have made all that much difference? You said he fired cannon balls. And you said cannon balls didn't work so good."

"But he didn't use balls. And he didn't use grapeshot. Grape wouldn't have carried that far. Not all the way across the river. He used canister, which was similar to grape shot, except that the grape stayed in the can until it arrived at its target, where it exploded."

"How come Jackson didn't use grape shot? He was closer."

"He did use grapeshot. He had to. He was almost out of balls."

"So how come Jackson's cannon didn't mow down the British? I thought the historians—"

"We talked about historians. The historians never stopped to properly analyze. They took for gospel what others had said before them. It was a very short battle, lasting only two hours. There was no way Jackson could have fired his few guns fast enough. There were simply too many enemy. He would have been over-run."

"Okay. So after the battle, Junior handed you the journal. How'd that fit in? Was it really written by Jean Lafitte?"

"It claimed to be."

"What'd you do?"

"What could I do? I thanked them for it, gathered up my cannon and maps and left. I read the journal on the train ride back home. I absolutely devoured that little book—very badly written and totally out of chronological order, it was often incoherent. My doubt about the book's veracity began to grow. Could a person who was presumably so well-educated have written as badly as this? Yet, I squirmed. It was so amateurish that it had a ring of authenticity about it. Surely, had it been prepared by a con artist, it would have been slicker, more methodical.

"The work with my practice began to pick up about that time, which was very frustrating, for my real interest lay with the journal, and not with Deeds of Trust. Still, the bills came in, and needed to be paid. Study of the journal became chaotic and incidental. But I did progress, and eventually, a pattern began to form. I outlined my strategy and fired off a letter to the Society, requesting a hearing.

"My letter went ignored; I wrote another. And another. I supposed that they felt that my case had been completely obliterated by the journal. Frantic, I sent a telegram. The Society at last responded and granted me yet another hearing."

CHAPTER 29
The Lafitte Society
Saint Louis, Missouri
February 6, 1970

The Society had changed.

The old faithful scrivener Choteau was gone, probably passed to his reward. Lionel Croft had moved up to the secretary's seat, and he scribbled furiously like his predecessor.

A new member named Frank Throckmorten had replaced Professor Hunt. Throckmorton glowered from within a face so dark and wrinkled that it appeared his maker might have created him within a skin intended for a larger person.

Steinbach reigned as chairman, if reigned be the word, for there was nothing about him that was powerful except his thick eyeglasses. He wielded the gavel as if it intimidated him.

And there was Junior, of course. As if his old butcher father had eaten so much baloney that the preservative had granted him eternal life.

Edward peered around at the changing faces and held high *The Journal of Jean Lafitte*. "Has the Society accepted this journal as authentic?" he asked. He set the slight volume on the table. A leaf turned of its own accord, revealing a sketch of Jean Lafitte on board a ship. He held a long, closed sword encased in an elaborate scabbard.

"Not yet." Junior smiled at him. "We don't react too swiftly, as you may know."

"But you must have some opinion. Do you believe it puts the lie to my testimony?"

"No doubt about that whatsoever, is there?" Junior glanced quickly about the table for confirmation.

"Or does it merely contradict?"

"However you want to put it."

"The wording's important. Unless the book has been authenticated as the actual writing of Jean Lafitte, it can't very well put the lie to my testimony."

"There is authentication. It's spelled out in the book, by the Library of Congress."

"I seem to recall reading that." Edward recalled very well. "Does the authentication constitute confirmation?"

Edward stood with his free hand on the edge of the table and one knee bent in the classic style of Thomas Jefferson arguing a point before the Continental Congress. "I would ask you to review page sixteen." He opened the book to that page and slid it across the table.

"The Society hasn't yet confirmed the book's validity. But," Junior said after opening his copy to the page, "that's where the book cites the authentication by the Library of Congress."

"Take a very close look," Edward said without losing his pose. "The Library of Congress makes no claim that it has authenticated the *book*. Merely that it has examined a leaf from an account book. We don't know which account book. Certainly, it does not claim to have authenticated the manuscript of the journal."

"Good point."

"The letter from the Library of Congress also refers to a 'small scrap which contains writing in French.'"

"It does."

"But nowhere is it stated that the 'small scrap' examined was a portion of the original manuscript of Jean Lafitte."

"Page sixteen," Junior replied patiently, "reproduces page thirty-three of the original manuscript."

"And the publisher would like you to believe that page thirty-three of the manuscript was not only from Jean Lafitte's original manuscript, but also a page that was authenticated. But does the journal actually say that?"

Junior studied the page. "It does not. Second good point."

"The portion of the original manuscript reproduced on page sixteen of the journal is written in French. Now," Edward said, staring about at the members' faces, "it has been frequently stated by reputable historians that Lafitte was conversant in many lanquages. It is said that he spoke English very well. He professed to be an American patriot. Why would he have written in French?"

"Perhaps," Junior offered, "he was merely accomplished in *spoken* English."

Edward laughed. "If the translation is any indication of his ability to write, he was not very accomplished in French, either."

"I suppose we should obtain a copy of the original manuscript."

"I have attempted that," Edward said. "The publisher says that he was provided only with an English translation. My attempts to find the original document have gone unfulfilled. But do you not see," he continued, looking at each member's face in turn, "that this uncertainty fortifies my theory of the *two Lafittes*?" The men stared blankly back at him.

"Furthermore, the letter states that the record from the account book examined by the Library could have been made 'in or about eighteen thirty.'" Edward relaxed his stiff pose. "According to the journal itself, Jean Lafitte had given up his privateering activities in eighteen twenty-six. Some four years before eighteen thirty, which the Library claims the record 'could have been made.'"

"I'm not sure," Junior said, "that even the Library of Congress could have determined the date so precisely."

"I'm sure you're right. Still, the Library avoided mention of any date for the account book itself. Why do you suppose they did that? That's only a small aside," Edward continued. "The principal question is, what significance does the leaf of some account book have to the authentication of the journal anyway? The Library goes on to say that the small scrap of paper referred to with French writing 'appears to be on a paper of somewhat earlier manufacture.'"

Edward rapped his knuckles on the table and began to rove about the room, peering into corners, at the ceiling, at the floor. "Let's move on. It is intimated that the 'small scrap of paper with French writing' was part of the original manuscript. Yet, it is claimed in the introduction to the journal that Jean Lafitte did his writing from eighteen forty-five to eighteen fifty. If that small scrap of paper was the paper on which Jean Lafitte actually wrote the journal," Edward said, spinning about on one toe, "he would have been writing on paper that was already more than twenty-five years old. Again, according to the journal, he had traveled about a great deal before he began the writing. Does it appear logical that he would have used an old batch of paper that he carried around with him for twenty-five years?"

"Good reasoning. But it doesn't prove anything."

"Quite right. It proves nothing. But the evidence would be substantial enough to give a jury pause. The question here is: is such a thing logical?"

Junior flung one arm across the back of his chair. "Do you claim that the journal wasn't written by Jean Lafitte?"

"No. I didn't say that. I merely pointed out that we have no evidence that the original manuscript was authenticated by the Library of Congress. Or that the dates add up. Or that Jean Lafitte would have written on such old paper."

"Is that it? Or do you have other points?"

"A great many," Edward nodded. "All of which indicate that the journal," he said, pointing to the book, "authentic or not, supports my position."

Junior closed the book and slid it along the table to Edward. "The mind boggles," he said, smiling. "I don't know what you're trying to prove, anymore."

"There is a very great possibility," Edward said, "that the journal actually was written by Jean Lafitte himself. Whether it was or not is of little importance. The fact remains that it is a badly-written piece of work and completely out of order chronologically. It contradicts itself on numerous occasions. It also contradicts much of accepted, proven history."

"Nothing much unusual about that. Sounds like your whole case." Junior didn't sound hostile, to Edward's gratification.

"I will point out a few of the most significant inconsistencies," Edward said, continuing his circling of the table. "Many others are contained in a report that I will leave with you.

"On page twenty, for example," he continued, citing from his well-rehearsed memory, "the writer states that he and Alexander first arrived in New Orleans on January nineteenth,

seventeen ninety-eight. On page thirty-six, he states that they
first arrived in March, seventeen ninety-nine."

"You said there were inconsistencies. According to your
own testimony, I think you once said that a minor fault would
not void a contract."

Edward was surprised. It was a legality he had related to
the elder Stratmeyer long ago.

"In—"

"That's only a minor detail," Junior said. "Irrelevant con-
flicts have nothing to do with the substance."

"Quite right," Edward said, delaying an instant to recover.
"But I will point out that the writer indicated in his foreword
that he needed to spend some years in research to collect the
necessary proofs of authenticity. 'Only in this way,' he said,
'shall I be free of contradiction—'"

"You indicated, if I remember correctly, that the journal
supports your position," Junior said. "If you tear it apart,
what difference does it make to you whether it supports you
or not? Why are we bothering with this?"

Edward stopped directly behind his chair. "Because I need
to prove to you that the journal may be used as a weapon in
my defense, whether you find it fake or not. I want to instill
the doubt of its authenticity in your mind. Its veracity is yet
to be proven. If it is finally called a fake, then it has no
bearing. But, if it is accepted, you will find that my argument
is supported."

"The mind still boggles."

"Let's assume for the moment that the work is legitimate,"
Edward said. "We'll assume that it was actually written by
Jean Lafitte. And," he said, beginning his pacing about the
room once again, "we'll begin at the beginning.

"The recollections of his boyhood are vivid. Right down to ages, dates, names. He was sixty-three years old when he began to write, but no detail of his young life was left out. He even has recollections from the age of three, which is most extraordinary. When he was six, he says, his grandmother began to teach him Spanish. When he was eight, Madame Raquel Geguria taught him arithmetic, history, geography and grammar. When he was fourteen, John Christopher Chauteys taught him navigation and map-charting. Fantastic, that he could so well remember names, such details."

"You seem to be doing very well with your powers of recollection," Junior said with a grin.

Edward nodded. "Only because I prepared myself for this presentation. I could not, however, recall the names of my early teachers. And, given the life that Jean Lafitte lived, he probably didn't carry a Daily Diary around with him. In fact, the foreword of the book states that he was far too busy most of his life to keep a diary, even if he had been inclined to do so."

"So now you're saying the *Journal of Jean Lafitte* is bunk?"

"No. Merely that his powers of recollection are far above average."

Junior tilted his head as if to say, "What does it matter?"

"Later, when he was nineteen years old and already well into his career of marauding, he cites an encounter with a Spanish ship. Not only does he remember the name of the ship, but he remembers precisely the *geographical position* of the encounter. 'Eighty-eight degrees fourteen minutes west longitude,' he says, and 'twenty-two degrees twelve minutes north latitude.' Extraordinary. There are other demonstrations of this power, all cited in my report. That ability continues until January, eighteen oh five. Suddenly, the journal changes." Edward paused, as if he had to do some recollecting of his own. "On that date, he says, 'we were caught by Spanish vessels and taken prisoner, losing all our property and money.'

"*In the very next paragraph*, he says that 'In March, eighteen oh five, we fought an audacious and reckless fight during which we captured seven vessels with only one small sloop.' No mention of the captivity, or any other detail of the capture. The very same sentence continues, 'after we had been set free in Cuba.'" Edward stentorously turned to face the Society. "I submit," he said slowly, "that Jean Lafitte was, at that point, held prisoner in a Cuban prison, probably Morro Castle. He remained there until January, eighteen fourteen." He paused to let the statement sink in.

"But the journal," Junior said, "describes in great detail his activities in setting up the base at Grande Terre before eighteen-fourteen."

"Alas," Edward smiled. "I'm afraid it does not. If you study the journal carefully, you will find that the details are sketchy at best. There is only the appearance of detail. Read the book closely. Bear in mind that this was the very period when he was at the pinnacle of his success. This time should be lavish with detail."

"But he does show great detail," Junior said. He dragged the journal closer and fumbled through the pages. "He lists, even, the names of his men. He lists the names of every ship—"

"And how is he able to do that?" Edward interrupted, holding a condemning finger high. "It was because he had in his possession the excellent account books of the operation. Account books—kept in precise detail—by none other than our ubiquitous Jean Paul."

Junior could not contain a chuckle.

"Is it so absurd? The journal rushes haphazardly through other periods which should have been vital to him. The encounter with the British Navy and Lockyer's offer. Tales of proposing duels not only to Governor Claiborne, but to Andrew Jackson. Then, his turning right around and offering help in Jackson's fight with the British. That entire segment is laden with contradictions."

"It sounds familiar."

"I'm only willing to contradict when logic indicates otherwise."

Junior quietly tapped a pencil on the table.

Edward resumed his pacing. "After the Battle of New Orleans, Lafitte resumed his practice of infinite detail in the writing. He also became a changed person: he is suddenly concerned about the common man; he opposes slavery; he travels to Europe; he contributes to the cause of Marx and Engels; he becomes a Communist, even before the term is coined."

"But you don't have any conclusive proof—"

Edward spun on his heel. "I was waiting for you to mention that." He hastened around the table to his briefcase.

"This," he said, holding high a sheet of paper, "is a memo from a distinguished professor of Linguistics at Loyola University." He slid the memo across the table to Junior. "The professor is a nationally recognized expert, not only in linguistics, but in calligraphy. I provided the professor with the journal, as well copies of the letters written by the leader of the Baratarians to Earl Blanque and to Governor Claiborne, which I obtained from the archives at Chalmette."

Junior studied the memo closely. "It isn't signed."

"It's a preliminary analysis. The professor will make himself known at the time of the final report."

"When will that be?"

"I'm not sure."

"And, until that time, we'll have to take your word for it?"

"Temporarily."

"Why didn't you have the final report ready for this meeting?"

"It—the idea—didn't occur to me in time."

"I must say."

"Please recognize," Edward said, "that the professor is one of the country's foremost experts. As such, he is extremely methodical. He only agreed to prepare this memo for me, even if unsigned, because I stated how vitally important it would be for this meeting. In any event, you may wish to get a second opinion. The professor compared the handwriting of the letters with the fragment of handwriting included in the book, the one authenticated by the Library of Congress. He also compared the syntax, the construction of sentences, the use of words. Linguistics."

Edward paused. He looked about the table at each of the members, locked their eyes before moving on. "He believes—though it's preliminary—that the letters were not written by the same person that wrote the journal."

The Society members sat without moving, without looking at Edward or each other, as if they were individually determining the significance.

"We will await the professor's final report with bated breath. However," Junior said almost congenially, "his report will speak only to the match in the handwriting. It may or may not prove The *Journal of Jean Lafitte* to be false. Anyway, as you have said, the veracity of the journal does not matter to you, so you must have more to support your greater position, some evidence much more substantive."

"How much," Steinbach asked, blinking behind his thick glasses, "did you pay the professor?"

So, not all the Society members were unmoved.

CHAPTER 30
New Orleans, Louisiana
February 6, 1993, 5:34 PM

The telephone rang in the study, jolting Edward into tense alert.

"I'll get it." Mickey scrambled to his feet before Edward could even gather up his cane.

"Hullo, Dad."

Oh, God. It was Charleton again. Edward tightened his trembling hands on the cane. He heard a tiny squawking, as if Charleton were shouting into the line.

"Just talking," Mickey said when the squawking temporarily stopped.

The squawking resumed and went on and on, rising and falling in pitch, the sound of Charleton scolding his son.

For what? For being with his grandfather?

Of course, Charleton would deny that he resented Mickey's spending the afternoon. There would be reasons, excuses. Things to blame. Always so much to blame.

"If that's what you want to do." Mickey's tone was hesitant, reluctant.

Sociologists liked to go back, find the root cause, build on it. They searched but didn't always find, however much they pretended to. However much they rationalized.

Problems didn't always fall into neat sociological niches.

Edward was convinced that, in Charleton's case, the problem
was a basic personality clash which had never been resolved,
and which deepened through the years. One that never improved. Only worsened.

He heard the receiver drop into its hook, cutting off the
squawks. He heard a jingle of the Pierce-Arrow keys, as if
Mickey had poked at them. He heard Mickey's scuffling shoes
re-enter the parlor. Edward gripped the cane so tightly his
knuckles hurt.

"I'm sorry if I got you into trouble with your father," he
said as Mickey dropped into the chair.

"It's okay. I was in trouble anyway."

"We went on too long. It isn't fair."

"He's coming over to pick me up."

"I gathered that." Hot blood rushed into Edward's cheeks.

"Boy." Mickey gazed into the fire. "Did I goof."

"Because you're here with me?" Edward lowered his bushy
brows until they rested on the top of his spectacles.

"More than that. But we said we wouldn't talk about it."

"Did we? Maybe we'd better, anyway."

"Won't do no good."

Maybe Mickey was right. He wasn't the problem, after all.
It was better said to the father, not the son, however much
Edward abhorred the thought of a harangue with Charleton.
A harangue that was too long postponed. Like a nagging tooth-
ache, it only worsened with time.

"Well, then," Edward said in a halting voice, "shall we continue with our discussion? About the Society?" He had lost all
interest in pursuing the case. It was over, through. But they
couldn't sit in embarrassed silence until Charleton arrived.

"Sure." Mickey kept his eyes diverted. He propped a foot

on his knee, waggling it furiously up and down. His interest was lost as well.

"Where was I?"

Edward was furious with Charleton for destroying the moment. It was what he always did. And Edward was always furious, but never said so. The nagging toothache had developed into real pain.

"You was before the Society. Talking about the professor."

"Ah, yes."

Charleton would arrive soon. He would burst into the house and destroy the warm bond that had developed between Edward and his grandson. The bond that would likely never be created again.

"Did you pay the professor?"

"What?"

"The professor. They wanted to know if you bought him off."

Edward felt himself drifting in a daze. He had no idea what Mickey was talking about.

"The professor. About the handwriting, and all that. Did you pay him?"

"Oh. The professor." Edward shook his head violently. "No. I didn't pay him anything. He contributed his time."

"Did you tell The Society that?"

The Society. The session about the journal. Edward struggled to concentrate on it. He remembered his feeling of apprehension when Junior handed him the mysterious brown package.

"I told them. But I don't think it did any good."

"Did you ever get a full report?"

"No."

He would have preferred to forget the Society. The entire Lafitte Case. But Mickey was relentless.

"Why not?"

"What?"

"Why didn't you get the full report?"

Edward strained to shift back to his frame of mind to the moment before Charleton's untimely telephone call.

"It was another of the lessons I learned from Clarence Darrow," he said. "Not to dissipate your energies running down details that wouldn't have a bearing on the outcome. It didn't matter to my case whether the journal was written by an imposter or not."

Like the sociologists do. Tracking down useless leads.

"Maybe you should have gone ahead anyway."

"No. I decided it was better to plant the seed of doubt and let it go at that. I could live with the journal, fraud or not."

"And they never asked for the rest of the report?"

"I only appeared at one more session after that, and we didn't discuss the journal. But I'm sure the subject will come up again. After all, it was presumably written by the very person they were studying."

"Did you ever prove that thing about the prison? In Cuba?"

Mickey's thoughts were wandering as Edward's were, rambling around, working to avoid the real subject, to continue the mindless patter about the case.

"Fidel Castro," Edward murmured quietly, nodding his head. He stared into the embers of the dying fire. There was unfinished business everywhere.

"What?"

"Fidel Castro. I wrote him a letter, asking for permission to do research on Morro Castle."

"And he said no, I guess?"

"I never got an answer." Edward let his head drift forward. He was very tired.

Mickey remained quiet for a few moments, as if he were thinking back, keeping the useless conversation afloat. "You said Jean Lafitte got out of prison. You didn't say how he escaped."

Edward heard the question, but Mickey's voice sounded as if it came from a far distance. "Nobody knows. The *Journal* didn't say, either. That's why I wanted to go to Cuba."

"How'd Lafitte get back to New Orleans?"

Maybe the idle conversation was a good idea, after all. Edward tried to pull himself together. "Another of those 'mists of history' things. It isn't important. In any case, it's an easy sail from Cuba to New Orleans. There have always been a lot of fishing boats in the Gulf. When he returned, he was a changed man. Prison does that to a person."

"But he still looked like Jean Paul."

Edward shook his head. "Not just like him. They were similar in appearance, that's all."

"Anybody know what Lafitte looked like?"

"Not actually. There were no decent pictures. Except in the journal, but those haven't been confirmed yet. No one was ever really sure what he looked like. In the journal, he claimed that 'no one knew who he was, but that he knew himself quite well.'" Edward laughed, in spite of himself. "Makes you think, doesn't it?"

"But Jean Paul was killed in battle, and they thought he was Lafitte. How could he suddenly come back to life?"

"The Baratarians didn't know he had been killed. Remember, he fired his gun from across the river. Only he and Manuel Perrin knew about that. The rest of the crew roared to New Orleans for a good long drunk. While they were enjoying themselves, Manuel quietly buried the body in the cemetery by the Bayou des Oises beside John Paul Jones."

Mickey pressed on. "So, after the battle, Lafitte started up the pirating business again? Or privateering?"

"Pirating, privateering. It depends on your point of view. I'm sure that pirates never thought of themselves as pirates."

"But Lafitte got a pardon because of the war."

"One of my better arguments."

"And he started in again."

"Not right away. When the real Jean Lafitte escaped from prison, he found nothing but ashes at Grande Terre. He went to Bayou LaFourche and stayed with friends. Word got out that he was back in business. The Baratarians looked him up."

Mickey laughed. "He must have been pretty pale, after being in prison for so long."

"Maybe. The sun in the swamps wouldn't take long to correct that, though."

"But you don't think they saw Jean Lafitte as a different person from Jean Paul?"

"Some of them probably did. But why would they have cared to rock the pirogue? They just wanted to get back to action. Here was their glorious leader. If he looked a little skinny, a little pale, so what?"

Mickey appeared to accept that, so Edward continued. "Two years later, the Baratarians decided Grand Terre wasn't any good anymore, so they sailed off to Galveston Island. Galveston was farther from the markets, but it was also farther away from Claiborne. It was one of my best arguments, that it didn't make sense to fight for the pardon and then go right back to the old ways."

"Doesn't make sense to me, either."

"Historians claim that Lafitte was angry because the government wouldn't pay him for the matériel he supplied to

Jackson, or the merchandise he lost when Patterson attacked Grande Terre."

"Maybe he should have been paid for the stuff."

Edward nodded. "Maybe. But he did get a pardon out of it. And it doesn't seem right that the government should have to pay. Police aren't required to pay the thief when the stolen loot is recovered. And, in the eyes of the government, it was stolen." Edward gazed hard at Mickey. "Are we all clear on that?" he asked. "Can we go to Galveston now?"

"On to Galveston."

Mickey was either a very good actor or he was better than Edward at forgetting his troubles.

"He set up a base on Galveston Island and called it Campeche, built a big red house, called Maison Rouge, with cannon mounted at the corners on the upper story where he lived. The downstairs was a warehouse. It was quite different from the way Jean Paul worked, which was to hide the merchandise, scatter it in case of attack. It was another of the differences between the two.

"They built quite a little village all around Maison Rouge, saloons, gambling dens, markets for the slaves they captured. That was different, too, more what you'd expect of a pirate's den, and not something that Jean Paul would have tolerated. Jean Paul was too much of a conscientious businessman for the debauched life."

Edward warmed to the subject. He felt his old enthusiasm returning. "There was another change in character that the historians gloss over. Before the Battle of New Orleans, the Baratarians attacked mostly Spanish ships. Yet, after he arrived in Galveston, Lafitte accepted Spanish gold for spying on the Mexicans, which further supports my two people theory."

"Why would he spy on the Mexicans?"

"The Mexicans were at that time revolting against Spain, 'throwing off the Spanish yoke,' as they put it."

"Sounds like he should have been on the side of the Mexicans, though. What does the journal say about that?"

"Just as I have recited it. That he deceived the Spaniards. But the Spaniards weren't dummies, after all."

"How do you explain it then?"

"I don't. It's one of the things that needs to be explored in Havana. In any event, that has little to do with what happened next."

"At Galveston?"

"A group of French army veterans arrived. Actually, they were a remnant of Napoleon's Imperial Guard, called the Grande Armée, with General Lallemand in command. They formed an organization called the Champ d'Asile. Ever heard of it?"

"No."

"Not many have. The Champ d'Asile had a noble goal: to free Napoleon from exile on St. Helena and reconquer Europe."

"There's lots of stories in New Orleans about rescuing Napoleon."

"This story wasn't from New Orleans. And it wasn't quite like the others. One of those veterans was an infantryman named Eugene Francois Robeaud."

"Never heard of him."

Edward shook his head. "Wouldn't have expected you to. He was one of those unfortunates that history likes to forget. He was Napoleon Bonaparte's official double."

"Another double. Does everybody have doubles?"

"I didn't say that Jean Paul and Jean Lafitte were doubles."

"Sorry."

Edward waved his hand. "Picture the scene. The remote island of Campeche. On the island is the headquarters of a big pirate base. Camped nearby is a group of French army veterans whose goal is to rescue Napoleon and restore him to the throne. One of those veterans is an exact look-alike to the former Emperor."

"Hard to believe."

"What's hard to believe?"

"That he was such an exact look-alike."

"Believe it. There's plenty of evidence. When he was Emperor, Napoleon grew weary of the tiresome need to appear at so many official functions. He preferred to spend more time with the ladies. They say he didn't have his hand in his weskit all the time."

Mickey laughed again. "Lucky he found the double, then."

"It's not so tough if you're the emperor. Napoleon told his Minister of Police, a fellow named Fouche, what he wanted, and Fouche found Private Robeaud. When they dressed him up in the general's uniform, no one could tell the difference. So it is recorded," Edward said heavily.

"And Jean Lafitte sailed to St. Helena and—"

"No. Jean Lafitte didn't go. He didn't care much about Napoleon. As a matter of fact, the notion of any sort of an Empire was contrary to his philosophy. After his time in prison, he was concerned about the common man, not emperors. He supported Marx and Lenin. He wouldn't have had anything to do with imperialists. Especially the biggest one of them all."

"But the New Orleans story goes that Jean Lafitte rescued Napoleon—"

"So does the newspaper story. But they're both wrong."

"Then—"

"It was Alexander Lafitte who may be history's most un-sung hero. He was responsible for bringing Jean Paul to Loui-siana, or else we wouldn't have had him there to help win the Battle of New Orleans for us. Alexander brought the breech-loader from France that Jean Paul used. Alexander was an avid Bonapartist, as avid as the old soldiers in the Champ d'Asile. Remember that he had fought with Napoleon's artillery. Now he was hobnobbing with a group of veterans that wanted to restore Napoleon to power. And he had just what the Champ d'Asile needed. A ship. All the necessary ingredients," Edward continued, relishing the opportunity to wax just a little bit eloquent, "were in the stewpot that was Campeche. Alexander loaded up Robeaud and sailed the good ship *Confiant* off to rescue Napoleon from St. Helena."

Edward thumped his cane three times on the floor. "Lis-ten carefully," he said pointedly to Mickey. "For in that rescue is the most important clue to the solution of the riddle."

Mickey's eyes glittered in the firelight.

"And," Edward said, "the substantive proof Junior wanted. Still wants."

CHAPTER 31
Saint Helena Island
August 21, 1818

PRES. BY Edw. Livingston, Esq.
FEBRUARY 6, 1975

"Robeaud, Robeaud. Why are you here?"

Napoleon Bonaparte stood warming himself before a crack-ling fire. He was in full dress uniform, and his famous cocked hat rested in the crook of his arm as if he were about to go out, rain or no.

Robeaud stepped forward. "I come from America, Sire."

Alexander waited beside the billiard table. Napoleon might still have been emperor, judging by his manner of dress. He wore white knee breeches, a green hunting coat with velvet cuffs and collar, the silver plaque of the Legion of Honour pinned to his breast, and of course, the cocked hat under his arm. He might have been ready for a parade down the Champs-Elyses.

"From America, is it? America is a very long way away." The emperor coughed.

Napoleon wore the trappings of an emperor, but he hardly looked the part. An overgrown paunch strained the buttons on his waistcoat. Squat chubby legs filled the breeches to capacity and beyond. A residue of snuff sprinkled down the front of him.

This was the commander that once had conquered Europe?

"And what is it you are playing at, Robeaud?"

Napoleon's breath swept across the billiard room to Alexander. He was reminded of rotten, sulfurous cabbage, overpowering even the smell of damp and mildew that filled the house called Longwood. His face had a yellowed jaundice look.

The emperor, Alexander thought, *is a dying man.*

"Sire, I have come to—"

Napoleon had dismissed his double. The intense blue-gray eyes flashed directly to Alexander, who stood twisting a wet cloth cap in his hands.

"You remind me of an old soldier," Napoleon said. "And your very appearance hints at what Robeaud here may be up to. Who, pray tell, might you be?"

Alexander stepped forward. At last he had his opportunity

to speak to Napoleon face to face. "Sire, I am Alexander Lafitte."
He shot a quick glance at Robeaud, who had only known him
as Dominique Youx. "Once of the Imperial Artillery."

Napoleon bowed his head, as if contemplating this last.
"Montholon!" he shouted in a drill ground command. "That
will be all!"

Lord Montholon stood before the open doorway of the
billiard room. Tall and courtly, clad in a worn uniform heavy
with gold braid, the Grand Chamberlain at once bowed his
curly head.

"Oh, Montholon." Napoleon's voice took on a more conversational tone. "Take that away." He waved dispassionately
at a saucer on the floor beside an aged piano.

Again Montholon bowed. He walked with grace and without sound to retrieve the saucer. He bowed again when he
backed through the door.

Napoleon coughed. "We feed the English rats. Grain and
arsenic." He pushed from the mantel and lay his hat atop
scattered maps on the billiard table.

Alexander heard the scampering of the rats within the
walls and wondered how their bodies might be removed after
an agonizing death from arsenic. He stole a glance at Robeaud,
who was perhaps less concerned with the poisoning of rats.

"Now tell me," Napoleon said suddenly, "how you come
to be here." He halted before a window streaked with rain.
Outside, a short distance away, a red-coated sentry huddled
beside a low stone wall. A prisoner as much as his prisoner.

They told the tale, the two of them chiming together at
times while the most-feared man in the world stared at the
poor sentry. They told of the Champ d'Asile, commanded by
Napoleon's own General Lallemand. Alexander thought he

detected a twitch of the imperial right arm at the mention of the general's name.

They told of the voyage across the Atlantic in *Confiant*, of the lying in wait for an East Indiaman steering south, for they knew that only ships of the East India Company were allowed to trade at St. Helena.

When at last one such ship was spotted by the topman, they told of being cast adrift in a gig, just the two of them, Alexander rowing strongly toward the Englishman while Robeaud retched over the side. Alexander thought he saw a trace of an imperial smile.

They told of their rescue by *David*, of their animated explanation of a need to repair a broken rudder on *Confiant*, then of that vessel's drifting away in a sudden wind, leaving them stranded and alone.

When the tale had finished, Napoleon ponderously turned from the window. "And how," he asked, "did you get past Sir Thomas Reade?"

Alexander and Robeaud looked at each other.

"The Chief of Police," Napoleon explained.

"The crates," Robeaud said. "From Lord Holland. On *David*. We—Alexander—bribed the purser."

Napoleon coughed, a long racking cough that appeared to accomplish little. "Lord Holland. My benefactor. My one friend in that unholy place they call England. He sends me food and wine." His voice grew loud. "Sir Thomas is accustomed to the delivery. But not," he said, softening his tone, "so accustomed to a drayman who so closely resembles his prisoner." He lowered his brow at Robeaud.

Robeaud withdrew a fuzzy dark fur-ball from his pocket. Napoleon puzzled at it, then smiled when his double formed

the fur-ball over his chin and fastened it behind his ears. The
false beard most adequately disguised his features.

"And the purpose of this elaborate charade?"

Alexander stepped forward. "We have come, Sire, to take
you to America."

Napoleon snorted sharply, as if snuff were trapped in his
nostrils. "And," he said, his voice booming, "you would conceal me within a barrel of rum? Load me on your English
ship and carry me away? Under the eyes of Sir Thomas Reade?
"No," he said, shaking his head. He paced a few steps from
the window, then turned slowly, as if uncertain his legs would
follow his command. "It is impossible. There have been count-
less escape plans and I have spurned them all. I cannot—will
not—submit myself to the indignity of a masquerade. It is not
the end I choose for myself. Not to risk discovery, to suffer
further humiliation. I have been mocked enough." He bent in
a racking frenzy of coughing. Alexander and Robeaud again
glanced uncertainly at each other. At last, the Emperor straightened and wiped his lips with the back of his hand.

"Call Montholon." His voice was choking. "He will take
you to your wagon. Return to your America."

"Sire." Alexander stepped closer, ready to extend an arm
for support. "We have ships, men, cannon—"

"Go! I will hear no more of it!"

Robeaud nodded in vigorous agreement. He appeared about
to apologize for even the conception of such a preposterous
scheme.

"Sire!" Alexander took charge. "It is said that your brother
will take the throne of Mexico!"

Napoleon visibly wavered. "Ah, Joseph," he said pleasantly.
He still lives in New Jersey, does he not? He will take Mexico?"

"So it is said."

Napoleon wavered again. He plucked the cocked hat from the table and pressed it on his head. "And how," he asked, "would you have proposed to get me on this ... English ship ... to America?"

Empty of its cargo, the wagon rattled on the rocky road to Jamestown. Alexander drove the horses, as before. Beside him sat a squat assistant as before. Fully bearded, dressed in drayman's clothing.

As they topped the last rise before the steep descent to Jamestown, the Royal Navy ships could be clearly seen through the light rain.

Alexander counted six brigs constantly guarding the island.

One cruised to windward, one to leeward. Four were anchored in the harbor, clustered around *David*.

When he drew up the wagon at the stone quay, a tall soldier watched them from a window.

They clambered down from the wagon, the bearded one stumbling a bit as if he might have tippled too much wine in the kitchen at Longwood. Alexander lent an arm, assisting him down the stone steps to the boat.

The soldier watched the little scene from his office, reluctant to step out into the rain. He would, Alexander hoped, simply note the time on *David*'s chargebill.

The soldier would not know that, under the rough teamster coat, the bearded one wore the silver plaque of the Legion of Honour.

Halfway to the ship, a distant cannon boomed from the island's interior. Alexander nervously splashed the oars at the sound, but was calmed by a quiet voice from behind the beard: "Only the cannon on Alarm Hill; it sounds at sunrise and sunset."

The final sentence was spoken so softly that it could hardly be heard above the slap of the waves against the side of the boat. "Or for the escape of Napoleon."

Resp. sub., J. Croft, Sec.
February 6, 1975

CHAPTER 32

New Orleans, Louisiana
February 6, 1993, 5:48 PM

A staccato of sharp knocks rang from the front door.

The sound was unlike Charleton's heavy hand, but Edward's spine tightened nevertheless.

Mickey bolted to his feet. His eyes darted about the parlor as if in search of a weapon or escape.

The knocking came again, followed by a muffled voice. "Pizza!"

Mickey laughed with obvious relief and started for the door. "Here," Edward said, reaching for his wallet.

The pizza was enormous and well encrusted with indefinable lumps on its surface that filled the parlor with spicy aroma. Edward watched as Mickey broke out the first piece.

"My favorite," Mickey said, raising the wedge high to sever a strand of cheese. "Everything on it."

Edward lay aside his cane and bent tentatively forward.

Mickey said, sucking air into his mouth to cool the hot pizza, "So Alexander rescued Napoleon. But it doesn't sound like he did much rescuing. They were still on an English ship, weren't they?"

"The *David*." Edward sat with the pizza in his napkin to

await cooling. "Alexander's ship lay just over the horizon from St. Helena. When *David* appeared, *Confiant* ran up alongside and asked after their missing crewmen."

"So they took Napoleon on board and whisked him off to America."

"Yes, but he never saw the shore. He died before the ship reached Barataria."

"Barataria? I thought they were headed to Galveston. Campeche."

"There was a great hurricane in that year. Alexander sought shelter in Barataria Bay. Manuel Perrin must have been very surprised when *Confiant* sailed in."

"Manuel Perrin was still at Grande Terre?"

"He was never a buccaneer, you know. He only guided the pirogues through the bayous to New Orleans. After the great battle, he returned to his old ways as a fisherman."

"So Manuel buried the emporer."

"In the little cemetery on the Bayou des Oises, where he had buried the others."

"What did Napoleon die of?" Mickey asked, through a mouthful of pizza.

"Arsenic poisoning."

"The rat poison?"

Edward nodded. He took his first bite of the savory pizza and found it delicious.

"Was it murder? You said this isn't a murder case."

"It isn't. But I said one of my clients was murdered. Two of them, actually."

"Who's the other one?"

"Robeaud."

"Did you get that from *a priori?*"

"No. Wheeler's book."

"Who?"

"Thomas Wheeler. Published in nineteen seventy-four. As soon as I read his book, the pieces fell into place. After I read it, I wrote to The Society and asked for another hearing."

"What'd Wheeler say?"

"He said what I said, mostly."

"That Napoleon ended up in Louisiana?"

"Wheeler was stumped when it came to that. He guessed that Napoleon went to Brazil because Rio de Janiero was *David's* destination."

"So you made up the part about Louisiana."

"There was other evidence, like Napoleon's memoirs."

"His memoirs said he went to Louisiana?"

They both jumped at a sound outside the front door. Edward waited, dreading Charleton's arrival. When no further sounds were heard, he took a bite of pizza to cover his anxiety.

"Napoleon," Edward continued, cautiously chewing his small bite, "wrote the *Memoirs* prior to eighteen eighteen, well before the rescue. The manuscript was lost for many years and finally turned up in a second-hand bookstore in Elwood, New Jersey. Fifty miles from Bordentown, where Napoleon's brother Joseph lived."

"That doesn't prove—"

"No one item of circumstantial evidence proves anything by itself. The chain must be considered as a whole. For example, the fact that Napoleon died of arsenic poisoning."

"Is there proof of that?"

"Tons of it. A Doctor Forshufvud published an article in nineteen sixty-one. He tested samples of Napoleon's hair and found a high content of arsenic."

"I don't ever remember reading that Napoleon was poisoned."

"I didn't just dream it up."

"And this doctor—whatever—proved he was poisoned?"

"There were more than one hundred and forty tests made of the hair, by irradiating samples with thermal neutrons in a nuclear reactor at the Harwell Atomic Energy Establishment at London. The tests were confirmed by the Police Toxology Laboratory at Paris."

"And you have the documentation."

"Some of the tests showed an arsenic content as high as seventy-six point six parts per million, almost a hundred times the normal content for human hair. Poison remains in hair forever, I guess."

"How'd they get the hair?"

"In Napoleon's time, it was common practice to give out locks of hair. Forshufvud advertised and got all the samples he needed."

"Was he sure it was Napoleon's hair?"

"No doubt whatsoever." Edward chewed an especially tasty bit of meat. "What's this on the pizza?"

"Blackened Cajun catfish, probably." Mickey grinned. "This's The New Orleans Special."

"Delicious." Edward swallowed before continuing. "In nineteen seventy-four, Ben Weider explored the possibility further. He fully confirmed Forshufvud's results. There's no doubt that Napoleon was poisoned."

"What did the Society say about all that?"

"They didn't. It was to have been my presentation today."

"Who did the poisoning? The English?"

"Not the English."

"How do you know?"

"It would have violated their innate sense of fair play. In any case, they wouldn't have wanted to create a martyr."

"Then who?"

"Count Montholon. Napoleon's Chamberlain."

"Montholon? Wasn't he Napoleon's man?"

"That put him above suspicion, didn't it?"

"But why—"

"St. Helena was a terrible place to live. And Napoleon's servants, Montholon included, were prisoners there, just as their master was."

"So Montholon poisoned the food?"

"Not the food. Napoleon had a food taster because he was always afraid of poisoning. But no one ever tasted the wine. Speaking of poison, what is this?" Edward fingered a lump atop the pizza.

"Crawdad. Why Montholon?"

"He had the key to the wine closet. And no one but Napoleon ever drank the emperor's personal wine."

"You think Montholon did it just so he could get off St. Helena?"

"That's probably a good enough reason. But the old boy might have been pretty upset because his wife shared Napoleon's bed, too."

"He must have been more upset when Napoleon escaped."

"He started the poisoning all over again with the new man."

"Why didn't he just report the escape? His problems were solved."

"He probably thought he'd be in hot water himself. Could be that the English would accuse him of being an accomplice, and he'd end up in prison. A real prison, this time. It was simpler to pretend that the prisoner hadn't changed. Stick with the original plan. Continue the poisoning."

A tough, chewy lump tasted suspiciously like alligator smelled, but Edward was afraid to ask.

"Nobody noticed the switch, not even the guards?"

"Robeaud was a good double, well-schooled in the mannerisms of his boss. Anyway, the guards never approached him closely. They saw him only as a distant figure in a heavy coat and a cocked hat, or a silhouette at a window."

"The other servants must have known."

"They looked the other way. They were prisoners too, you know. But Napoleon didn't have so many servants left by the end of eighteen eighteen. And, with the exception of those few, no one who had ever seen him close up prior to eighteen nineteen saw him alive again."

"And nobody suspected anything."

The sudden grind of a passing streetcar shook the parlor, making them glance apprehensively at the front door. Charleton's specter hung in the room like a cloud, intimidating their every thought.

"They suspected plenty. The new man didn't take snuff, for example. And, beginning in eighteen nineteen, the prisoner seemed to recover from his illness. He went out into the garden, started a whole new series of planting and landscaping. Robeaud was a consummate actor; in his mind, he actually became the exiled emperor himself. He lived out the greatest of fantasies."

"Like *a priori*."

"Like that."

"Until he died of poison."

"He lasted a little over two years after the switch."

"Was there an autopsy?"

"There were no signs of arsenic poisoning, if that's what you're getting at."

"The autopsy was rigged?"

"Robeaud was given several strong doses of laxative shortly before his death, which would've flushed the poison out of his body. Neither the English nor the French would have cared to reveal any signs of poisoning. There was no point in making things difficult for themselves."

"What did the autopsy say he died of?"

"Cancer of the stomach. The doctors ignored the fact that there were no prior symptoms of cancer. He grew fatter and fatter before he died, but cancer victims grow thinner and thinner. Those symptoms, as well as the fact that the liver was greatly enlarged, indicate positively that he was poisoned."

"But it wasn't Napoleon, you say. It was really the other guy."

"Robeaud. Yes. There were other inconsistencies, too, like the scars. Several of Napoleon's known wounds weren't reported. Others were found for which he had no history. Wounds more likely inflicted on an infantryman that once engaged in hand-to-hand combat with a bayonet. Like Robeaud."

"Maybe Napoleon had more wounds than they knew about."

"Not on a person so important as him."

"The Society's going to love it."

"There's more," Edward said. He lay the pizza on the table and wiped the alligator from his fingers. "After the autopsy, the remains were buried on St. Helena. Later, the French exhumed the body. They wanted to take him to Paris. That's where the story gets chilling. They opened the casket," Edward said slowly, drawing out the words mysteriously, "and found the body in a state of near-perfect preservation."

He tapped the cane on the floor. "Sounds like the opening of the casket of John Paul Jones, doesn't it? The plaque of the Legion of Honour lay on his body, badly tarnished. His clothing was so badly decayed it fell away from his body. Yet, the body itself was perfectly preserved. Almost as if the emperor had merely fallen asleep." He leaned back in the chair. "How," he asked, "could that be accounted for?"

Mickey chewed, watching him closely.

"It could only have been the arsenic. Museums use arsenic to preserve flesh."

Mickey's mouth was so full his words were hardly intelligible. "Sounds like you proved it."

"There's one more thing. The witnesses were astounded by the body's apparent youth. When Napoleon died in eighteen twenty-one, he would have been almost fifty-two years old. Now, Robeaud was born in seventeen eighty-one, which would have made him only forty years old. Robeaud was twelve years younger."

Mickey's capacity was amazing. He reached for more pizza. "So. It's Robeaud at Paris. Not Napoleon."

"Pretty convincing evidence, isn't it?"

Edward looked up sharply at choking sounds from across the table as if too much pizza had been stuffed into Mickey's mouth too quickly. He relaxed when he saw a beatific expression envelope Mickey's face.

"The Legion of Honour." Mickey chewed animatedly.

Edward waited. His grandson had just solved the riddle.

CHAPTER 33

New Orleans, Louisiana
February 6, 1993, 5:56 PM

Edward stiffened when a quickstep thunder across the front porch shook the house and rattled windows. His breath caught when the door burst open and Charleton plunged through like a gunslinger looking for a fight.

Dressed in a blue work shirt and blue jeans wet with rain, Charleton thudded high-heeled cowboy boots across the parlor directly to Mickey, who reeled back in his chair as if expecting to be attacked.

"We got to go home." Charleton breathed heavily through his nose, hands loose at his sides, exuding impatience. The soggy ponytail plastered its drooping yellow ribbon to the rounded shoulders.

Edward's hands quivered on the cane. His mouth worked. "Mickey and I were talking," he said quietly into the heavy silence. "We haven't finished."

Charleton turned to look at his father as if surprised that another person was even in the room. His gaze dropped to the low table where the pizza box lay empty but for a single slice.

"You been talking all day."

"Only for the afternoon."

"Mickey's supposed to be at work."

"He went to his grandmother's funeral." Edward dropped the reproach between them like a clattering sword.

"He should've called in to say he'd be late."

It was vintage Charleton. Hiding his sins behind the sins of another.

"That's my fault." Edward let him get away with it. He

glanced at Mickey to see how he was coping with the exclusion from the conversation as if he were a small child.

"We've nearly finished, haven't we?" Edward said to his grandson, trying to include him.

"Finished with what?" Charleton wouldn't let go.

"With what we were talking about. Before we were interrupted." Edward gripped the cane as if he meant to lash out with it.

Mickey fled the chair. Head bent, he scurried to the fireplace, took up the poker, jabbed at the fire.

Edward pushed himself to his feet. He stood uncertainly, leaning on the cane, shaking his legs to restore their circulation. He was close to Charleton, close enough to smell the mud of Carrollton on his boots. A wave of resolve swept over him, a resolve not to be dominated by his son, whose petty fiefdom didn't extend this far. Not to this house. Not anymore.

"Sit down," Edward said crisply with the voice of command, a tone he had never before used on Charleton. He pointed the cane at Mickey's empty chair.

Charleton stared at him incredulously, hands wavering just above his hips. After several moments, he dropped his hulk into the chair like a truck. To hide his surprise, Edward levered himself across the parlor to the bay window where the geraniums lined up on the wide ledge.

"You may proceed, Mickey," Edward said pleasantly, recovering from his astonishment.

Mickey straightened before the fireplace, the poker in his hand. "I guess I don't want to talk about it no more," he said in a rush, his voice tight.

Edward bent to inspect the underside of the flowers, although he couldn't see well in the semi-dark. "You were on the verge of discovery."

"Get it over with," Charleton muttered from the chair.

Charleton filled the room with his mass, his smell, his heavy breathing. It was unfair to ask so much of Mickey, Edward decided. He turned slowly, a withered geranium blossom in his free hand.

Charleton stretched his legs straight and crossed his ankles, nudging bits of mud to the floor. "The sooner you're through, the sooner we can go," he said. "Just figure I'm not here."

The sagging blossom held foolishly in his hand, Edward poled himself across the parlor and stopped directly before Charleton's chair. He stared down at the fruit of his loins. *How could anyone figure he wasn't there?*

The aging hippie's cheeks were in need of a shave, his hair in need of a barber. He looked up at his father as if in challenge and laced his fingers over an obscene bit of belly showing between the strained buttons of his shirt.

Edward hobbled away, across the room. He tossed the geranium blossom toward the fire and frowned when it fell short. Charleton was too old, too dug into the mud of Carrolton, to change his ways. And Mickey followed in his father's footsteps, too fearful to rebel. Just as Edward had.

After Father died, Edward couldn't believe that the world could continue without him; he was mildly surprised to see that the sun knew to come up; that the birds still knew how to fly; that newspapers could still be printed; that streetcars could run.

When Charleton was born, the age of permissiveness had just made its appearance. Edward seized on it; determined not to follow in the path of his own dictatorial father. He gave Charleton free rein; let him wear the clothes he wanted to wear, choose the friends he wanted to choose, drop out of school when he wanted to drop out.

And that method, too, had been a failure.

Edward circled the parlor, keeping to the gloom beyond the firelight. He halted before the wall of Father's leatherbound library. He sagged on his cane and bowed his head. The genes had skipped a generation; Charleton was Father all over again.

And Mickey the new victim.

Silence lay in the room like a fog over the swamp.

"We will," Edward said boldly, caning himself back to his chair, "hear what Mickey has to say. He was about to solve a riddle, I believe." He sat on the edge of the chair and propped both hands atop his cane. "The riddle of the long-lost medal of John Paul Jones."

Mickey's eyes darted uncertainly between his father and his grandfather.

"Let's hear it," Charleton muttered, opening his lips but not his teeth.

Edward nodded his head vigorously, urging his grandson on. At last, Mickey mumbled in an unwilling voice, "I think maybe the medal's buried with John Paul Jones' body."

Edward stifled a rush of exhilaration, the bitterness with Charleton forgotten. "Why," he asked, "would you guess that?"

"Because of what you said about Napoleon." Mickey returned the poker to its holder, keeping his eyes downcast, safely away from his father.

Edward rose and began to circle the room again, swinging the cane like a country gentleman on an afternoon stroll. "And what was it I said about Napoleon?"

"You said he always wore his medal."

"The plaque of the Legion of Honour."

"Yeah. You said it was important to him."

Edward halted before the books. "I said it was his proudest possession, didn't I? He never went anywhere without it. Probably pinned it to his pajamas at night. What does that have to do with John Paul Jones?"

"Well, you said that when Napoleon died, the plaque was buried with him."

Edward wanted to dance. He wanted to shout that Mickey had just won a 1928 Pierce-Arrow Saloon. Nearly new. One owner.

"And," Mickey said more exuberantly, "John Paul Jones' medal was just as important to him as the plaque was to Napoleon. So it must have been buried with him. That's why they haven't found it, because they haven't dug up the right body yet. Except," he added regretfully, "Napoleon probably wasn't buried with his plaque."

"Why not?" Edward swiveled sharply.

"The double. The double would've worn the plaque if he wanted everybody to think that he was Napoleon, wouldn't he? When he died, he would have been buried with it."

"Don't you suppose," Edward said, strutting around the chairs to stand beside Mickey, "that Napoleon had more than one plaque? Don't you suppose that, as Emperor of France, he had a whole box? After all, many had been awarded."

"Maybe so." Mickey shuffled his feet and kicked the geranium blossom into the fire, where it blazed briefly. "But, just because those guys were buried with their medals, what does it prove? That doesn't have anything to do with Jean Lafitte. Or Jean Paul."

Edward returned to his chair. He settled deeply into the cushions and lay the cane across his lap. "It has a great deal to do with Jean Lafitte and Jean Paul. One more piece of the mosaic. Quite a big piece, perhaps the biggest piece discovered so far. Remember what I said about everything fitting together?"

"But—"

"If those bodies by the Bayou des Oises are ever dug up, one will be wearing the Plaque of the Legion of Honour. Emperor Napoleon Bonaparte. Another, the Congressional Medal. Admiral John Paul Jones. We'll make him an honorary admiral," Edward said, smiling.

"And the third. Why, the remains of the third will be broken and shattered by the explosion of a cannon. But his broken bones alone would be meaningless without the supportive evidence of the other two. You see how important it is? You see how you've provided the definitive proof?"

"I provided it? But you did it. Not me."

Edward shook his head. "I gave you the clues. About the riddle, the missing medal. You took the clues and sorted it out."

Mickey lifted his hands in protest.

"Maybe it was *a priori*," Edward said, cutting him off.

CHAPTER 34

The Lafitte Society
Saint Louis, Missouri
February 6, 1997

CORRESPONDENCE
RECEIVED

Dear Chairman Stratmeyer,

This is to inform you that my grandfather, Mr. Edward Livingston, Esquire, passed away in his sleep on February 6, 1993, at the age of ninety. It may interest you to know that, in accordance with his Last Will and Testament, his ashes were scattered in the place known locally as "The Lafitte Cem-

etery," at the point of intersection of Big Barataria Bayou and
the Bayou des Oises.

I offer my sincerest apologies for not communicating with
you earlier. I trust that after reading this most difficult of
letters, you will understand the reasons for my delay.

Just before he died, Mr. Livingston (please permit me to
respectfully refer to him in this manner) urged on me full
responsibility for prosecution of the action known to him as
"The Lafitte Case." Accordingly, I reviewed his voluminous
files, for I felt I needed to completely familiarize myself with
all the ramifications of this lengthy and most incredible tale
before making a presentation to you.

Mr. Livingston stated that the Society required a single
piece of substantive, irrefutable evidence that would clinch
the final solution of the case. That bit of evidence, held by
him to be the consummate proof, was discovered just before
his death. Although he insisted that I take the credit, you
must understand that it was his finding, and his alone.

Perusal of his notes indicated additional avenues of explo-
ration for primary information that he had been unable to
obtain in his lifetime. Since his death, I have collected much
of that additional data, and it has added to the validity of the
case. If there was doubt before, there is none now.

During this period of review and investigation, I complied
with another of Mr. Livingston's entreaties and entered Tulane
University, majoring in history. (What else?) I have been accepted by their Law School, which I will enter in the Fall. There
will once again be a Livingston Law Office in New Orleans.

I tell you this because I would have you know the change
of direction in my life. The courses in history have caused me
to look at The Case in a whole new light. Should this history

be re-written? Of course, history has repeatedly been re-written as new information has come to light, and properly so. New caves are found that extend the age of man. Hieroglyphs are uncovered that speak of Egyptian kings in dynasties unknown before. A belated confession frees an innocent man from prison.

But what is to be gained from the re-writing that The Lafitte Case would engender? Will men be set free? Will kings be found? I think not. I think only consternation and confusion can result. And I think we have enough dissension already in our fragile world. (I also studied sociology.)

The several nations honor their several heroes, justified or not. France, Britain, and America each have their icons; each properly, if perhaps too ostentatiously, entombed.

Now, we would say that those tombs honor not the real heroes, but imposters. Not John Paul Jones, but an unknown Frenchman. Not Napoleon Bonaparte, but a simple infantryman. Could the clamor, the outrage even be imagined? And what purpose would be served? What good might be accomplished?

But it is the truth, you say. And history should reflect that truth, whatever the consequences. Perhaps. But I am not convinced.

I further realize that "The Lafitte Case" represents Mr. Livingston's life work, his pre-eminent purpose. On his very death-bed, he entrusted to me its completion. It is that consideration, above all, that has made my decision most wrenching.

I tell you now that I have decided to hold the matter in abeyance. I hope that when Mr. Livingston looks down from above, he will not see it as a violation of my charge. As God knows, I have wrestled long and hard with the decision. I have not destroyed the evidence. It all waits there, in his Secret Room.

I have double-locked the door; no person is permitted to enter. Not even myself, lest I falter. Perhaps the day will come when I will think better of my action and unlock the door. Perhaps some new circumstance, unknown to us now, will demand that the truth be revealed and thrust upon the world.

But until that day, I will put the matter aside. I ask that you do the same. Think no more of two Jean Lafittes or of breech-loading cannon. Please allow those ancient secrets to lie with those ancient bones, whoever it is that those bones may once have belonged to.

I will not correspond with you again unless I determine that I must unlock the door to that Secret Room.

In the manner of Mr. Livingston's closings,

I remain,

Yr. most humble and obed. servant,

Michael Livingston, L.L.D. (Futurus)

RESP. SUB., J. Croft, Sec.
FEBRUARY 6, 1997

EPILOGUE

Following the destruction of Campeche, Jean Lafitte (The Real) and his brother Pierre continued to marauder in the Caribbean until 1826. Jean then moved to St. Louis, Missouri, where for a time he operated a gunpowder shop. He died May 5, 1854 and is buried at Alton, Illinois.

Pierre Laffite moved first to Silan, Mexico, then to the Sabine River in Texas before joining his brother Jean. He died March 9, 1844 and is buried at St. Louis.

Alexander Lafitte (alias Dominique Youx), did not stay with his brothers on Campeche, but lived out his days in New Orleans and drank excessively. He died November 14, 1830, and is buried at New Orleans.

Eugene Francois Robeaud was a light infantryman of the Third Regiment of Voltigeurs. Rumored to have been born in the little village of Baleicourt near Verdun, his name has vanished from all official registers of births and deaths.

Despite extensive searches, neither the bones of *BonHomme Richard* nor her cannon have been located.

The medal authorized Commodore John Paul Jones by Act of Congress in 1787, struck by Augustin Dupré, has never been found.

The three mysterious graves still exist in the Perrin Cemetery on the point beside the Bayou des Oises.

SELECTED BIBLIOGRAPHY

Arthur, Stanley Clisby. Jean Lafitte, *Gentleman Rover*. New Orleans: Harmanson, 1952

Bienvenu, Lionel J. *The Story of Jean Lafitte*, New Orleans: Lafitte National Historic Park, 1986

Brooks, Charles B. *The Siege of New Orleans*. Seattle: University of Washington Press, 1961

Chidsey. *The Battle of New Orleans*. New York: Crown, 1961

Core, Jesse. *War of 1812 Battlefield Gazette*, New Orleans: News Replicas Ltd., 1984

de Grummond, Jane Lucas. *The Baratarians and the Battle of New Orleans*. Baton Rouge: Legacy, 1961.

Engleman. *The Peace of Christmas Eve*. New York: Harcourt, 1960

Forshufvud, Smith & Wassen, Drs. *Arsenic Content of Napoleon 1's Hair*. Goteburg: 1961

Fourner. *Napoleon the First*. New York: Holt, 1903.

Lafitte, Jean. *The Journal of Jean Lafitte*. New York: Vantage, 1958

Martineau. *Napoleon's St. Helena*. New York: Rand McNally, 1966

Morison, Samuel Eliot. *John Paul Jones*. New York: Time Inc., 1959

Porter, Horace. *Commemoration at Annapolis*. Washington: General Printing Office, 1907.

Saxon, Lyle. *Lafitte the Pirate*. New York: Century, 1930

United States Naval Records. *Admiral John Paul Jones*. Chicago: Elliott-Madison, 1951

Walsh. *Night on Fire*. New York: McGraw-Hill, 1978

Weider & Hapgood. *The Murder of Napoleon*. New York: Congdon & Lattes, 1982

Wachter & Trussell. *Journal of the American Statistical Association*, New York: Vol. 77, No. 378, 1982

Wheeler, Thomas G. *Who Lies Here?* New York: G.P. Putnam's Sons, 1975